21j £3.50

The Heart's Desire

Book One of The Briarcrest Chronicles

Anna Furtado

Yellow Rose Books

Nederland, Texas

ISBN 1-932300-32-5

First Printing 2004

9 8 7 6 5 4 3 2 1

Cover design by Donna Pawlowski

Published by:

Yellow Rose Books
PMB 210, 8691 9th Avenue
Port Arthur, Texas 77642-8025

Find us on the World Wide Web at
http://www.regalcrest.biz

Printed in the United States of America

Acknowledgments

A big thank you to my editor, Sylverre, for helping me bring this story to the world in its most intelligible form, and for keeping me "honest" about the many details.

I especially want to acknowledge all the help and hand-holding offered by Lori Lake as we journeyed on this path to getting this book into print and to Cathy LeNoir for allowing me the opportunity to have the first of "The Briarcrest Chronicles" published.

To all the friends who read, edited, commented and critiqued over time and the evolution of this story, thank you! I especially want to acknowledge Judy Z, Carol and Michelle, Jackie and Chris, Joan S, Marge W, Monique C, Robyn D and Connie C. If I've forgotten anyone, it's not for lack of appreciation, but rather for lack of memory. Additionally, there were many others along the way who gave their encouragement and support who deserve my sincere thanks. Consider it done.

Most of all, my heartfelt thanks to my partner, Earlene, for her love and encouragement of me as a person and as a writer. She has given me the gift of time over and over again. Without it, this first of Catherine's and Lydia's stories would never have been told.

~ Anna Furtado

To Earlene,
without whom this story would never have been told.

Chapter
One

The Eve of the Feast of St. Remi
September 30, 1458
Willowglen Township, England

CATHERINE COULD NOT forget the woman's eyes. That grey-green gaze had probed into the depths of her soul and left her overwhelmed with puzzling emotions.

She tried not to dwell on it, not with all the preparations to make for the start of Willowglen's Harvest Fair. However, try as she might to ignore her feelings, it just was not possible. Catherine trembled. She felt bewildered because of a woman — a mystery woman that she could not erase from her mind — a stranger with compelling eyes capable of sending shivers dancing on the surface of Catherine's skin.

How had one look banished the melancholy that she had endured for the seasons of a year? One look had cracked open the cold, impenetrable shell that surrounded her, bringing the first hint of joy in life since her father's death.

As Catherine pulled open the shutters of the old shop window and breathed in the new day, a ray of morning sun sparkled on the window sill. It made her smile, and evoked the memory of the woman standing outside her shop. Catherine tingled with excitement. Questions raced through her mind. *What was this new passion that woke in her?* Her chest pounded when she thought of the woman. The dull ache that had not left her since she'd first seen those eyes was almost too much to bear.

As the sun rose, the light became more intense, crisper. The familiar cupboard of rich, dark wood spanning the far wall almost glowed. Stoneware jars and small wooden boxes of herbs seemed luminescent. Carefully arranged linen, brocade and velvet, neatly piled on shelves, shimmered. Catherine saw it all with new eyes.

The thick-planked worktable in the middle of the room held

last-minute preparations for the fair, reminding her that she did not have time to linger. Moving across the room, she negotiated the large baskets of herbs harvested from her garden. As she passed a small wooden chest containing her most costly and exotic spices, she ran her fingertips across the lid and smiled. The contents of the box came from places Catherine had only seen with her mind's eye. When she was young, her father had let her stay and listen to stories told by traders who came from far-off lands; now, some of those same men told their tales to her.

As a youngster, Catherine had been careful to be quiet and well behaved so that she would not be banished from the room during those sessions. Her father would never do such a thing, of course, but the presence of a girl-child might be frowned upon by some. As she approached womanhood, Catherine Hawkins developed into a tall, stately individual. She commanded attention when she entered a room, even when she did not intend to be noticed. Both her parents had encouraged her to be confident and self-assured — odd for a young woman in this time and in this place. Her teachers, the women of Wooster Abbey, also fostered this attitude.

Catherine reached for the hem of her outer skirt and deftly folded it up into her waistband. Plucking a well-worn broom from the corner with a large, slender hand, Catherine opened the door and stepped outside. Every morning, she performed the same ritual. It started with sweeping the front step of the spice shop.

Catherine whisked the cobbles in front of the building and smiled. She loved the old shop that held the herbs and spices she sold. When her father added the fabric, sturdy wool, linen and extravagant brocades and silks, she happily included them on the shop shelves. But it was the herbs that she especially favored, because she used them to heal.

"No time for daydreaming," Catherine chided herself softly, plunging into her chore again. She thought of the woman's eyes as she swept.

A customer had come to the shop before she opened for business the previous morning, seeking Catherine's special blend of herbs to ease his wife's aching joints. She packaged the ingredients and watched from the doorway as he hurried off with the bundle tucked under his arm. Turning to go back inside, she noticed the young woman in the street opposite the shop. By her dress, Catherine deduced that she was a woman of means, perhaps of title, but the beauty of the fabric was as nothing compared to her eyes. Excited and uneasy, Catherine puzzled over the episode. *Who is this stranger and why is she in the street, unescorted, so early in the morning?*

In the end, both had shied away without speaking. A rush of heat that she couldn't explain stole across her face, and, surprised by her feelings, Catherine stopped sweeping. To try to overcome her uncharacteristic awkwardness, she attacked the cobblestones with her broom. She was unsuccessful in sweeping away the emotion she felt.

When she gained control, Catherine went back into the shop. Gathering up rosemary sprigs and several small baskets, she took everything outside to try a display for the fair the next day. After setting it up on the shelf beneath the shop's open window, she stepped back to assess her creation, but she was distracted by a commotion down the street.

A group of women laughed boisterously as they waited outside Edward the silversmith's shop. Catherine chuckled to herself at their liveliness. *Such a rare thing for ladies of title to be so rowdy in public. It does my heart good to see them enjoy themselves like that. They must be waiting for Edward to give them a preview of his work before the fair.*

The door opened and the revelry stopped. The women jostled around in the street moving toward the opened doorway. As they did, they resumed their chattering.

Catherine saw *her* watching her from the edge of the crowd. A flood of emotion washed over her; she turned away and stumbled back to the shop window sill. Pretending to fuss with the sprigs of herbs, she held on to the shelf with one hand until the disabling dizziness passed. Regaining her composure, she gathered up her baskets and started back to the shop. Almost involuntarily, she slowed and glanced sidelong down the street. To her disappointment, she found it deserted.

"Mind your wits, Catherine," she scolded herself. "You have herb packets to prepare. A fair is about to begin. There are a great many things that need your attention. Back to work with you, now."

CATHERINE SAT AT the worktable half-listening to the activity in the street and wondered again about the women. She thought they must be from another town, and remembered seeing two of the older ladies at another fair. The rest were strangers, newcomers to the celebration. One thing was certain. *If I had seen her before, I would have remembered those extraordinary eyes...*Catherine shivered and forced herself back to her small fabric bundles. The street grew quiet.

She started as a sharp voice shattered the silence just outside her open window.

"There you are. I wondered where you had gotten off to."

Catherine looked up in time to see a short, plump woman with greying hair and the young lady with the grey-green eyes disappear from view, the older woman pulling the young noblewoman along. She strained to hear more.

"Come along now, dear. Your Aunt Beatrice wants you to see the new silver candlesticks she just bought. Mind you stay with us, Lydia."

The name was like a beautiful melody to Catherine. She felt the sound caress the ether as she breathed it forth. "Lydia." Then she spoke the question she longed to have answered: "Who are you?"

Chapter
Two

The Feast of St. Remi
October 1, 1458
The Shoppe of Hawkins & Hawkins

CATHERINE AROSE IN the pre-dawn darkness, thinking of Lydia. She lit a small candle and waited as the taper flared to a luminous orange, brightening before it settled to a soft yellow glow. She dressed in her linen shift and underskirt, poured water from a pitcher into a well-worn basin and washed her face. After brushing her dark brown hair with long, deliberate strokes, she captured its silkiness in a net cap and tied it up securely. From a peg on the wall, she took a smooth, brown linen kirtle to put on. Over the top, she donned a black bodice embellished with bright embroidery, a gift from her father following a trip north. She laced and tied the front of the vest, feeling the pressure of the cloth against her breasts.

She discarded the water from her basin out the second-story window overlooking her garden. The water cascaded to the ground and splashed on some winter beans climbing a trellis against the house wall. The plants would be glad of the moisture, for the autumn ground was unusually dry.

As she started down the steps to the shop, her shadow danced beside her on the whitewashed mud-and-straw wall in the candle's glow. The leaping phantom called her to come and join in its frolic. Although Catherine could make merry with the best of them, she was not prone to flights of fancy, especially in the midst of such a busy time. For a moment, though, she was tempted, even if she could not say why. The fragrance of the herbs and spices wafting up the stairway called her back to her duties; she turned away from the beckoning darkness with some reluctance.

Reaching the bottom of the stairs, Catherine heard a soft rap on the door to the street. She slid the long, wooden latch back from the heavy door. Sarah, her young assistant, stood outside with her younger brother, Andy.

At Catherine's encouragement, Sarah had gone to help her uncle's family bring their goods to the fair. The family was the only kin the young girl had left since, several years before, Sarah and Andy had lost their parents to a devastating illness that swept through the poor hamlet-dwellers. Catherine had tried to minister to the ailing folks with teas and potions, but to no avail. After her parents died, Catherine took Sarah in to apprentice with her in order to save the remainder of the family from the burden of another girl-child. Andy still lived with his aunt and uncle.

Once her brother had gone, Sarah joined Catherine in tying up some sprigs of fresh mint. As they worked, Catherine inquired about Sarah's uncle and his family.

"They are fine, Mistress, but my uncle's family is so large and noisy. It is good to be back in the quiet of the shop."

"Still, Sarah, I'm glad you went. I'm sure they appreciated your help."

"Oh, I have no doubt of it, Mistress Catherine."

As they waited for the first light of morning, they talked of the fair and the herbs and spices they were readying. Lydia was uppermost in Catherine's mind all the while, but she did not mention the oddly compelling woman. By the time the sun started to peek above the hills beyond Willowglen, they were ready to set up their wares outside.

ACTIVITY IN THE street grew while Catherine and Sarah decorated the shop front with garlands of fresh herbal boughs and arranged their goods on temporary stands outside. Soon fair-goers would be spilling down the street, their enthusiasm bubbling over. The merry throng, led by banner-bearers, accompanied by musicians and singers, would overrun the temporary booths and shops. Another Willowglen fair was about to begin—and with it came an excitement that Catherine had not felt since childhood.

The Grouse & Pheasant Inn

AS DAWN BROKE, Lydia opened her eyes and stretched sensually in her small room at the Grouse and Pheasant Inn. She lay in bed thinking of her encounters with the herbalist until she heard movement in the tiny enclosure next to hers, the two separated by a thick tapestry. Marian was stirring.

A scowl spread across Lydia's face. She wanted to be alone to savor her thoughts of Catherine. Although Lydia did not understand her feelings completely, she thought that if she were to fall in love, it would feel very much like she felt now.

A shudder ran through her.

AS MARIAN DRESSED, flashes of Lydia's childhood scurried through the passages of her mind. She always took refuge in these thoughts when concerned with her young charge. Lydia had been in Marian's care since she was a baby. The child's laughter echoed through Marian's memory in recollections of a game of Fox and Hen, with Marian in pursuit of the toddler, Lydia giggling with delight as she ran on unsure legs. Recalling those happy hours brought a smile to Marian's face. She had tried to be like a mantle around Lydia's shoulders over the years, covering her with love, trying to make up for the loss of her mother and the lack of affection from her father.

The Earl of Greencastle had always been too busy with some affair of his office to spend any time with his young daughter. He was often away from home, and he did not seem to know how to express affection when he was there. In his defense, the death of Lydia's mother had left Lord Wellington devastated, so he spent his lonely days growing bitter, preoccupied by status and wealth. By the time his grief might have been healed, he was so embittered that he could not, or would not, change. So he continued to entrust his young daughter's nurturing to Marian, and her education to the priest, Isadore.

Marian scowled at the thought of the priest. Now, that cleric — that poor excuse for a holy man of God — *he* wanted to spend time with Lydia. A sound of contempt came from Marian's throat unbidden.

Rather than leave the young child alone with her tutor, although Isadore suggested it often, Marian contrived a story about enjoying the lessons herself and finding them so interesting that she did not want to miss a single one. In reality, although Marian did appreciate the opportunity for learning, it was more that she did not trust the seedy little priest.

"Vile little man," muttered Marian.

Isadore had a way of making Marian feel surrounded by dark winter storm clouds. Marian shook off the thoughts and called through the curtain gently. "Lydia, dear, are you awake?"

"Yes, Marian."

"Shall I come and assist you at dressing, then?"

"No, Marian, I shall dress myself this morning."

Lydia heard the sound of soft leather padding against smooth wood, then silence. Marian was probably off to the kitchen to get some light refreshment for them to start their day. In the quiet, the young woman returned to her musings.

In the silversmith's shop the day before, with her companions out of earshot, Lydia had inquired about Catherine. As she leaned over a creation of Edward's and admired his handiwork, she'd remarked casually that Willowglen seemed a town of very creative people.

Then she said, "I have heard said, sir, that the herbalist down the street has some excellent goods. Is it true?"

"Yes, My Lady, it is true. Mistress Catherine has a fine reputation. She grows and processes most of her herbs and they are most excellent. Her spices are the best around and her prices fair for treasures that come from so far away. She also carries fabrics, linens and velvets — lovely things. I am sure the quality would interest a lady of your fine taste."

"You seem enamored of this shopkeeper, sir. Does her husband know you think so highly of her?" Lydia chided.

Edward chuckled at Lydia's suggestion. He only cared about Catherine as he would his own daughter. He had responded that she was only just a little older than his own two sons. In fact, his children had spent a great deal of time with Catherine in childhood. Edward and Catherine's father had been fast friends and it was Edward who had joined with Catherine's father to petition that she become a member of the Spice Vendors' Guild in her own right.

"No, My Lady, I am just an old man who admires the hard work of a friend's daughter. She has made an excellent name for herself by her good work and skill. But I have no worry of my admiration being misunderstood. The mistress Catherine seems to have no need of a husband. Her father once confided in me that she was far too independent to be tethered to a man, and that such companionship never interested her — but, forgive me, My Lady. I should not go on so."

But it was enough. Lydia was intrigued.

While Edward and Lydia conversed, Marian busied herself examining the jewelry in a small case nearby. She seemed to be too preoccupied with the ornaments to hear the discussion but, in fact, she listened to every word. She wondered why Lydia had so special a regard for this herbalist — why she disappeared down Market Street at every opportunity — and why she inquired about this woman now.

LYDIA REMOVED HER linen shift from a hook next to her bed and slipped the garment over her head. She stood up, smoothing the soft cloth over her breasts, lingering there for just a moment before moving her hand down to her stomach and across to her hips. All the while, she was aware of the cool fabric against the warmth of her body.

She donned her dress, brushed her thick auburn hair quickly and pinned it up with exquisite gold combs. Then she walked over to a stool in the corner of the room and pulled on the long, thick stockings she liked to wear with her soft leather traveling boots. As she smoothed the cloth against her thighs, she wondered how someone else's caresses might feel.

Catherine's face came to her. Lydia's heart pounded. Bewildered and breathless, Lydia stamped both feet firmly on the floor and stood, throwing her dress hem down emphatically. She took a deep breath and tried to collect herself. She needed a distraction. She headed downstairs to look for Marian.

Willowglen Township Square

THE BUZZ IN the town square died down as the officials climbed the temporary platform. Their opening speeches promised a marvelous celebration beyond anyone's imagination. Enthusiastic cheers punctuated their words. However, in the midst of the festivity, one young woman found herself quite wearied by the opening spectacle.

Unlike Marian, who hung on every word, Lydia fidgeted and sighed. The Ladies, Beatrice and Hilary, listened with mild interest and seemed to take no notice of Lydia's fretting. To the young woman, the speakers seemed to drone on and on, until she could not endure them for one more moment. Finally, she leaned over and whispered to her companions. "These speeches are so tedious they give me a headache. I need to get away from this din."

Marian made a weak attempt to stop Lydia, but she knew the young woman all too well. Once she made up her mind to do something, there was no stopping her. In the end, Marian offered to accompany her, but Lydia insisted that she wanted to be alone.

"Marian, you do so love the splendor of a fair's opening. I would not dream of taking you away from it. Let me go alone. I can manage just fine."

Marian opened her mouth to protest, but Lady Beatrice intervened.

"Marian, let the child go. Everyone is here in the square, save for a few merchants busy about their fair preparations. She can go back to the Inn and rest awhile. Go on, Lydia, dear, meet us later. We will start our browsing on Market Street."

Somewhat reluctantly, Marian agreed.

Lydia headed in the direction of the Inn. In order to reach it, she had to pass Catherine's shop. As Catherine's booth came into view, Lydia saw that the shopkeeper was engaged in animated conversation with another young woman.

Catherine did not see Lydia.

The young noblewoman slowed her pace as anxiety overtook her. She steeled herself against the urge to turn and run away. She looked up toward the thick board hung above the shop entrance and took a deep breath. The sign was uniquely different from most shop signs. Ordinarily, a picture or symbol of a shop's wares or a design representing the name of the establishment sufficed. This sign contained an innovation. It had lettering that read:

Hawkins & Hawkins
purveyors of herbs, spices & fine linens

Above the words, the emblem of the Spice Vendors' Guild, the mortar and pestle, gleamed in gold. Lydia stared at the sign trying to compose herself. Her legs trembled, keeping time with her racing heart. Although she did not look in Catherine's direction, she knew that the shopkeeper had turned around and was staring.

Lydia's imagination ran wild. Catherine would think her mad to be approaching once more, unaccompanied and without introduction. *And to what purpose? Only that I am drawn to this woman as a moth is drawn to candlelight.*

Plucking up her courage, Lydia looked directly at Catherine and tried to read her expression. What was it? Puzzlement? Curiosity? Distress?

The two women studied one another. Then Lydia gulped and forged ahead. Her eyes still held the spice vendor's when Lydia stopped in front of her.

Catherine spoke first.

"Good day, My Lady. Welcome to Willowglen fair. May I help you in choosing a spice, or perhaps some fine cloth?"

Lydia struggled to find her voice. "No. I mean, yes, I... What will you show me in a linen? Something bright that I may wear riding or hawking." She looked aside shyly.

Disappointed that the young woman had turned away,

Catherine tried not to let her voice betray her. "I have some finely dyed reds and purples inside, My Lady. Please follow me and I will show them to you."

Lydia was glad for the chance to move into the shop, to leave the street and be alone with Catherine. She had no idea what to say next, but she knew that it must be something more than idle prattle about fabric.

Inside, the shopkeeper moved to the far end of the room and removed large, neatly folded pieces of fabric from the shelves. The colors were the most vibrant Lydia had ever seen. As Catherine spread the cloth out on the workbench, Lydia thought the reds and purples, greens and golds shone like some deep rainbow. However, she only saw them out of the corner of her eye, for she was more interested in watching Catherine's ebb and flow.

Catherine reached above her head to take yet another measure of cloth down. As she did, her loose sleeves slipped to her elbows and exposed her tanned forearms. An image of the woman putting her hoe to rows of plants, moving from one green stalk to another with sleeves rolled up to expose supple arms to the day's warmth made Lydia breathe hard. Her fantasy played itself out in her mind until Catherine's voice shook her from her reverie as she repeated her question. Did the Lady find any of the fabric to her liking?

In an instant, Lydia formed a plan and launched into a proposal, hoping that the shopkeeper would hear her out. "Mistress...Catherine, is it not?"

Catherine smiled and nodded. *So, she knows my name, as well.*

The shopkeeper's smile reassured Lydia. She continued, "Mistress Catherine, I have become very interested in the processing of herbs of late. I have actually come to engage you as a tutor so that I might learn about the cultivating of this art. I will remain in Willowglen if you would be willing to do so."

Catherine stared. Lydia looked away quickly, afraid Catherine would see the real reason that she was drawn to her and refuse her request. How else was Lydia to spend time with Catherine, to get to know more about her? It didn't matter that she would have to get Marian's permission to do so. She didn't even think about the fact that her father might be opposed to such a suggestion. She would have her way.

Out of the silence, Catherine responded cautiously. "I have but one question, My Lady. Why it is that you come to me for this instruction?"

Lydia walked around the table nervously and stammered

her response. "I...have heard that you do much of your own growing and drying of special herbs, Mistress. I am interested to learn all I can about what you do here. I am at a loss to be instructed in herbology otherwise and I know little about spices — or cloth, for that matter. I would find this knowledge most useful. And I have heard that you have a good reputation."

Catherine's mind raced. Her heart battled to keep up with her head. If she wanted to spend time with Lydia, getting acquainted, finding out more about her, why not do so? *In truth, there is nothing to stop me — nothing at all. I am free to do as I please. If I want to take this woman as my pupil, I can. I have no one to answer to but myself. So why not?*

A smile blossomed on Catherine's face. "Agreed, then. Shall we begin right after the fair ends, one week hence?"

Lydia replied enthusiastically, "Yes, after the fair, that would be most agreeable!"

"I shall see you then, Lady Lydia."

Lydia's eyes widened, surprised at hearing Catherine say her name. *How did she know it? Could it be that perhaps she has felt this drawing, too? Has she learned all she could about me, as I have about her?*

Lydia stammered, "Perhaps I shall come back to discuss the particulars of my studies while the fair is going on?" She did not want to seem too eager, so she made a conscious effort to slow her words down. "If that would not be too much of an inconvenience to you, Mistress Catherine."

Catherine had felt immediate disappointment to think that she would have to wait an entire week before meeting with Lydia again. Yet knowing that she would be weary each evening of the fair, Catherine grappled with her own practicality. Her shadow — the one that had called her to come and dance in the flickering light on the stairway — caught her eye on the opposite wall. She imagined struggling with it in some mock wrestling match until she allowed it to win, and thought it odd that she gave in so easily.

"The fair does get busy at times, My Lady, but perhaps we could talk at the end of the day when everyone has closed up and gone home to rest. Would you find that satisfactory?"

Lydia could barely contain herself. "Yes, very satisfactory. I shall see you — perhaps tonight at supper time?"

"Yes," said Catherine. She hoped she concealed her eagerness. "Tonight."

Lydia smiled sweetly, and Catherine thought, *She is the most beautiful woman I have ever seen.*

Lydia felt her cheeks flush with embarrassment under

Catherine's gaze. "I must go," she said. She started toward the shop door, turned back and smiled again. "I am off to the fair, now — until tonight!"

CATHERINE WATCHED LYDIA glide down the street as if carried by unseen angels. She could hardly believe that the encounter had taken place. From the corner of her eye, Catherine caught a glimpse of something moving. It was as if a shadow was doing cartwheels across the shop wall. When she turned, though, there was nothing there. Catherine thought it must have been her imagination...*but the beauty of Lady Lydia's eyes — that is not my imagination. And she is interested in learning the herbal art. Why does she want to learn from me? Does she not have other means to learn about herbs?*

Catherine's questions went unanswered. At that moment, the din of the approaching parade pierced her thoughts. From her window, Catherine could see a huge crowd moving down Market Street. Large, colorful banners fluttered in the autumn breeze. Flute players, bell ringers and drummers led the happy, noisy throng. The colors, the music, all seemed more beautiful than she had ever experienced. The fair had begun like many other fairs, but this one was different.

Turning back into the room, the sight of the fabric pieces lying on the table made Catherine laugh out loud. *So, the Lady Lydia never meant to look at cloth.* She quickly returned the textiles to the shelves and hurried outside.

To look at her, anyone would have thought that Catherine was especially enthralled by the celebration this year. Sarah even remarked, much to Catherine's surprise, that she was glad to see her mistress so happy. There was no way Sarah could have known that it was Lydia who brought such a look of joy to Catherine's face. Lydia had captivated Catherine's heart.

Chapter
Three

The Feast of St. Remi
Eventide

BUSINESS THE FIRST day of the fair had been brisk and profitable.

In the evening quiet, Catherine sat down to tally the days' receipts. Just as she finished, she heard a delicate knock on the door. Realization dawned slowly. *Lydia. I have been so busy since we parted company this morning that I forgot she was coming back...for supper, she said. Oh, dear, and I have nothing to offer her to eat but bread and dried meat.*

The rapping came again, more purposeful this time. A voice called from the street, "Mistress Catherine, it is Lydia. I have come to sup with you."

Catherine headed for the door, her distress growing. The knocking resumed. When Catherine pulled open the door, she almost met Lydia's fist.

Lydia stood before her holding a large cloth-covered basket. Behind her, a young man carried a pewter pitcher. A large leather pouch hung from his shoulder. Catherine recognized young Will from the Grouse and Pheasant Inn at the end of the street.

Lydia said, "Good evening to you, Mistress. I had begun to think you were not at home this evening. Since I invited myself to supper, I thought I should provide something to eat. Will you allow us to set out the food?"

Catherine, embarrassed and grateful, opened the door wide and gestured toward the next room. The pair walked past her, through the shop, toward the kitchen. Catherine followed.

Will placed the pitcher carefully on the table and helped Lydia unpack the basket. They set out fresh-cooked meat, potatoes, carrots and warm bread. Will produced autumn grapes and a slab of cheese from the pouch. The young shopkeeper's eyes widened as the feast materialized.

When they were done, Lydia handed the young man a coin with her thanks. She asked him to return later to escort her back to the Grouse and Pheasant.

"Thank you, Your Ladyship," Will responded shyly. "I shall call for you after we clean up from the evening meal at the Inn."

"That will be fine, Master Will, thank you," Lydia said.

He gave Catherine a shy smile as he passed her heading for the door. Halfway, he turned, as if something had just crossed his mind. "Is Sarah about, Mistress?"

Lydia added, "Yes, would she like to join us? I have brought enough."

"I am afraid the bustle of the fair did Sarah in. She has gone to bed. No doubt she is already sound asleep."

Will looked disappointed. He turned and plodded toward the door, but just before he put his hand on the handle, Catherine called to him.

"Will, perhaps you could come by tomorrow during the day and visit Sarah at our booth. Tell Master Elbert I asked if he might spare you for awhile. I need you to help me move a barrel of herbs that is too heavy for me."

Will reeled around. His face had brightened into a broad grin. "Yes, mum," he said with enthusiasm. "I am sure he would let me come to assist you. Tomorrow, then."

He pulled open the door. As the door closed with a soft thud, Catherine turned back to Lydia.

"Is Sarah the young woman who was with you earlier today, Mistress?" Lydia asked.

"Yes," Catherine replied. "She is my assistant. Young Will, there, fancies her, I suspect. Don't you?"

Both women laughed.

The initial tension was broken. Catherine invited Lydia to sit down and she served the meal on plain wooden plates that she produced from a chest in the kitchen. Almost as soon as Catherine joined Lydia at the table, the tiredness seemed to melt from her shoulders. Lydia's presence and the aroma of the food renewed her. Whenever her eyes met Lydia's, Catherine felt a fluttering sensation in her stomach. For that reason, she kept her attention on her plate. It allowed her to eat in spite of her feelings. Catherine had not eaten all day and now she realized how hungry she was.

Lydia watched her scoop the food up from her plate, pleased that she seemed to enjoy the meal.

Shoveling the last morsels onto her spoon, Catherine said, "It was so kind of you to think of all of this, Lady Lydia."

As she spoke, her eye caught movement on the stone

hearth—a shadow. Was it the flickering firelight playing tricks, or a fleeting phantom that danced merrily across the stones? *Curious*, Catherine thought.

When she looked at Lydia, she was immediately caught up in the spellbinding grey-green eyes. Thoughts about those eyes, her lips, her face, her hair, swirled wildly in Catherine's head. No matter how much she pushed against them, they would not go away. Finally, Catherine let go and dove into the grey-green sea. Feelings washed over the young herbalist. Time stood still.

CATHERINE REALIZED THAT she had no idea how much time had passed when she saw how low the fire in the hearth was. They had talked long into the evening. Catherine felt giddy and light-headed, almost as if the wine had been too much for her. Yet she knew she had not drunk a full goblet.

"Lady Lydia, you left before you told me if any of my fabric appealed to you earlier today," Catherine said.

Lydia hesitated, then confessed, "I did not really want to look at fabric."

Catherine laughed. "That was most apparent by the time you left this morning, My Lady," she said in a teasing tone.

Lydia blushed and replied, "I only wanted to speak to you alone. I wanted to ask you about...tutoring me. I was afraid you might not agree to take me as a student." *I was afraid that you might refuse my request and I might never see you again.*

Catherine stifled another chuckle. "Oh, I see, My Lady."

Lydia felt embarrassed. She searched for a change of subject, pleading, "Mistress, please, let us not be so formal. Will you call me Lydia?"

Catherine felt more and more mischievous. She looked over at the stone fireplace. *Ridiculous. How can a shadow be smiling?*

"I will agree only if you will consent to my condition, M'lady." As Catherine spoke, the room started to turn, slowly at first; then, faster and faster. She tried to ignore the dizziness, but it was very disorienting.

"...and what would that condition be, Mistress?" inquired Lydia for a second time.

Catherine willed the movement of the walls around her to stop. She took a long, deep breath, grateful when the movement finally began to slow down.

As if from down a long tunnel, she heard Lydia's voice. "...the condition?"

"Oh, yes, the condition." The spinning finally stopped. Catherine took another deep breath and said, "You must not call me Mistress. My name is Catherine."

"Yes," replied Lydia shyly, "I know."

"Oh, yes, of course you do," stammered Catherine. She waited. Would the room start turning again? Thankfully, it did not.

Lydia pronounced, "Agreed, then."

"Agreed? Oh, yes, let us dispense with titles. We have no need of them here." The mischievous twinkle returned to Catherine's eyes. "And do not trouble yourself about the fabric." She leaned forward now, boldly meeting Lydia's gaze. "Tell me, Lydia — what is it that you wish to learn about herbs?"

Lydia replied excitedly, "Everything, Catherine." Holding her new teacher's gaze, she suddenly felt shy, yet added, "I want to know everything." *About you.*

AS THE EVENING wore on, the women became more comfortable with one another and shared many things. Catherine spoke of her love of tending to people's illnesses and injuries. Lydia gave Catherine a glimpse into the days she spent at Briarcrest with her aunt Beatrice and her companion, Hilary. They made plans for Marian, Lydia's former nurse and current companion, to join them for dinner the following night, and arrangements for the remainder of the fair. Lydia insisted on bringing the evening meal to share with Catherine and Sarah at each day's end.

At first, Catherine objected. "Lydia, I cannot have you provide our meals. Surely, you will let me supply the food, for you are my guest."

But Lydia had made up her mind. When she said, "Please, let us not quarrel over this, Catherine," the shopkeeper agreed and said no more about the matter.

The hours passed almost unnoticed. Both women blushed whenever their eyes met again. Catherine got up from the table and busied herself stirring the kitchen hearth back to life. Lydia watched her, admiring the outline of her body against the fire's glow.

After a while, Lydia broke the silence. "What of *your* parents, Catherine?"

Catherine turned back to her visitor. "I lost my mother at the age of twelve. My father has not been dead long. It is still difficult to think of him gone. He was an exceptional man and I feel his loss deeply."

Lydia noted the pained look in Catherine's eyes. "He is the other Hawkins, then? On the sign, I mean."

"Yes," Catherine said, "this shop belonged to him and to my mother. He built up this trade from nothing. He gave me the benefit of his livelihood when I was a child and I continued the shop with him as an adult.

"I apprenticed with my father and I was taught by the nuns of Wooster Abbey. They taught me all the customary subjects: reading, ciphering and how to keep books. They also instructed me in needlework and music. Since I already knew a great deal about herbs, they also saw to my education in the healing art.

"Some people these days frown upon such an ability, preferring to think that only learned men can be healers, but I know that I am destined to use this skill. I have been fortunate. In Willowglen, the people are accepting of my ways. I know they think me a little odd, but they say nothing against me and they are grateful for my help with their illnesses."

Later that evening, when she was alone, Catherine would reflect on how unusual it was for her to reveal so much of herself to anyone, let alone to someone she had so recently met. Yet, she felt that she could tell Lydia anything. Well, *almost* anything.

THE KNOCK AT the door meant that Will had come to escort Lydia back to the Grouse and Pheasant. Both women felt that the evening had passed far too quickly. Their only consolation was in knowing that they would be able to see each other again the next night.

The young man helped Catherine and Lydia pile leftovers into a basket and walked ahead while the women said their reluctant goodnight. Catherine stood outside her shop and watched Lydia's silhouette as she walked down Market Street. When she disappeared into the Inn, Catherine went back inside.

The two women's hearts were so full that each of them found sleep elusive that night. They had so many questions and so much to share with one another. When weariness finally overtook them, it was in the wee hours of the morning.

Chapter
Four

October 1458
Willowglen Fair continues

EARLY ON THE second day of the fair, before the crowds began to gather, Lydia, Marian and some other women appeared at Catherine's stall. Lydia introduced Catherine to her companions.

As Catherine had surmised earlier in the week, she recognized the Ladies of Briarcrest, Beatrice, Duchess of Briarcrest, and Lady Hilary, from a previous Willowglen fair. Beatrice and Catherine discovered that they shared a mutual fondness for a refreshing tea made from mint leaves. Catherine had her own blend of mint varieties that she combined with lemon balm. The Duchess purchased several fresh bundles from Catherine.

Lady Hilary found a dark brown linen cloth with an elegant weave that appealed to her. She bought all that Catherine had and eagerly showed it off to Lady Beatrice. Catherine heard the Duchess say to Lady Hilary, "You'll stir up some talk with that garb, my dear," and chuckle as they walked off down the street.

Lydia and Marian lingered at Catherine's stall awhile longer. The shopkeeper took advantage of the early morning lull to engage Marian in conversation.

"Are you enjoying Willowglen Township's Fair, M'lady?"

Marian replied, "Oh, my dear, I am. Why, yesterday I saw a performance in the square that was truly delightful."

The portly woman launched into a retelling of the comic story, shaking with laughter as she recounted some of the play's lines. However, she was not so distracted by her merriment that she did not remember to scrutinize Catherine. The nature of her questions regarding Catherine's business dealings made it clear that Lydia had informed Marian of her plan.

Though they'd only just met, Catherine was certain that the older woman would only allow her charge to be placed into the most trustworthy of hands. Catherine, normally a woman who cared little of what others thought about her, found herself eager to gain Marian's approval.

The second day of the fair promised to be another busy one for Catherine and Sarah. Crowds of fair-goers began to swell in the street. Catherine might be called away at any time to attend to business, so she wasted no time in asking Marian to accompany Lydia that evening. Marian flushed with pleasure and accepted the invitation.

Catherine watched as Lydia moved off down Market Street with Marian. Before the pair was devoured by the crowd, Lydia turned back and smiled at Catherine. It took the young shopkeeper's breath away for a moment. When she turned back to the booth, Sarah was staring at her.

THAT EVENING, CATHERINE felt more tired than she had on the one before. Still, she could not contain her excitement at the thought of Lydia's return.

Sarah had fared much better, having retired nearly as soon as the fair ended for the day and gotten a good night's sleep. Although she was tired from the bustle of the day, she was able to join the group for dinner. She could not, however, overcome her nervousness in the presence of Lydia and her companion. When Marian asked Sarah a question, she stuttered her response and turned a bright crimson.

Marian chuckled at Sarah's befuddled state. Then, remembering a day when she had been more like Sarah, she tried to put the young girl at ease. Marian, too, had come from a poor family, she said. When she first went to Greencastle to care for Lydia, she was quite bashful and she was reluctant to speak up. She did not mention that she had quickly learned to be bold in order to protect Lydia.

Marian offered, "Deep down in my heart, I am still a peasant woman, you know, Sarah."

Peasant woman? Catherine did not think so. Marian was quite a lady, indeed.

When the meal was over, Marian engaged Catherine in an intense discussion. It was apparent that Lydia's companion had gathered a great deal of information about the young shopkeeper. She seemed to know about her family history and her upbringing. She questioned Catherine extensively about her knowledge of herbology, about her business endeavors, and about her philosophy of life in general. Catherine knew that it was more than Marian's curiosity that prompted her questions. She felt as if she were being tested. She tried to answer Marian confidently, in spite of the fact that, at times, she felt as if she were trembling visibly.

"I believe it will be good for Lydia to take lessons from you, Mistress," Marian pronounced finally. "I think that they will be most beneficial to her. You have a great deal that you can teach her. Perhaps she may have something to teach you, too."

Outwardly, Catherine smiled. Internally, it took every ounce of self-restraint she had not to grab hold of Marian and embrace her enthusiastically. In an effort to stay calm, Catherine understated, "I am pleased that you have decided to allow me to tutor Lydia, M'lady."

Pleased? Not exactly. Overjoyed? Ecstatic, that was more like it.

She looked over at Lydia, who had remained very quiet during the whole ordeal. The grey-green eyes sparkled as she grinned from ear to ear. If anyone had looked up at the ceiling, they would have seen not one but two shadows swirling around in the flickering lamp light, and might have imagined their leaping as the young women's emotions were given form.

Marian had some stipulations to her agreement. First, she felt it was important for Lydia to learn *all* aspects of the business, from planting and harvesting to keeping the books. Catherine agreed without hesitation. She was more than willing to teach Lydia everything she knew.

"In addition," Marian said, "Lydia will stay at the Grouse and Pheasant during her studies. She is not used to the labor involved in your work, Mistress, and she will need a place to retreat and rest at the end of the day."

The Inn was not a typical lodging of the time with a tavern-like atmosphere. It had a reputation as a refined, honorable establishment. It was known as a place where ladies would not have to contend with the bawdiness found in some inns of the day.

Catherine agreed with Marian, acknowledging her insight. It was wise to have a place for Lydia to get away from the duties of the shop and be able to rest. Catherine couldn't help but wonder what other perceptions and intuitions the older woman had.

In actuality, Marian did know that something significant was happening between the two young women. The ever-strengthening bond between them did not escape her watchful eye as she observed Lydia and Catherine together that night. She decided that it would be best not to interfere.

With their business completed, the conversation turned to the women's common interests. Marian and Catherine found that they enjoyed each other immensely.   Although neither Catherine nor Lydia was aware of it, this helped make Marian's next decision a little easier: She would not stay with Lydia in Willowglen.

Lydia's father had made it clear that the new husband he intended for his daughter would provide maids and attendants from his own household in France. Callously, he had informed Marian that her service would no longer be needed then. It was a good assumption that her days were numbered at Greencastle, too.   When Beatrice had learned of this, she was furious. Concerned for Marian, she had immediately extended an invitation to her to make Briarcrest her home.

Although Lydia's Aunt Beatrice wielded a great deal of power, she could not prevent her brother from sending Lydia away. He alone held the right to decide his daughter's future. Beatrice had considered herself fortunate to have convinced her brother to allow Lydia to attend Willowglen's Fair with her.

Beatrice, Hilary, Marian—even Lydia—knew the Earl's motives in his search for a husband for Lydia.   He sought someone of high rank and title to increase his own status and prestige.   No pact had been made yet because Lord Wellington had not decided on the alliance that suited his needs.

Although Lydia did not want to marry anyone, she was helpless against her father's wishes. She and her father had argued about it more than once and, each time, Marian had intervened to smooth over their ill will.   By arguing that the Earl's young daughter would make a far better wife if she were given more time to mature, the older woman had bought Lydia some time. However, her father would have to make a decision soon, or he might lose his opportunity altogether. Toward that end, the Earl was out of the country again and could not interfere with Lydia's latest plan.

Before going to Catherine's that evening, Marian had consulted with Beatrice about the situation. The Duchess had agreed. They would not interfere with Lydia's plan as long as Marian approved of Catherine.   Now, Marian made another decision. She would take Beatrice up on her offer to go back to Briarcrest with them. The decision was bittersweet for Marian. Lydia was no longer a child and Marian felt that she had to allow her a life of her own—even if her father would not give her the same consideration.

FOR THE REMAINING evenings of the fair, Lydia came to Catherine's alone. Sarah joined them for supper but preferred to retire early, leaving Catherine and Lydia alone after the meal.

On the night the fair closed, Beatrice and Hilary invited Catherine and Sarah to dine with them at the Inn. Although Marian had made Sarah a little more comfortable in her presence, and it had become easier and easier for the young girl to talk to Lydia, she still could not overcome her nervousness in the presence of the Ladies of Briarcrest. She shook whenever she thought of the evening to come.

During a pause in activity on the last afternoon of the fair, Catherine questioned her. "Is something troubling you, Sarah? You are not yourself today."

"No, Mistress Catherine," Sarah squeaked.

Catherine decided that she could not continue to allow Sarah to be in such agony. "Are you troubled about dinner this evening, Sarah?"

Sarah's anxiety spilled out like liquid from a tipped bottle. "Oh, Mistress, I wish I did not have to go. All those fine Ladies make my tongue feel as if it is upside-down in my mouth. If they ask me a question, I shall die from fright before I think of an answer."

Catherine looked into the girl's eyes. Sarah knew the workings of Hawkins and Hawkins almost as well as Catherine did herself. When Catherine's father could no longer carry on in the shop, Catherine took Sarah in as her apprentice. This had allowed Catherine time to tend to her father's needs in his illness and took some of the burden from Sarah's uncle and his family. It took only a short time for Catherine to realize that the young girl was extremely bright, and determined that she would not let her ability go to waste.

Catherine taught Sarah to read and write a little and she familiarized her with a variety of duties. Eventually, Sarah began assisting customers. She managed very well. She had no reason to feel so nervous in the presence of the Ladies of Briarcrest, but Catherine knew she would not be able to convince Sarah of that. Perhaps it was better to give her a way out of this dinner than to allow her continue in her torment.

"I am sure that the Duchess does not want to cause you anxiety over her invitation, Sarah. She seems a kind and understanding woman. I do not think she will be offended if I ask her to excuse you tonight."

Sarah breathed an audible sigh of relief. "I would be so grateful if you would do that, Mistress Catherine. I would rather stay in the shop and begin putting things away after the fair."

"You may stay, Sarah, but you have worked hard enough all week. Take the evening for yourself. We'll put things away together in the morning."

Sarah smiled and whispered, "Yes, Mistress Catherine."

Tomorrow, Catherine mused, there would be another pair of hands in the shop—Lydia's.

The end of Willowglen Fair

CATHERINE DINED AT the Grouse and Pheasant with the women of Briarcrest. Lively topics during dinner spanned politics in the Court of London to styles of dress for women. They talked of other fairs in other towns, of commerce and travel. Catherine felt a sense of pride to be among women who conversed with such intelligence, wit and insight.

At the end of the evening, Lydia and Catherine decided that Lydia would begin the following day at the shop. The day after the fair closed was always something of a holiday for the shop owners; it gave them time to reorganize, take stock, and rest a little. Catherine could not bear the thought of a day without seeing Lydia, however, so she told Lydia that she was most welcome at the shop.

"Sarah and I planned to put the shop in order. It will be a good time for you to study the wares on the shelves and ask any questions you may have."

Lydia had responded that she would be there first thing in the morning to begin her course of studies.

Catherine then thanked the Duchess for her hospitality, and for understanding about Sarah's absence, and she bid the group goodnight. Making her way down Market Street, Catherine found that she looked forward to the next day eagerly—largely because of Lydia.

THE NEXT MORNING, Lydia's aunt and her company departed early for Briarcrest. At Marian's insistence, Lydia promised to join them before the feast of St. Nicholas. If she delayed any longer than that, the journey might not be possible. The roads deteriorated quickly once the rains began, making carriage travel difficult at best.

Marian did not want Lydia to miss the Christmastide feast at Briarcrest. The two had often spent the winter months there, for the Lord of Greencastle did not abide much keeping of the Yule season. He considered it a frivolous waste of his treasury.

Lydia's Aunt Beatrice, on the other hand, believed the season was meant to be enjoyed with as much gladness and feasting as possible. This was a prime example of why the Earl of Greencastle had little use for his sister. He considered her nothing but a foolish woman, and much too unconventional for his liking. He tolerated his daughter's relationship with Beatrice for only one reason: She had more holdings, inherited from her dead husband, and more friends in higher places, cultivated on her own, than he did. In short, his sister was far more powerful than he was. Yet, in spite of her wealth and authority, Beatrice insisted on mingling with commoners and peasantry. He did not understand the woman. She had friends in the Court of London, which was more than he could boast, but she did not seem to understand her place. There were times when he worried that Lydia would be found lacking by a potential husband if they got wind of Beatrice's influence. Still, she was family, and she did dote on the child.

Christmastide was special at Briarcrest. Lydia, Marian insisted, must be there. Lydia agreed reluctantly. At least she had the coming weeks with Catherine. She wondered what they would bring.

Chapter
Five

Lessons at the Spice Shoppe
Willowglen Township

LYDIA AND CATHERINE settled quickly into a routine. For the first few days, Lydia arrived each morning to find Catherine in the kitchen enjoying her first cup of mint tea. Before the week was out, however, Lydia arrived before Catherine came downstairs. Sarah would let her into the shop and she would go directly to the kitchen to prepare Catherine's tea.

When Catherine came to the kitchen each morning, she protested Lydia's ministrations. The shopkeeper was uncomfortable with this attention, imagining the servants Lydia had at Greencastle and Briarcrest.

For her part, Lydia ignored Catherine's protests, which went on for days. Gradually, though, Catherine came to look forward to finding Lydia in her kitchen at the start of each day and she no longer objected to her performing this morning ritual. The women would sit talking about the day's duties over their cups of tea before they joined Sarah in the shop.

Lydia flourished in Willowglen. For, although she loved her time spent at Briarcrest, there was something much more enlivening about her life with Catherine. She was happier than she had ever been.

The autumn harvest over, Lydia learned that there was still much to do. Herbs needed to be tended as they dried. Winter plants had to be started and patches of the garden had to be cleared and prepared for the next spring's planting. Lydia became comfortable amid the herbs and soil and burlap bags. She learned more about spices than she had ever imagined possible through Catherine's exotic tales of the cultures that yielded them. Catherine wove stories about her father's dealings with people from all over the world, people with whom Catherine still dealt. Her trade was so well established that new spices found their way to her shop with little need for her to travel as her father had once done. Lydia listened to Catherine's stories, spellbound. It never occurred to her that anything Catherine had to say would have held her attention for hours.

ONE DAY, LYDIA asked about Catherine's parents.

The shopkeeper offered, "When my father and mother married, they had a small plot of land at the edge of town where they planted an herb garden and began to sell their wares. They worked hard and did well. My father began to travel to acquire other goods to sell. By the time I was born, they had this shop. My father put the sign up outside when they opened for business. From the first, he had wanted my mother to be his partner, not merely an assistant. When I think of it now, it was a remarkable gesture to include a woman as a business associate. He told me later that the people of Willowglen thought little of it, however, since he already had a reputation among his fellow guild members as being somewhat unusual. Little did anyone know he was paving my way into the Spice Vendor's Guild at the time.

"I'm sure you have noticed that the shop sign is quite extraordinary, Lydia. He insisted that it bear script. I remembered him telling me more than once, 'A day is coming when every commoner will be able to read. People will not be kept in the dark forever. Those who are most ignorant will rise up and demand to be delivered from their illiteracy, for in knowledge there is liberty.'

"My father was an educated man," Catherine continued. "More than that, he believed that everyone was entitled to an education. He taught my mother to read, and he saw to my schooling as well. My time at Wooster Abbey was happy, although I missed my parents when I was away. I spent summer and winter months of the year with the nuns and I came home during the busiest seasons to help with planting and harvesting.

"In the spring of my twelfth year, my mother died. I did not return home for the spring planting that year because there was none. My father closed up the shop and traveled for long periods, trying to avoid the pain of losing my mother.

"I, too, felt her loss, of course. However, there were marked differences in our grieving. I had found a mentor in one of the nuns, Lady Anne. My father had no such confidant. It took him much longer to overcome his grief. One thing he could not bring himself to do was to change the sign. To him, it would have been as if he were banishing the spirit of his beloved wife.

"After my mother's death, Lady Anne and I spent many long hours talking of my sorrow. In addition to missing my mother, I felt helpless at seeing my father so aggrieved. To help me overcome my sadness, Lady Anne built upon my knowledge of herbs by instructing me in their use for healing. The medicinal use of plants and herbs fascinated me, and it gave me a positive focus at a difficult time in my life. I discovered, during those days, that I have a gift to recognize illnesses and insight to know how to heal them. I recalled many treasured moments we Hawkins women spent together when I was home discussing such things.

"Often I would read aloud to my mother as she worked. My father bought books during his travels. Sometimes, the reading evoked lively discussions between us. We did not always see eye to eye, but I delighted in these debates. I came to realize that my mother did, too. She always tried to encourage me and listened to what I had to say."

Lydia sat engrossed in Catherine's narrative.

"For two years after my mother died, I watched my father grow tired and bent by his grief. I only saw him briefly during that time, but I recognized that his sorrow was consuming him. Finally, I decided to take matters into my own hands. I informed him that I was about to begin a formal apprenticeship with him in his business. He would need to stay home, reopen the shop, and work closely with me.

"At first, he would not hear of it. Then gradually, he became accustomed to the idea. By the time the day arrived for me to bid the Abbey good-bye, he seemed delighted with the prospect and was a great deal less disheartened.

"When I left the Abbey, Lady Anne gave me a gift — a small medicinal bag — but over the years I have found that she gave me so much more. For she gave me the skill to use the bag's contents to heal many afflictions that would have consumed a number of people in this town.

"On my fifteenth birthday, my father announced that the sign above the shop door no longer signified his partnership with my mother. It now meant Master and the young Mistress Hawkins. I rejoiced in the announcement, for I knew it meant more than a full partnership with my father. It meant that he had finally accepted my mother's death and let go of his grief."

Almost wondering out loud, Lydia inquired, "Did your father not want you to marry?"

"He talked about finding a husband for me," Catherine replied. "But I told him I had no desire to marry each time he brought it up. We discussed whether or not he would be failing in his duty as a father if he did not find a suitable mate for me. My reply usually soothed his concern because I maintained that a father's duty was to provide for a daughter after his death. By providing me with a thriving enterprise, he was more than fulfilling his fatherly duty to care for me. After a time, we no longer discussed it. I think father grew accustomed to our lives together and he could not imagine them to be any different. It pleased him that I had found my place among the townspeople, too."

"And your father—he has not been gone for more than a cycle of seasons, has he?"

"Two summers ago, his health started to decline. He was ill for quite a while and in the end, he faded in and out of wakefulness. During one of his better days, he told me of his confidence in me. He told me that he knew I had the respect of many of the good people of Willowglen and that I would continue after he was gone. He said that he could give up his life with no concern of failing in his fatherly duty. He died at summer's end a year ago."

Both women worked quietly for awhile. Then Lydia asked, "Why did you tell him that you did not wish to marry?"

Catherine gave Lydia a curious look, then smiled her crooked smile, one side of her mouth turning up more than the other. "I am not sure I can answer you," she replied. "I only know I do not wish it. I feel no desire to be bound to a man. I see how women in this town, and in other places I visited with my father, do not have the same alliance with their husbands as my mother did with her spouse. My father was a rare find. I suppose that if I ever found someone like him, someone who believed in equal partnership, perhaps then I might change my mind. Still, in reality, I do not think I would want a husband."

"I feel many of these same things, Catherine, but I haven't been so fortunate to have a father like yours. I fear that I will never find such understanding or acceptance from him. His reasons for finding me a husband are not as noble as your father's were. He sees my pairing as a means to amass more wealth and status for himself and he wouldn't give up his opportunity. It distresses me, but I am at a loss over what to do. Being here with you these weeks, though, makes me more determined not to allow him to betroth me for his own gain when I want no betrothal at all."

Then, looking into Catherine's eyes, she added shyly, "Except, perhaps, that which I may choose for myself."

There was a long pause. The air hung heavy in the room. Each woman sat alone with her thoughts.

Catherine wondered at the strength of her own desire to fulfill Lydia's dream of finding a partner in life. Yet somehow, Catherine couldn't imagine the young Lady finding contentment with a man.

Lydia struggled with the fantasy that Catherine was a rich and powerful nobleman to whom her father would happily betroth her. Frustrated at realizing that her thoughts were merely a daydream, Lydia shook them off, asking another question. "Was it difficult for you to be accepted as a member of the merchant's Guild?"

"Yes, my father and Edward, the silversmith, fought hard for my admittance."

"Are there no other women who are members of the Guilds in Willowglen?"

"Yes, but everyone is married with a husband in the Guild, or older and widowed. The Guild Masters found it difficult to accept a young, unmarried woman likely to become the sole proprietor of Hawkins and Hawkins one day as a member of their order."

"How did you win them over? Although I imagine your considerable charm could do it."

The crooked smile appeared again. "Charm, indeed," Catherine scoffed. "It was only after Edward's son was on his deathbed with fever and I was able to help him by my ministrations with herb teas and baths that Edward stepped in and spoke on my behalf. My father was very influential in the Guild, but he still spoke as a father in the Guild Masters' eyes. Only when Edward finally joined with him did the Masters allow them to present my skills. Once I was accepted, though, I was able to prove my own merit. No one ever spoke again about whether or not it should be so. I pay my Guild fees and continue in the manner of my parents, and everyone seems to accept it."

Lydia offered, "You have gained more than acceptance into the Guild, Catherine. I have heard some of those men when they come into the shop. They seek your counsel. They hold your opinions in very high esteem."

Catherine brushed Lydia's accolades aside. "Oh, they have learned to appreciate my views as an honest, hardworking Guild member, but you give me more credit than is my due, Lady Lydia."

Catherine's formality brought a smile to Lydia's face. She had come to realize that the shopkeeper now only used her title when she was embarrassed or uncomfortable with a conversation.

The women held each others' gaze and Lydia thought, *I, too, bestow admiration, and more than mere admiration, so much is my fondness for you. Dare I call it love? Yes, I dare.*

The conversation ended there. Each woman spent time deep in thought as they cleaned up the shop after the day's work.

Their time together passed with only small interruptions. People came into the shop to make purchases. Occasionally, Catherine went to the home of one or another of the townspeople to bring some fabric for them to examine or certain spices for them to buy.

When Catherine was consulted with regard to ailments and illnesses, she skillfully recommended remedies of leaf or root, this plant or that or several together. If someone could not obtain what she recommended and she had a supply of it, she gave it freely, never taking payment for the medicinal plants and counsel she dispensed.

As the days flowed one into the next, the two women shared more and more of themselves with one another. Lydia's love for her aunt was apparent as she revealed treasured memories of time spent at Briarcrest. She told Catherine the story of her aunt's betrothal to the young Duke of Briarcrest—as much as Lydia knew of it. To Catherine, it seemed a curious tale.

Beatrice had been given in marriage by her father, Lydia's grandfather, at the age of fifteen. Lydia did not know of her aunt's feelings toward the Duke. She said Beatrice had never discussed them. On those rare occasions when she spoke of the Duke at all, she was always gracious. Some time after their wedding, the young Duke went off to fight for Henry VI in France, leaving his bride to oversee his house and lands.

The Duke had been taken up with endeavors for political and personal gain much as Lydia's own father had been over the years. However, the Duke was quick to realize that Beatrice was gifted in the management of Briarcrest. He saw to it that she was well supported in her efforts. When he did not return from his final campaign, it mattered little to those who pledged their steadfastness to Briarcrest. Beatrice, a fair administrator, ruled wisely and gained the respect and allegiance of those in the service of Briarcrest quickly. The Duke had been gone so often, and for so long, that to them, loyalty belonged to Beatrice alone upon his death.

During Beatrice's husband's last effort in France, a friend of the Duke brought his daughter to Briarcrest, to stay with Beatrice while he went off to join her husband. Hilary and Beatrice had met once before only briefly. At first, Beatrice considered her hospitality to the young Hilary to be merely for the sake of her husband's friendship with Hilary's father. As time passed, and the two women became better acquainted, their friendship deepened.

One year later, the Duke and Hilary's father were killed in the same battle. When word of their loss reached Briarcrest, the two women decided that Hilary would stay on. For Hilary, one year Beatrice's junior, had become her trusted associate.

LIFE AT THE spice shop went on in its usual, uneventful way until a week before the feast of All Saints. Then Lydia began talking about going to the Hallow's Eve observance in the town square. Catherine almost dropped the kettle she was holding when first Lydia voiced the idea. She didn't want Lydia to go. She knew it was dangerous, and the whole idea of the gathering angered her. The passing of days did nothing to change her mind.

She could not explain her reaction to her friend beyond saying she'd been once before. During childhood, Catherine had feared the gathering. When she was old enough to realize what was really going on, she became infuriated. People would be admonished to live good lives, then they would do as they pleased anyway; fueled by drink and inspired by the "demons" they had just seen, they would do things they might otherwise not.

The fire in Catherine's eyes stilled Lydia's tongue for awhile, but the young noblewoman still intended to go to the square. As the day drew near, Catherine tried to wear away at the other's resolve, but the lure of the unknown was too strong to be ignored.

Catherine's hand shook, and she bit her lip as she fastened her cloak. She closed the shop door and followed Lydia out to the street. Dusk had fallen. All Hallow's Eve had begun.

Chapter
Six

All Hallow's Eve
October 31, 1458
Willowglen Township Square

A PENETRATING DAMPNESS hung in the air as the two women hurried down Market Street. Their foggy breath mimicked the clouds hiding the stars in the night sky. Catherine shivered and wrapped her heavy cloak around her tighter in an effort to seal out the biting cold—and her feeling of apprehension.

Earlier, the persistent rain had given her the hope that Lydia wouldn't want to go to the square. However, just before dark, the storm passed and Lydia announced that she still intended to go. Refusing to let her venture out alone, Catherine now reluctantly stepped along the cobblestone path at Lydia's side.

A faint pinpoint of light from a single lamp at the center of the square drew them. They joined the other gathering townspeople. The subdued crowd murmured in low tones. Catherine dreaded what would happen next. The apparitions— spectral saints and netherworld devils—would come as if unbidden. More than any other night Catherine could remember, she wanted to be at home in front of a warm fire— preferably with Lydia beside her.

"Please, Mother, please, please *let me go to the square tomorrow night," the little girl whined.*

"Your father and I do not think it a place for a child. We are not even sure it is a place for adults. No, we will not permit it. You will not go."

The little girl skulked away, but later that evening, she climbed onto her father's lap and nuzzled his bearded cheek, fully aware that she was up to no good. She wanted to go to the celebration in the square and she knew her father could seldom resist her.

"Father, I especially want to go to All Hallow's Eve tomorrow night. Will you take me?"

"Why would you want to go to that spectacle, child? It is the Church's miserable way of keeping the rabble under their thumb by scaring them half to death. We have no need of that sort of trickery." His voice was firm, but very quiet; he'd explained to her before that his views would not be accepted in the town.

"I want to see, father." She leaned so close to his face that she felt the warmth of his skin. She whispered, *"James said there are devils — "*

"There are no devils — I told you already. If there are devils in Willowglen, they certainly do not show themselves so blatantly that we can recognize them in the street. Demons are much more discreet. Sometimes, they even come disguised as men of the Church." Even with their heads close together, Catherine had barely been able to hear that last remark.

Still, the little girl persisted. Finally, her father reluctantly gave in.

He took the girl to the square the next evening, held her hand as they waited for the costumed creatures to arrive. What followed unsettled the child and gave her nightmares for weeks afterward. Her parents vowed never to allow her to attend the event again, but they had nothing to fear. Young Catherine never asked.

Catherine still failed to see the value in such fiendish displays; why spend so much energy in telling tales? She would rather try to help people, to ease their pain, cure their illness. Stave off death. The nuns at Wooster Abbey had told her that faith involved a relationship with a good and loving God. Catherine could only conclude that a spiritual life and religion seldom had the same goals. As an adult, she rejected the Church almost entirely, refusing to participate in the town's expressions of piety. The clergy made their disapproval of her attitude be known, but the townspeople accepted her rebelliousness as part of the Hawkins family idiosyncrasy.

As people arrived in the square with their children in tow, Catherine cringed and wondered how many weeks and months of horrifying nightmares would follow for these little ones. As they stood in Willowglen's square, waiting, Catherine tried once again to shake the anxiety that permeated her being.

Lydia, for her part, had found Catherine's bitterness difficult to understand. She had been deeply disappointed when Catherine so emphatically refused to participate at first. Although Catherine had tried to make Lydia understand that her concern was for the nightmares that would be imposed on the children, the young noblewoman couldn't understand. Lydia simply wanted to experience something that had a forbidden quality to it; she didn't understand Catherine's vehemence. To her, it was a party, nothing more.

Catherine had not been able to bear the silence and tension their disagreement caused, so finally, she gave in and went along. It took all her will to keep her from running back to the shop. She knew that if she left, Lydia would never follow. So she stayed, feeling overwhelmingly protective, her feelings perplexing her.

THE CROWD DREW in a collective breath as the lamp in the square was extinguished. Darkness seemed to swallow them up. The first devilish creatures approached, announcing their arrival with screams and laments. When they reached the crowds, they clawed at them. They grabbed at their clothes and poked them with what felt like sharp, fleshless fingers.

Catherine wanted to shut out the howls by covering her ears. She wanted to slap away the unwelcomed contact. Instead, she stood stoically by Lydia's side and wondered if her companion was disturbed at all by the display.

If she could only see Lydia's face she would know if the other woman was frightened or not — but in the inky darkness of the moonless night, Catherine could see nothing. As the agonizing shrieks tore through the blackness, Catherine set her jaw firmly against the night. Her refusal to leave Lydia's side became her armor against the awfulness of her surroundings and the fury the ritual provoked.

After an eternity, the ghoulish howling turned to moaning and whimpers. Relief washed over Catherine. She let out a breath.

Flickering lantern light gradually illuminated the square. Saints and martyrs dressed in white garments and the garb of monks and nuns drove the evil beings to cringe and moan in a huddled mass away from the crowd. A welcome quiet descended on the square. Then the bellowing voice of the presiding clergyman rang out, announcing that good had, once again, triumphed over evil. The citizens of Willowglen were to pattern their lives after these holy men. Catherine wondered how he had not noticed that some of the "saints" portrayed were women.

The speech over, saint and devil alike formed a procession around the gathering. Catherine was grateful that the ghoulish figures were more ordered and well-behaved in the presence of their holy counterparts. They no longer seemed so dreadful bathed in the soft glow of lantern light.

The villains and the virtuous led the townspeople toward the Governor's Hall for a service in the chapel. The pious among them followed. The less devout took the opportunity to go in other directions. Some headed for home; others made for the local tavern, despite the cleric's earlier admonition.

The monotone bell in the chapel tower clanged its metallic prayer for the souls of the dead. Catherine and Lydia waited until the end of the procession before winding their way behind the crowd.

When the women reached Market Street, they broke from the line. At Catherine's insistence, Lydia would not return to the Grouse and Pheasant. Instead, she would stay the night with Catherine rather than be out on the street alone. Lydia had agreed, not wanting to risk another quarrel.

They moved quickly through the darkened street with only the light shining through a few scattered windows reflecting off the still-damp cobblestones. Catherine and Lydia engaged in an animated debate about the Hallow's Eve event. They were halfway to Catherine's shop when a hooded figure leaped into their path, fingers curled in their faces menacingly, growling and threatening to do them harm.

At first they thought the person had merely meant to play a Hallow's Eve prank on them, but they soon realized that they were wrong. The monster grabbed Lydia with one hideous hand and stifled her cry with the other, then quickly dragged her into the alley. Catherine frantically looked around for help. The street was deserted. The quiet was broken only by the pounding of Catherine's own heart in her ears and the din of the chapel bell driving itself like a wedge into her consciousness.

Anger quickly replaced Catherine's alarm. She scrambled back toward the alley, wondering how she would save Lydia. Running down the narrow passageway, Catherine tripped over an old, discarded ax handle. As she regained her balance, she grabbed the makeshift club.

The figures were barely visible in the dark, yet Catherine somehow knew where Lydia was. She charged at the dim, ghoulish figure just as it was lifting Lydia's skirts above her shoulders. Catherine wrapped her hands tightly around the handle and raised it over her head. Taking a deep breath, she slammed the bludgeon down with all her might as she exhaled, aiming for a spot high on the attacker's back.

The monster gasped and released Lydia. Entangled in leggings twisted down around its knees, the fiend reeled, then

fell to the ground and scrambled, crawling off into the darkness.
Catherine could hear gasping and choking.

Lydia stood unable to move. Catherine pushed her out of
the alley with one hard shove. Out on the street, she grasped
Lydia's hand as tightly as she could and broke into a run, pulling
the young woman along with her.

When she reached the shop, Catherine flung open the door
and hurled Lydia inside. She yanked the door shut and pulled
the bolt across with a mighty heave. Plopping onto a workbench
seat, Catherine plunged her face into her hands and let out an
agonized sob.

Lydia staggered to Catherine and fell beside her on the
bench. Tears flowing, they held one another until Catherine
finally felt the fear and anger drain from her like poison from a
wound.

No longer lost to her panic, she felt awkward holding Lydia.
How many times had she dreamed of embracing Lydia? But her
fantasy had contained nothing of this type of distress. This was
not how she'd hoped to find her arms around the other woman.
Self-conscious, and worried that the gesture might be
misinterpreted, Catherine pulled away. "Are you all right,
Lydia?"

"Yes."

"Did he...hurt you?"

"Only my arm, when he pulled me into the alley. I am sure
it will be fine, Catherine."

Anger welled up again. Catherine spit out her words. "This
is not a celebration. It is a mad, evil event. A poor excuse to
subject people to things that should never occur. 'Good
overcoming evil,' indeed."

Catherine's rage ballooned until it overwhelmed her. She
clenched her fists on the table in front of her as she envisioned
herself running down the street, searching for the devil that had
tried to violate Lydia. In her mind's eye, she carried a sharp,
pointed stake in her hand. When she found the demon, she
called to it. It turned and met her with a hideous smile. Without
hesitation, she drove the implement through the villain's chest
with all her strength and almost felt the flesh and bone giving
way under her hand as she did.

Horror quickly replaced satisfaction when she realized that
anger had made her envisage killing another human being. She
was a healer, committed to preserving life, not a murderer. She
wailed.

Lydia put a tentative hand on Catherine's arm.

When Catherine's tears finally stopped, Lydia conceded,

"Perhaps Hallow's Eve in the square is not such a good idea. I should have listened to you. I'm sorry."

With trembling hands, Catherine lit the lamp on the table. Lydia's tear-stained face appeared in the soft glow. Catherine's heart ached at the sight. She said, "I should have been more insistent about not going. Are you sure you are all right?"

"Yes, please believe me, Catherine. I am unharmed."

"I could not live with myself if you had gotten hurt—or worse, Lydia."

Lydia stared at her hands without speaking for a moment. When she looked back at Catherine, she spoke almost inaudibly. "Thank you."

"Please, do not thank me—"

"But you rescued me."

"I allowed you to be put in danger."

"Catherine, it was not your fault. I insisted on going. I should have listened to you." She tried to catch Catherine's eye. "Forgive me?"

Now Catherine turned away. *I just realized that I could kill someone rather than let anything happen to you, such is my great care for you. I have never felt like this about anyone before in my entire life. How can I tell you my real feelings?*

Lydia repeated, tentatively, "Catherine, will you forgive me?"

Catherine faced her. "Oh, Lydia, of course I forgive you." *My love.*

She turned away again, embarrassed by her thought, and the two women sat together in the subtle glow of the small lamp for a long time without speaking. Finally, Catherine rose from her seat. "Would you like some tea before we go to bed, Lydia? I left the kettle over the fire."

"Thank you, Catherine, but suddenly I am very tired. I would like to go to bed, if you don't mind. Have some tea yourself, though, if you would like."

"No, I am quite tired myself. Come with me upstairs. I shall show you where you will sleep."

Lydia's haggard face revealed the toll the ordeal had taken on her. Catherine fought the urge to snatch her into her arms. She picked up the lamp and headed for the stairway. Lydia pulled herself up slowly and followed.

Upstairs, Catherine led Lydia through the main room that had been Catherine's parents' bedroom before it was her own. Next to it was a small, enclosed area that had served as Catherine's childhood bedchamber. She lifted the heavy tapestry that hung in the doorway and motioned Lydia into the tiny room.

Catherine found it difficult to leave. She stood frozen, unable to move, waiting for her desire to take Lydia in her arms to pass. "I shall leave you to your rest, Lydia. Goodnight. Sleep well."

"Thank you, Catherine," Lydia sighed.

In the next room, Catherine undressed down to her undergarments, then went back to the tapestried doorway and listened for movement. There was none. She moved the curtain aside. The lamp sat on a stool beside the bed, still lit. Lydia was sound asleep on the cot, fully clothed. Catherine let the curtain drop.

Even in the darkness, Catherine found the carved chest at the foot of her bed with ease. Years before, her father had brought it back with him from the Far East. It was made from the smooth, warm wood of the camphor tree. A unique pastoral scene had been carved into the lid. Catherine could not make out the details of the design in the moonless night, but she felt the grooves under her fingers as she lifted the lid.

Stories of a race with smooth, round faces whose eyes looked different from her own passed through her mind. Her father had told her of meeting people who stood ankle-deep in water to harvest their grain from wet fields.

Catherine found what she was looking for — a thickly woven covering. She took it back to the small room and laid it gently over Lydia. The young woman stirred only slightly but did not awaken. The ache in Catherine's heart surfaced as she watched Lydia's face in the flickering lamplight. On the wall behind her, as if waiting for her to take action, Catherine's shadow swayed back and forth with the flickering light.

With great effort, Catherine finally tore herself away, taking the lamp with her. Back in her own bedchamber, she blew out the flame and climbed into bed. Fatigue overcame her quickly and she slept fitfully, chasing demons all night long.

Chapter
Seven

The Feast of All Saints
November 1, 1458
Willowglen Township

THE SKY WAS still dark when Catherine woke. She dressed quickly in the dim lamplight and went to check on Lydia. Catherine lingered in the doorway watching her guest sleep before letting the tapestry curtain fall gently across the opening.

Downstairs in the kitchen, Catherine stirred the kitchen fire awake and added more wood to the embers. She watched the logs ignite. The warmth slowly spread into the room. She busied herself by rearranging some pots until the water in the kettle boiled then made herself some tea. Taking her steaming cup to the window that overlooked the garden, she watched the day dawn through a fine mist.

WHEN LYDIA FINALLY came into the kitchen, she surprised Catherine out of a daydream.

"Oh! Lydia, how are you feeling?"

"I am rested, Catherine, thank you. I slept very soundly. I was very tired, indeed, after last evening."

"Yes, I think we were both worn out after last night." Finding it painful to think of the experience of the prior evening, Catherine changed the subject. "Would you like something to eat, Lydia?"

"I shall join you for tea. Master Elbert told me there is to be a celebration at the Grouse and Pheasant this morning. I told him that I would be there and that I would ask you to be my guest. Will you come?"

Catherine replied shyly, "Yes, Lydia. I shall come, if it pleases you."

"It pleases me. Very much."

At the Grouse & Pheasant Inn

THE ROOM WAS abuzz with lively conversation as Catherine entered the Grouse and Pheasant Inn. Several of Willowglen's merchants, as well as many of the town's officials, were already partaking of the harvest abundance served by Master Elbert, the Inn's proprietor. Catherine recognized James Hall, a merchant trader who had been well acquainted with Catherine's father, among the visitors. The elder Hawkins and Hall had traveled together on many trade journeys, but it had been more than three years since James Hall had come through Willowglen.

He called to Catherine, "Mistress, I am so glad to see you. Please, come. Sit here." He gestured opposite him with a large roasted drumstick.

Catherine sat on one of two empty stools. "Thank you, Master Hall," she said. "How have you been keeping?"

"I have been well, Mistress; and I must say that you look as if you are doing quite well, too."

Catherine smiled and nodded shyly.

When Lydia came over and took the empty seat, Catherine introduced her to Master Hall. He gallantly rose from his seat in greeting, all the while keeping his grip on the poultry leg.

Catherine said, "Your travels must have kept you quite busy, sir. We have not seen you for quite some time in Willowglen."

"Too long, Mistress." He turned to Lydia and added, "Why, the last time I was here, Mistress Catherine had just been accepted into the Guild. Her father and I embarked on a trading excursion together soon after."

"Yes, and that trip proved most successful for Hawkins and Hawkins, Master Hall."

"And you, Mistress, no doubt proved yourself very capable of running the little shop on Market Street in your father's absence?"

"I suppose I did, sir. Yes," Catherine answered.

"I must apologize for waiting so long to return to Willowglen. The news of your father's death saddened me, but circumstances did not permit me to make my way here until now. I had planned to stop by your shop later to pay my respects. But now, it is my good fortune to have you dine with me." He raised his tankard in Catherine's direction and added, "To the memory of your father, Mistress — and to you, fine lady."

Catherine raised her tankard, smiling uncomfortably.

A murmur of ascent rattled around the room and everyone

stared in Catherine's direction as she turned crimson from her neck to her cheeks. She looked down at her lap.

In fact, James Hall admired Catherine. He had once entertained the thought of asking for her hand in marriage, but her father had discouraged him. He knew both James Hall and his daughter well enough to know that it would not have been a marriage made in heaven. Master Hall had long since dismissed the idea of taking Catherine as his wife, but he still held warm feelings for her.

The conversation then turned to local events. One of the other town merchants launched into the strange tale of a peculiar little man seen limping out of town that morning. The authorities had stopped and questioned him, judging him to be someone of doubtful reputation, but he only cried out that he wanted to be as far from Willowglen as he could be, as fast as possible.

"He had a long, bloody gash across the back of his tunic. When the magistrate questioned him about his injuries, he babbled like a madman and refused all offers of help. Since he didn't seem much of a threat to anyone in his condition, he allowed him to be on his way. No one seems to know who he was or what his business here might have been. His injury is a mystery, too, but the magistrate is convinced he was up to no good. I, for one, would like to meet the man that imposed the likes of his injury on him, though. I can tell you that."

Everyone laughed — except Catherine and Lydia. They only exchanged knowing looks. Neither of them said anything, and conversation among smaller groups along the table started up as people speculated as to who the mysterious man could have been.

Lydia tried to shrug off her unpleasant feeling about the previous evening by leaning toward Catherine and saying in a low tone, "I do have something to tell you. When we came into the Inn earlier, Master Elbert gave me a note from Briarcrest. My aunt is sending transport for me."

Catherine's heart sank. She had known it would happen. Now, she was more surprised by her own reaction than she was by the news itself. Her voice sounded like a helpless kitten when she responded, "I see."

Catherine's reaction magnified Lydia's own feelings of concern and confusion. She had given her promise to Marian to return to Briarcrest before the roads became unfit for carriage travel, yet she did not want to leave. "You knew I would have to go," she said. "I promised Marian. I cannot go back on my pledge."

"I know. I just did not realize how quickly this time would pass." Catherine could barely cope with the agony she felt. It was difficult to get the words out. "When will you leave?"

With a voice full of pain, Lydia replied, "On the feast of St. Andrew. If I do not leave then, I may not be able to get back to Briarcrest once the winter storms start."

"Yes, that's true. I only wish..." Catherine looked into the grey-green eyes, remembering the first time they had enraptured her. It seemed so long ago, yet somehow, like only yesterday. Conflicting emotions flooded in, leaving her disoriented. In her thoughts, she heard herself cry out: *Do not leave me, Lydia.*

Panic set in. She could not allow the words to slip from her mind to her lips. She could not give voice to her feelings. Catherine pushed her stool back with a loud scrape. All heads turned toward the sound. "Forgive me," she blurted out. "I must leave."

She turned and bolted for the door.

Market Street

OUTSIDE, THE LIGHT rain had turned to a downpour. The dark sky lit up for an instant. A loud clap of thunder followed.

Lydia ran into the street after Catherine shouting, "Catherine, wait!"

When she caught up with Catherine a few doors from the spice shop, she spoke her name again. Catherine turned. She looked tired and drawn. She backed away, trying to keep Lydia from seeing the state she was in. Lydia came close in an effort to be heard above the storm. Tiny rivulets of water streamed down Catherine's hair onto her face, meeting and mingling with tears on her cheeks. She stared past Lydia.

"Catherine, please, let's get out of this rain."

Catherine dared not move. She battled for control of her emotions and the thoughts she dared not speak.

She thought, *How can you leave me? I have fallen in love with you.*

She said, "How can you leave? We have only scratched the surface of what there is to learn about herbs."

Lydia struggled to keep from voicing her own conflict. She loved Marian like a mother, but her feelings for Catherine were compelling—oh, so much more compelling—yet she had given her word. After a long silence, Lydia said, "I find that I am torn, but I must keep my promise to Marian—and my aunt is expecting me."

She thought, *Oh, Catherine, I do not want to leave you — ever — but I need to hear you say that you want me to stay for more than the study of herbs. Please, Catherine, ask me to stay because you need me — because you want me.*

There was an edge in Catherine's voice when she replied, "Yes. Well, you *must* keep your promise."

Lydia did not conceal her own disappointment, but Catherine did not notice. She had looked away — in the direction of the sound of running feet squishing water between leather and cobblestones. The feet belonged to James Hall, who stopped when he reached them. Rain streamed from the wide brim of his hat in several places as he spoke. "Ladies, do you require assistance?"

Lydia replied, "No, sir, we were just so involved in our conversation that we took no notice of the rain."

"No notice?" Hall asked incredulously. "That must be quite a subject, but I suggest you continue it indoors — " He raised his voice over a deep roll of thunder. " — it does not look as if this storm will stop any time soon."

"Quite right, Master Hall," Lydia acknowledged. Turning to Catherine, she said, "Mistress Catherine, let's continue this at your shop, shall we?"

Unsure of her own voice, Catherine merely nodded. Lydia bid Master Hall a good day.

James Hall, noting a look of sadness on Catherine's face, said no more. He bowed to the ladies and broke into a run down the street again.

The two women headed for the shop in silence. Their wet dresses weighed upon them as heavily as their thoughts as they walked.

The Shoppe of Hawkins & Hawkins

CATHERINE SENT LYDIA into Sarah's room to remove her wet clothes. The house was still warm, but Catherine went into the kitchen and added a log to the fire. Then she plodded up the steps to her own bedchamber. In her room, Catherine peeled out of her wet clothing and dried off hurriedly. She put on an old, soft dress and tied a sash around her waist. She took her best — and warmest — dress from its hook on the wall and carried it downstairs.

Through the curtain separating Sarah's small room from the storeroom, Catherine called, "Lydia, here is something for you to wear until your clothes dry out."

Lydia opened the curtain. She stood wrapped in the covering from Sarah's bed. Lydia looked at the garment and then at Catherine. "This is your best dress, Catherine, I cannot wear this."

"Please, Lydia, put it on. Anything else I have is in tatters from use in the garden."

Lydia's tone was indignant as she replied, "I am not ashamed to wear your work clothes. I have toiled side by side with you in the garden for weeks now. Some of my things are beginning to look the same way."

Catherine said, "Still, take this. It is what I would like you to wear — just until your own things dry."

Lydia sighed and took the dress from Catherine. It was useless to try to argue, she knew.

Catherine stood in the doorway as Lydia walked back to Sarah's cot. With her back to the entrance, she let the bedcover drop to the floor, exposing her bare body. Catherine felt a thrill rush through her. She could not take her eyes from Lydia and followed the youthful lines, tracing the alabaster skin of Lydia's shoulders, down her back to her buttocks. *How graceful she looks. How beautiful her thighs.* Catherine tried to absorb the sight of Lydia's exquisite form. Her breathing grew deep and labored.

When Lydia pulled the dress over her head, it seemed to Catherine as if a tapestry had been pulled across the gates of heaven and she could no longer see in.

As Lydia turned around, Catherine's mood changed and she burst out laughing, uncertain if it was a release from tension, or if it was the comical sight before her. Catherine was considerably taller than Lydia. The sleeves of the dress Catherine had lent her hid Lydia's hands well past her fingertips. The hem of the frock lay on the floor, twisted around Lydia's legs, in appearance rather like an old, disheveled mop. To Catherine, she looked like a small child wearing her mother's dress to play a game of pretend.

Lydia looked down at herself and realized what she looked like. She laughed, too. When she took a tentative step toward Catherine, she stumbled and the two women laughed even more.

Catherine moved toward Lydia and took her hidden hand in her own. She rolled up the sleeve. When she finished, Lydia presented Catherine the other hand. Catherine shivered under the gaze of the woman with the grey-green eyes. Lydia looked away, not wanting to reveal her own inner feelings. Catherine and Lydia stood motionless. Catherine thought, *I do not want you to go. I fear I shall never see you again.*

Without warning, Lydia threw her arms around Catherine

and laid her head against her breast. Catherine's dry dress absorbed the water from Lydia's wet hair quickly, but she did not mind.

"I shall miss you," Lydia whispered.

Catherine pulled Lydia closer and said hoarsely, "And I shall miss you."

THEY SPENT THE rest of the day in the front of the fire, their wet clothing draped all around the kitchen to dry. Steeped in each other's presence, they found little need for conversation. Finally, as the grey day showed signs of turning to night, Lydia got up and gathered her clothes together.

"I should get back to the Grouse and Pheasant. It will be dark soon." *Ask me to stay the night with you again, Catherine. Please, don't let me go.*

The feelings Catherine had experienced while she watched Lydia dress came back to her in a flood of emotion. She looked into Lydia's eyes. It was unwise to invite Lydia to stay.

"Yes, you should go, or it will be too dark to venture out alone."

I wish I could ask you to stay, Lydia, but I cannot trust myself. I am so confused by my own feelings. Confused...and afraid. How can I go on without you? Yet you are leaving. Leaving me. Oh, Lydia, if I asked you to stay, would you? And if you stayed, what would happen? No. You must go back to the Inn.

As Lydia turned to go into Sarah's room to change, she looked disappointed. Catherine read the look as fatigue. A bent shadow-figure reflected on the wall opposite Catherine.

Chapter
Eight

St. Martin's Day, also called the Feast of the Plowman
November 11, 1458
Willowglen Township

THE DAYS PASSED far too quickly. Often, Lydia joined Catherine as she cultivated delicate stalks in the garden. Occasionally, Lydia would stop under pretense of needing to catch her breath. She would stand back and watch Catherine, following her movements as she worked her way around the rows of herbs and medicinal plants. Catherine's sleeves, rolled up to her elbows, exposed her forearm muscles, taut under the tanned skin as she worked her rake or hoe. It was just as Lydia had imagined that first day of the fair.

From the time Lydia had announced her imminent departure until the day before she was to leave, an intensity grew between the two women, although few words were exchanged regarding it. They were often quiet and introspective when they were together. It was as if they needed the stillness to soak in each other's essence, trying to commit it to memory for the absence that would follow.

Late one afternoon, as Lydia and Catherine worked in the garden, Sarah waved Lydia to the back door of the shop. After a brief exchange with the young assistant, Lydia called back to Catherine that she had to leave for the day. "I shall finish in the morning, Catherine."

Catherine motioned to Lydia to go and responded, "There will be more to do tomorrow."

Lydia disappeared into the shop.

Catherine found herself struggling again, as she often did these days, in an attempt to distance herself from Lydia, not wanting to stand in the way of her decision to leave Willowglen. Catherine had to fight not to reveal how difficult their separation would be for her.

Lydia felt the strain, too. She knew that, when the day came for her to leave Willowglen, the pain would be unbearable. However, the more the women tried to detach themselves from one another, the stronger their bond became in spite of themselves.

Chapter
Nine

The Eve of St. Andrew's Feast
November 29, 1458
The Shoppe of Hawkins & Hawkins

THE NIGHT BEFORE Lydia's departure, the three women ate their evening meal in Catherine's kitchen. Sarah, ever attuned to her mistress, excused herself to attend to some chore in the storeroom. She asked Catherine to call her to accompany them when Lydia was ready to go back to the Grouse and Pheasant.

Alone with Lydia, Catherine produced a package from the cupboard and presented it to her. When Lydia unwrapped it, she found a woolen, hooded cloak, lined with a beautiful soft silk. The color of the outer cloth was a deep, rich purple, more splendid than Lydia had ever seen. The fabric shimmered in the firelight.

Lydia correctly surmised that it had cost Catherine several months of her earnings. Catherine had bought the material from James Hall before he left Willowglen. Storing the cloth out of sight, she had worked on the garment each night after Lydia left the shop. She cut and stitched by lamp and firelight after a hard day's work so that she would have the cloak ready before Lydia's departure.

Lydia tried to contain her emotion, but tears flooded her eyes and flowed down her cheeks. Between her tears, Lydia whispered her thanks to Catherine.

Catherine made light of her reaction, careful not to reveal her own thoughts. *I love you. I wanted to make the most beautiful thing I could for you. It is the only way I know to convey what I feel. I hope you understand that, my beloved.*

To Catherine's surprise, Lydia had a gift for her, too. From deep within her sleeve Lydia produced a small package wrapped in soft cloth.

Catherine fumbled with the wrapping, protesting that Lydia

should not have done anything for her. When she folded back the fabric, she exposed a beautifully etched golden medallion. It contained a detailed relief of a mint stalk superimposed upon a mortar and pestle. Catherine turned the medal over to reveal an engraved message on the back. It read:

CH
gratefully
LW

Catherine stroked the design with her fingers. She tried not to betray her emotions, but when she spoke, her voice quivered. "Lydia, it's beautiful. You should not have done such a thing. It cost you far too much—"

Lydia interrupted. "Do not concern yourself about the expense, Catherine. I have paid a very small price to express my gratitude to you. You are very special to me. It is difficult...to say good-bye. I hope you will wear this and keep good thoughts of me in your heart."

Tears welled up in Catherine's eyes. "I shall wear it gladly," she murmured. Then, trying to sound detached, she asked, "How did you come by such a splendid piece, Lydia?"

Lydia confessed, "A few days ago, I left early. You remember. Sarah called me when we were in the garden. She told me that Edward had come by and asked her to tell me that this was ready. His work is so elegant. I wanted you to have something special from me."

"You mean you had this made especially for me?"

"Yes, Catherine," Lydia admitted shyly.

Catherine stared at the gold medallion. Then, as they embraced, Catherine struggled with her thoughts. *If I asked you to stay, would you?* Instead, she said nothing. Her shadow was barely visible in the corner of the room, a forlorn, hunched-over shape.

Lydia was not without her own conflict, wrestling with her own thoughts. *If only you would tell me to stay, not for any other reason but that we should be together. Perhaps I could be persuaded...*

But Catherine broke their silence by calling for Sarah. It was time for Lydia to go back to the Grouse and Pheasant.

SARAH AND CATHERINE said their good-byes at the door of the Inn. The carriage had arrived from Briarcrest that afternoon. Lydia was to leave before dawn the next morning. She clasped the folded cloak tightly to her breast and, as she turned to go, Catherine saw tears in her eyes.

The two women hurried back down the street to the spice shop. No matter how fast Sarah walked, in an effort to catch up to her Mistress, Catherine kept two steps ahead of her. That way, her young assistant would not see her tears.

Catherine clutched the gold medallion in her hand. The more the tears welled up, the tighter she squeezed it, as if the discomfort of the metal cutting into her hand could distract her from the miserable pain in her heart. How would she carry on with Lydia gone?

Chapter
Ten

Feast of St. Andrew
November 30, 1458
Market Street

A SLIVER OF the moon cut a small notch in the darkness of the pre-dawn sky. Two men emerged from the Grouse and Pheasant Inn. They hurried to the stables to hitch two horses to an enclosed carriage bearing the shield of Briarcrest on each side.

The coach pulled up in front of the Inn and stopped. The attendants sat silently in their seats, waiting. The horses stood, stamping their hooves, their nostrils emitting clouds of steamy breath.

A figure appeared in the doorway wrapped in a dark cloak, the hood blocking the wearer's face from view. One of the men jumped down, opened the small carriage door and bowed as the woman passed him. He latched the door and swung himself up onto the seat beside the driver. The sound of his voice echoed down the quiet cobbled street. "Ready," he declared.

With a clicking noise and a flip of the reins, the driver signaled the horses. They pushed against their leather harnesses and the carriage began to roll. The darkness swallowed them quickly.

Standing outside the shop, Catherine strained to hear the fading sound of the jingling traces until the noise died out. The moon, although it was thin, had given enough light for Catherine to make out the arrival of the carriage. She had watched the figure exit the inn, had seen her enter the carriage without a sidelong glance. Catherine had barely been able to make out the cloak the woman wore, but she knew it was a rich, deep purple wool, lined with silk. Choking back her tears, Catherine grasped the gold medallion hanging around her neck on a cord and turned from the street. When she put out her hand to open the shop door, it gave way too easily, causing her to stumble. Sarah stood on the other side of the entrance with a lit taper in her hand.

Catherine blurted out, "She's gone, Sarah."

"Will she be back, Mistress?"

"I do not know."

Without another word, the young girl turned and led the way back into the shop. Catherine plodded up the stairs in the dark. She needed no light to negotiate them for she knew their every unevenness.

Sarah went back to her own room and, although she returned to her cot, she could not sleep. The sight of her mistress with red, swollen eyes rimmed by dark circles haunted her. The only other time she had seen Catherine look like that was right after her father had died.

Catherine also found sleep elusive. As she lay in her bed upstairs, a swirling, sinking feeling overwhelmed her. She felt as if she were drowning, and she heard Lydia's name echoed over and over again in her mind to the rhythm of a dull ache in her heart. Just before dawn, Catherine fell into a brief, exhausted sleep.

Chapter
Eleven

Feast of the Epiphany of Christ
January 6, 1459
Hawkins & Hawkins

AS CATHERINE SAT alone in the shop during the late winter afternoon, the shape of her shadow on the wall behind her moved as if heaving a deep sigh. Sarah was making a delivery to a customer and would, no doubt, be gone longer than necessary. Lately Catherine's young assistant took every opportunity to stop by the Grouse and Pheasant to talk to Will.

Catherine shook her head and smiled. *Young love.* But her smile vanished quickly. She tried to ignore the ache in her heart by concentrating on rearranging her herb shelf. She didn't succeed. Images of Lydia bobbed to the surface like corks in her watery consciousness. She struggled until the sound of the shop door opening ended her private battle.

"Back so soon, Sa—?"

It was not her young assistant.

The stranger stood just inside the door of the shop and scrutinized Catherine. He looked dusty and tired from a long, hard ride. Tentatively, he inquired, "Mistress Catherine Hawkins?"

"Yes. How may I be of assistance to you, good sir?"

The doubt and fatigue lifted from the man's face. It was replaced by a gentle smile. He plunged his hand into a leather sack and pulled out a thick, folded piece of paper. A red wax seal held the overlapping sheet together.

"I have come from Briarcrest, mum," he said. "This is from the Lady Lydia Wellington. She told me I should give it to none other than yourself. She said I was to come here directly and that I should wait to see if there was a reply. My horse is stabled with the smith. I will be staying with him tonight. I could come back in the morning, mum, if you please."

Catherine's heart raced. She moved toward the note, trying

not to seem too eager. Her hand trembled ever so slightly as she reached for the paper the man held out to her. Feigning composure, she asked, "Whom shall I thank for bringing news of the Lady Lydia to me, sir?"

"They call me Henry, Mistress," replied the man shyly.

"Thank you, Henry. You have done well. Let me fetch you something for your trouble."

"Oh, no, mum. I could take nothing. I was asked by the Duchess herself. *'Lady Lydia will tell you where to take the note,'* she said. *'Please take it for her,'* she said. The Duchess is always so polite, you know, a real Lady, she is. And what the Duchess asks, Henry does willingly, mum. She and Lady Hilary are so good to my family and me. If it were not for them, I do not know what would have become of us—" He paused, checking his speech. "Excuse me, mum. I should not go on so."

"Do not trouble yourself, Henry," Catherine said. She moved to the counter where she kept her funds and removed a coin from a plain wooden box. She pressed it into the messenger's hand. "Now, Henry, since you will be staying here in Willowglen tonight, would you not like to be able to have a tankard or two of ale at the tavern? Please, take this and enjoy yourself. I shall look for you in the morning."

Henry smiled a sheepish grin, pleased by her kindness. He tipped his cap, saying, "Thank you, Mistress. You are most kind. I will come by first thing tomorrow. Good day to you."

"Good day, Henry."

As soon as the door closed, Catherine sat down by the window. She breathed deeply in an attempt to calm her trembling hands. Almost as if in a dream, she heard the faint *tick* of the wax yielding under her fingers. Tilting the note toward the fading light outside, she read the message written in Lydia's delicate hand:

Octave of Christmas

Dear Catherine,

I have been thinking of you so much and so often that I must send you word. I miss our days together in your shop and your garden. I wish I were there with you now. We celebrated Christmas by exchanging gifts. Marian, my Aunt Beatrice, and Hilary, as well as the rest of the household, all joined in, as is the custom at Briarcrest. As much as I enjoyed the gifts I received, I treasure the beautiful cloak you made for me most of all. Its fine workmanship has brought many compliments. Whenever I wear it, I think of you.

> *I shall be journeying back to Greencastle, as my father has sent word for me to return. I do not wish to go, for my days here at Briarcrest are happy ones, at least, if I cannot be with you in Willowglen. But I am afraid I cannot hold back fate and so I must return to my father. I beg you, please send word back to me with my aunt's messenger. I must hear from you. I shall try to send you word again from Greencastle when I arrive there. Everyone that you know here at Briarcrest has asked me to send regards to you.*

With a true heart,
Lydia

Catherine closed her eyes and raised the paper to her nostrils. It smelled of lavender and roses. It smelled of Lydia.

She inhaled deeply. Her heart pounded. Then a shiver ran through her body. She felt the ache and a sadness similar to that which she felt after her father's death. She longed for Lydia's presence. She yearned to tell her of her feelings for her, but she feared she could not.

Just then, the shop door burst open and Sarah rushed in looking flushed. She stammered excitedly, "Mistress, I was at the Inn — uh, that is, Will said, that is, um..."

Catherine shook off her sorrow. Sarah looked like a peasant cat caught with the royal pet bird in its mouth. The young assistant fidgeted with a small thread at her waistband. She wouldn't look at Catherine. Catherine struggled to contain a chuckle, unsuccessfully.

"Sarah, do not be concerned. I know that you and Will have eyes for each other, and I know that you visit him when you go out. Why do you think I send you on so many errands lately?"

Sarah stopped fussing with the filament and looked up, wide-eyed.

Catherine continued, "Now, tell me, why are you in such a dither?"

A look of relief crossed the young girl's face and she began again. "I was at the Grouse and Pheasant, and a man came into the Inn. Will told me that he heard him say he was looking for your shop. He said he was from Briarcrest. I told Will that I needed to get back right away to see if, if everything was all right. With the Lady, I mean."

Catherine gave her young helper a penetrating look. *Is she concerned about Lydia, or about me? How much else does she know, I wonder? More than she lets on, I think.*

In an effort to ease Sarah's mind about the message, Catherine said, "Lydia has sent word that she is about to leave Briarcrest and return to Greencastle."

"Oh," said Sarah disappointedly. "I thought she might be coming back to Willowglen."

"No, Sarah, I am afraid not. At least not for now."

A long pause ensued. Sarah peered at the floor. Catherine knew that Sarah had more to say.

She waited, and when the young girl continued her silence, she added, "I shall be sending a note back tomorrow, Sarah. Is there anything you would like me to tell Lady Lydia for you?"

Sarah scrutinized the floor again. When she finally raised her head, she wore a determined expression. "Tell her I wish she could come back here to stay. Tell her..."

"Yes, Sarah?"

"Tell her you were happier when she was here. She was, too, no doubt."

Sarah's blunt honesty stunned Catherine. She stared at her assistant blankly.

Sarah felt that, perhaps, she had said too much. She exclaimed, "I am sorry if I spoke out of turn, Mistress. It is just that it troubles me to see you so low in spirit. You were so happy when she was here. You smiled and laughed easily. So did Lady Lydia. There was a feeling of delight in this house that left when she went away."

Slowly, the enormity of what Sarah said seeped into Catherine's understanding. "Sarah, you are a wonder. When did you become so wise?"

Sarah blushed and stammered, "I am not wise at all, Mistress."

"Oh, but you are, Sarah. Wise and bold. I do not know if I shall be able to be so bold myself as to write such things to Lydia, but I shall think about what you have said. I shall try to be honest with her."

Sarah pronounced a single, emphatic "good." Then she turned on her heel and marched into the kitchen. Catherine stood rooted to the floor, staring after Sarah in disbelief.

WHENEVER CATHERINE FOUND herself alone that afternoon, she pulled out Lydia's note and read it again. She held the letter close to her face and breathed deeply. The aroma of lavender and roses brought with it the image of Lydia's face, and she felt the sadness and the longing more intensely. Yet this ritual somehow strengthened Catherine. By it, she became more determined to set her true thoughts and feelings on paper, just as Sarah had recommended.

With the day's work done and the shop closed for the evening, Catherine and Sarah ate a simple meal together. They did not speak of their earlier conversation about Lydia, but Catherine decided to broach the topic of Sarah's feelings for Will.

Reluctantly, Sarah admitted that they were in love, but Will was only a kitchen lad at the Inn and his pay was meager. With Sarah's parents dead and her only family a younger brother, and her uncle and aunt and their six children, Sarah would have no dowry. It would be a long time before she and Will could wed, she said, if they were able to do so at all. Catherine wanted to help the young couple and resolved to think of a way, but she said nothing to Sarah about it.

IT WAS CATHERINE'S custom to remain in the kitchen by the fire for a while each evening after supper to read or to work at some project. Often, she spent her time consulting a well-worn book on medicinal herbs given to her by Lady Anne. Both Catherine's father and the nuns at Wooster Abbey had instilled in Catherine a love of books early on in her life. She even owned one of the new typeset books, and she still had her favorite *"The City of Women"* by Christine de Pisan. However, on this particular evening, she would neither read nor sew. Instead, after cleaning up from supper, she retired to her bedchamber, taking with her writing implements and a sheet of paper.

Upstairs, Catherine placed everything on a small oak table located at one end of the bedchamber and drew up the stool from beside her bed. She adjusted the small lamp so that the circle of yellow light illuminated the blank page. Removing the stopper from the ink bottle, she inserted the quill to the proper depth. Then she put the pen to the paper and began writing in her bold hand:

January 6, Epiphany

Dear Lydia,
    It gladdened my heart to hear you are wearing the cloak I made for you. I hope that you find it protection from the winter cold. I was sorry to hear that you would not be able to stay at Briarcrest for an extended period. I know that you enjoy your aunt's home immensely.

Perhaps I shall be able to see its charm myself, one day.

Sarah heard that you had sent a messenger from Briarcrest and she wanted me to tell you that I miss you and that I wish you could be here, too. I find it difficult to tell you that which is in my heart, mostly because I do not understand it myself. I only know that, as Sarah said, I laugh more when you are near.

The pendant that you gave me is around my neck to remind me of you daily. It is, indeed, a beautiful treasure to me. I never take it off. I do have an advantage over you in that, do I not? For you cannot always wear your cloak. People would think you most peculiar and you would find it most uncomfortable in the summer's heat, I am sure.

Safe journey to you, my Lydia. I do wish you were coming to Willowglen instead of going to Greencastle.

As ever,
Catherine

The gritty powder made dull tinkling sounds as she sprinkled it onto the paper. She waited for the powder to soak up the ink, then blew it away. After reading the letter once more, she folded it, making careful, even creases. She removed the chimney from the lamp and used the flame to melt the small piece of brown wax cradled in a tiny metal spoon. When it was melted, she allowed the liquid to drip onto the overlapping edges of the folded paper and watched the wax pool into a round mass. Lifting a seal with an embossed mortar and pestle on it, she positioned it over the liquid wax and pressed firmly. A few seconds later, she pulled up on the seal and felt its unwillingness to let go. It reminded her of her own reluctance to allow the letter to leave her hands.

CATHERINE RESISTED THE urge to call Henry back to retrieve her letter as he walked out of the shop. The determined look on Sarah's face the previous afternoon was all she had to prevent her from doing so. She had to admit to herself that what she had written was as it should be. Like the seal letting go of the wax, she let the messenger—and her written words—go.

Chapter
Twelve

February 20, 1459
The Shoppe of Hawkins & Hawkins

The Octave of Candlemas, February 10
at Greencastle

Dearest Catherine,

I find it difficult to be in my father's house these days. He talks of nothing but the plans he is making with a Grand Duke in France for my betrothal. I cannot bear it. At least he has not made a pledge for me as yet and Marian has been able to convince him, once again, that I need time to get used to the idea. He has, at least, consented to allow me to go back to Briarcrest once the roads become more passable for one final celebration of the May. I suspect Marian had something to do with his willingness to grant this request, although she will not admit it.

Before I left for Greencastle, my aunt told me that I must invite you to Briarcrest as soon as travel conditions become better, so I have a plan. Marian and I are to leave Greencastle after Easter and will go to Briarcrest. Marian will stay on with my aunt, for she finds long journeys difficult these days. From there, I shall come to Willowglen to take you back with me for a visit. It may well be our last chance to do such a thing, although I pray it is not. You are invited for the May celebration. I trust you will be able to leave your shop in Sarah's charge for a few days, since you have said she is quite capable. Please send word to Briarcrest accepting my invitation. Be ready three days before May Day.

I think of you every day and I miss you profoundly.

You have my heart,
Lydia

Catherine sat by the fire in the kitchen and read the letter for the second time since it had arrived that day. One of Lord Wellington's men had appeared at the shop door that afternoon. Sir Stubius, a stern-looking man, said that the Lady Lydia had sent him. He held out a note to Catherine, stiffly, in his gloved hand. Catherine thanked him politely and took it. She thought it not prudent to ask him to bear a response back to Lydia and he did not offer. He was curt in his manner and gave her the impression that he found it irritating to do the bidding of his master's child — and a woman at that. Something about him annoyed Catherine, but she couldn't say what. Only interested in Lydia's letter, she was happy to take it from him and watch him go. Her irritation dissipated quickly as she focused on the letter in her hand.

Chapter
Thirteen

The Eve of the Feast of the Annunciation
March 24, 1459
Willowglen Township

WEEKS AFTER LYDIA'S letter, written at Candlemas,
arrived, Catherine still mulled over leaving the shop in Sarah's
care to go to Briarcrest for the May celebration. She knew Sarah
could take care of business for a few days, but ever since the
incident on Hallow's Eve, Catherine had become particularly
cautious. She felt uncomfortable leaving Sarah alone, especially
at night. Finally, she hit upon an idea.

Of late, Sarah's brother had not been able to work because of
an injury, but he was still strong, and a good man. Catherine
would ask him to stay at the shop with his sister during her
absence. She then took her ink and quill to the room above the
shop and wrote to Lydia:

March 24, Our Lady's Annunciation Eve

Dearest Lydia,

*I received your note and invitation to Briarcrest for
the May Day celebration. My heart jumped for joy at the
thought of seeing you again. I am glad you will come to
Willowglen and allow me to travel back to Briarcrest with
you. I look forward to the May feast there. Please extend
my thanks to your aunt for her most gracious invitation. I
shall be glad to see her, Lady Hilary and Marian again. I
have no doubt that Sarah will do well in my absence. I
hope to enlist Sarah's brother to stay at the shop with her
while I am gone. I will feel better if she has the
companionship.*

I can hardly believe that I shall be seeing your beloved

Briarcrest soon.   I await your arrival with happy anticipation.

As always,
Catherine

THE FOLLOWING MORNING, Catherine went to the Governor's Hall to hire a messenger to take her letter to Briarcrest. The road was not fit for carriage travel as yet, but a horseman could easily make the journey in a day if no new storms developed.

As Catherine inquired about a courier at the Governor's Hall, John, the silversmith's son, came to her. "Mistress Catherine, I heard you inquiring about a messenger to Briarcrest. I leave to go there myself tomorrow morning. The Lady Hilary has commissioned some silver goblets for the May celebration and I have some sketches to show her for her approval. I shall be glad to take your message with me when I go."

"I would be most grateful, John." She handed him her note, sealed with brown wax.

"Tell me, Mistress, do you expect a response to your message?"

"No, the message is for the Lady Lydia, who will be along later. I will be happy to have the note waiting for her there when she arrives. I thought that it might take some time before I found someone going in that direction. I am most grateful to you, John."

"I am happy to do it, Mistress Catherine — but excuse me, if you will. I see the man I am to meet over there." He put her note in his sack and started toward a group of men at the far end of the hall. Before he disappeared, he called back over his shoulder to her. "I shall deliver your note safely, Mistress."

WHEN CATHERINE RETURNED to the shop, she informed Sarah of her plan and asked her to enlist her brother to come and stay with her. Sarah said her brother would probably find the arrangement most agreeable since his injured arm did not seem to be healing very well.

Catherine insisted, "Sarah, you must tell him to come to me and I shall see if I can help him."

"I told him that, Mistress, but he is proud and says he will not come to you because he cannot pay."

"You know I charge no one when I dispense medicines,

Sarah. Have you not told your brother this? If I don't ask him for money, it's not to demean him; it's my way with everyone who has a need."

"I told him, Mistress, but he is young and stubborn."

Catherine tried to keep from smiling. He was young, but Sarah was only his senior by a year. More and more Catherine realized her assistant was older than her years. After puzzling with the problem of the young man's obstinacy for a moment, Catherine thought of a solution.

"Tell your brother I intend to pay him to come and stay with you while I am away. He may compensate me later, if he insists. But tell him he must come for care now, before he gets a fever in his wound."

"I shall tell him, Mistress. Do not be concerned. This time, I shall make him come."

Satisfied, Catherine set about the business of the spice shop. Sarah arrived with her brother in tow the following day. When Catherine examined his injury, she scolded him for waiting to come for help, for it was badly inflamed. She set about bathing his arm in a comfrey tea and gave him some calendula to apply as a poultice for the inflammation. She made him promise to continue with the treatment.

The days that followed passed far too slowly for Catherine. She could hardly wait to see Lydia again, and this time, she resolved, she would try to be more forthcoming about her feelings toward the young noblewoman. The thought frightened her, but she tried not to allow it to lessen her determination. Could she do it?

Chapter
Fourteen

Within the Octave of Philip, the Apostle
April 29, 1459
The Shoppe of Hawkins & Hawkins

A DEAFENING CLANG sent Sarah racing inside from the garden. When she reached the shop, she found Catherine stooped over a large copper pot. The scent of bay filled the air. In the middle of the room, dried leaves lay strewn across the floor. Catherine scooped them up and returned them to the container.

"Mistress Catherine, are you hurt?"

Catherine waved her off. "No, no—I am not hurt. Do not concern yourself, Sarah. Go back to what you were doing. I can manage."

Catherine had been agitated all morning. Sarah noticed, but decided not to speak of it. She knew the source. Lydia had been due to arrive the previous day and she had not come. No word had arrived concerning her delay, either. As the day wore on, Catherine had become more and more distressed. Now, Sarah decided she could no longer keep her concern to herself.

In an effort to soothe Catherine's anxiety, she ventured, "Mistress, I am sure that Lady Lydia will be here. There are still two days left until the May celebration. She might have been delayed coming from Greencastle. Everyone says the roads have been good for traveling for weeks, but Greencastle is a long way and perhaps no one from Willowglen has traveled that way of late." Then Sarah added, not feeling completely convinced herself, "She will be here today, Mistress. I am certain of it."

Catherine was taken aback once again by Sarah's perceptiveness. She felt embarrassed to be so obvious to her young helper about Lydia. Words came only after a struggle. "Yes, I am sure you are right, Sarah. I must try to keep my composure. It's just that I am so eager to see her, and a little concerned that she didn't arrive yesterday. But I'm fine now.

Truly! Go back to the garden. I can clean up here."

Reluctantly, Sarah left her mistress kneeling on the floor gathering up the spilled herbs, battling dark thoughts and trying desperately not to succumb to her growing panic. *What if she does not come? What will I do if something has happened to her? What if she has been hurt? How will I know? What if her father has gone back on his word and has forced her to go to France now?*

This last thought horrified Catherine, for here was something she had no control over. If Lydia was sick, she could administer healing herbs and, hopefully, she could overcome the illness. However, if Lydia were forced to leave England, to marry someone of her father's choosing, Catherine would be helpless to do anything. In the midst of her increasing alarm, Catherine did not hear the shop door open. As she continued stuffing the container with dried plants from the floor, a familiar voice broke through her uneasy thoughts.

"When I was a student under the tutelage of Mistress Hawkins, it was considered most inappropriate to sort herbs on the shop floor."

"Lydia!" Catherine jumped to her feet, spilling the pot's contents again.

"Catherine! I thought I would never get here. I am sorry I was delayed. I had to wait an extra day before my father would make transport available for Marian and me, but I am here at last."

Catherine wrapped her arms around Lydia and sighed with relief. She whispered into the fiery hair, "I am so glad you've finally come, Lydia."

The two women were still holding each other when Sarah came into the shop. When she saw Lydia, she squealed with delight. "Lady Lydia. Oh, Mistress Catherine, you see, I told you she would be here today." Sarah embraced Lydia warmly. "I am so glad you have finally come."

"Thank you, Sarah. I'm glad to have gotten here at last, myself."

Turning back to Catherine, Lydia asked, "Can you be ready to leave for Briarcrest in the morning? We only have two days before the May celebration and Aunt Beatrice asked me to get you to come as early as possible."

"Well," Catherine said, turning to her assistant, "Sarah, you had better fetch your brother so that Lady Lydia and I can leave in the morning. We must not disappoint the Duchess, now, must we?"

"No, Mistress. I shall go and fetch him now. I am sure we can be back by this afternoon."

After Sarah left, Catherine turned to Lydia, and said, "It seems like so long ago since you left. Yet, now that you are back, it is as if you were only gone briefly. I want to hear everything that has happened — and I hope that you will stay with me tonight, Lydia."

"Yes, Catherine, I will stay," Lydia said shyly. "Let me tell the carriage men that I will not go to the Grouse and Pheasant and that they may call for us here in the morning."

Lydia disappeared out the front door. Catherine stood in the middle of the shop for a moment, catching her breath. By the time Lydia returned, Catherine had put the last of the herbs into the metal pot once more.

Lydia stood in the entrance of the shop and inhaled the warm, spicy-sweet aroma of the herbs and spices. Catherine could not help but admire the beauty of the woman standing there. She wore a fine purple cloak. Her hood was thrown back, exposing auburn ringlets of hair that framed her grey-green eyes. Catherine beamed.

Lydia smiled back sheepishly. "It smells wonderful in here," she said. "I have missed the fragrance of your shop so much — and my daily cup of fresh mint tea, Mistress. Do you know where I might get a cup?"

Catherine laughed lightly, then harder once Lydia joined in. It felt so good to have Lydia back. "Right this way, my dear," said Catherine.

As she led the way to the kitchen, Catherine thought, *Sarah was right. I do laugh more when she is around. I believe she may be right about Lydia laughing more, too.*

Catherine stopped short in the doorway. She turned around and met Lydia's face three fingerbreadths from her own. They did not speak. They held each other's gaze until, after great effort, Catherine turned back to the kitchen. Lydia trembled as she followed Catherine into the next room.

Trying to sound casual, Catherine said, "I am so glad you are here, Lydia. I have missed you."

Lydia replied, "I have missed you, too." *My love.*

Catherine hung the brewing kettle over the hearth. She was glad for something with which to busy herself. Lydia watched Catherine's every move from her vantage point at the kitchen table and allowed herself to admire the curve of Catherine's hips as the herbalist prepared their tea. Catherine stirred the fire. It flared up brightly and cast a shadow on the wall: a figure with its head thrown back, laughing joyously.

IT TURNED OUT to be a quiet day at the spice shop. The two women passed the hours straightening up. While they worked, they talked about Lydia's trip to Willowglen and the next day's plans. Neither of them wanted to bring up the subject that troubled them most—Lydia's impending betrothal. Instead, they spent the time delighting in each other's company without inviting that dark cloud upon themselves just yet.

Sarah returned later in the day with her brother. As soon as Andy set foot in the shop, Catherine examined his arm. She questioned him to make sure he had continued with his treatment. Satisfied, she pronounced that he would have full use of the limb in another week or so. Andy grinned when he heard the news. Lydia watched Catherine at her ministrations with a look of admiration on her face.

Andy and Sarah ate early and set up his cot in the corner of the shop. After Catherine and Lydia ate, Catherine led the way to her quarters upstairs.

Reaching the main bedchamber, Catherine said, "It seems such a bother to make up the small cot in the other room. Perhaps you would not mind sleeping in here with me, since it's just for this evening."

Lydia repeated shyly, "Since it's just for this evening."

Neither woman looked the other in the eye.

Catherine inspected the weave of her dress as she spoke. "Shall we retire, then? The carriage will be here early. We should get some rest."

Lydia studied her feet. "Yes, I suppose we should, Catherine."

"You may put your clothes on the hook over on that side of the bed." Catherine pointed to the opposite wall.

Lydia looked up just in time. "Yes, thank you," she replied self-consciously. She walked around to the other side of the bed.

The two women undressed with their backs to each other. They hung their garments on the hooks on the wall and ducked under the covers quickly, each careful to keep to her own side of the bed.

Catherine pulled herself up on her elbow to blow out the candle sitting on the stool beside her. As she leaned forward to quench the light, she felt the coolness of the medallion on her skin. She lay back down in the darkness and smiled. Neither of them spoke for a while, until Catherine finally chanced the question that was uppermost in her mind. "Has your father made any progress with your betrothal?"

There was a long silence before Lydia answered. "He left for France as we left for Briarcrest. He thought the time was right to make final arrangements, he said. He suggested I accompany him. We fought about it, and Marian interceded. She persuaded him that I should be allowed to spend one last May time with my aunt."

Another long pause.

"Catherine?"

"Yes, Lydia?"

"Hold my hand."

Catherine slid her hand across the mattress. The straw crackled as she did. She met Lydia's hand and grasped it firmly. It was cold — as cold as metal in winter. "Your hand is so cold, Lydia."

"I am afraid. I do not want...to be betrothed." *At least not to anyone other than you. If only that were possible.*

"I know. I am afraid, too. Perhaps we can think of something. But, try to sleep, now. Do you think you can?"

"Perhaps."

"Try, then. Do not worry. At least we are together for now."

"Yes. We are together. At least for a time."

"Good night, Lydia." *My dear, sweet love.*

"Good night, Catherine." *How I love you.*

The fatigue of an emotional day overtook them quickly and they slept, holding hands all night long. Even in slumber, they would not dare cross the invisible line that divided the bed in two.

Chapter
Fifteen

The Eve of May Day
April 30, 1459
Willowglen Township

THE FIRST HINT of light through the upstairs window roused Catherine. In her sleepy fog, she could not remember if Lydia had actually arrived the previous afternoon or if it had all been a dream. The mist rose from her mind. She felt Lydia's hand on hers. It was true. Lydia was there beside her. Catherine blinked. She slowly slipped her hand from under Lydia's. The sleeping woman did not stir. Catherine watched as the covers moved up and down in rhythm with Lydia's breathing. *She is so beautiful. Her lips, so inviting. Kissing her would be...*

Her unfinished thought jarred her. She pushed herself out of bed and wrenched her clothes from their hook. Turning away from the bed, Catherine tried to compose herself as she dressed. *Calm yourself, Catherine. This cannot continue. You must stop. You might lose her altogether if you do something rash.*

Still, she could not deny herself another look at Lydia's lovely face. When she turned around, Catherine found the grey-green eyes open. She blushed and struggled to regain composure. "Did you s-sleep well, Lydia?"

"Yes, very well, thank you, Catherine," Lydia answered.

Catherine battled her desire to take Lydia in her arms and kiss her. *Distraction, Catherine. You need a distraction.* "We had better get ready for our journey, Lydia. I was just going to gather a few things to bring with me."

"Mmm, yes, I suppose we should," Lydia responded dreamily.

Come on, then, Catherine. Move your feet. Stop acting as if you're fixed to the floor. But instead of moving, she just stood while words escaped through her lips without her consent. "Shall I help you get dressed first, Lydia?"

What are you saying? She does not need your help. Why do you want to help her? Oh, Catherine, you cannot look at her body, that beautiful, wonderful body! You cannot. Remember the last time you saw her? You almost fainted with the joy of it...and you wanted so much to...to touch her, caress her, kiss her.

Before Catherine could protest her own suggestion, Lydia said, "Yes, perhaps you could help me." She sat up, allowing the bedcovers to fall to her waist.

Catherine immediately felt her body respond with something like a shooting pain that ran the entire length of her body. She breathed deeply and forced her feet to start around the bed. Lydia threw off the covers and stood naked before Catherine. It was almost more than Catherine could bear. She lost her footing. She stumbled, then turned to stare at the floor behind her in disbelief. Had some imaginary bump risen during the night to trip her? Nothing looked out of place. She turned back to Lydia.

A wordless dance of sensual pleasure followed as Catherine slowly gathered up each item of clothing and Lydia held out her arms to receive the garment. They moved as in a dream. Time seemed to suspend itself. Catherine had no idea how she was able to move amidst the sweet ache she felt. Each piece of clothing slipped onto Lydia's body effortlessly. Finally, when she fastened the front of Lydia's dress, Catherine's hand brushed against her soft breast captured inside the linen garment. Catherine thought she might faint from the sheer delight of the brief touch.

In the end, Catherine managed a hoarse question. "Shall we have some tea before the carriage arrives?"

Lydia replied with great effort. "I will go and put the kettle on, Catherine. You get your things."

"If you do not mind, Lydia...I shall join you downstairs later."

Catherine watched Lydia leave, trying to memorize her beauty before she disappeared down the stairway, finally exhaling only when the other woman was no longer in sight.

Thoughts and feelings bombarded her in a chaotic jumble. She opened the ornate chest at the foot of the bed and took out a cloth sack. As she stuffed her things into it, her composure gradually returned. When her shaking eased, she stood straight, eyes scanning the room, checking to be sure what she needed had been packed. On the wall behind Catherine, a shadow seemed to lean into the corner, heaving deep, panting breaths.

THE CARRIAGE ARRIVED just as Catherine finished giving Sarah some last minute instructions. The two women boarded the coach and heard the latch click as they settled onto padded leather seats. As they started off down Market Street, Catherine thought happily, *This is so different from Lydia's last departure.* For now, they were going to Briarcrest together. She peered out through the small slit at the rear of the carriage and caught a final glimpse of Sarah and Andy standing in the street, waving.

"She will do well, Catherine," Lydia offered.

"I know she will. I am glad Andy is staying with her, though."

"He seems like a good boy, in spite of being a little rough around the edges. What happened to his arm?"

"A hunting accident, he said—but he would not tell me more. He may have been in Lord Brunswick's forest. I hear that some young men from around here are suspected of taking game. I should not be surprised to find that young Andy has been among them. Some of the lads do it just to boast that they have gotten away with a hare or a quail. But Sarah's uncle is so poor and his family so large, I have no doubt that they have been desperate for food at times. If he were to be caught, though... Well, I prefer not to think of what could have happened to him. It looks as if he tore his flesh on something sharp. I think the reason it was difficult for Sarah to get him to come to me was that he thought I might turn him in. He was very scared, but he was also too proud to ask for help for himself. His arm will be fine, now, though. The worst is over—and I hope he has learned a lesson."

"They are very lucky to have you, Catherine Hawkins. Not unlike me."

Catherine's cheeks darkened.

Lydia extended her hand. Catherine took it gently in her own. They smiled at each other broadly.

The carriage turned off the road from Willowglen and took the fork that led to Briarcrest. They would ride all day to reach their destination before dark.

The Journey to Briarcrest

THE CLATTERING OF the harnesses, coupled with the sound of beating hooves against hard-packed dirt and wheels grating against the uneven road, made conversation impossible for most of the trip. Catherine and Lydia bounced continuously until, as the sun melted into the horizon, the road smoothed out.

Briarcrest materialized in the distance, prestidigitated by some invisible sorcerer. The road wound to and fro, back and forth, as if to tease the vast towers in the distance.

Now Catherine understood one more of Lydia's attractions to Briarcrest. Not only did she love its inhabitants, but the place itself was enchanting. The vast structure was surrounded by trees reflecting the waning fireball in the sky. The stones of the walled edifice shone with a soft, pink luster, looking like the stuff of childrens' fairy tales.

Small thatch-roofed cottages clustered around Briarcrest to the east, seeming to pop up out of the ground like spring daisies. The road swung wide past the dwellings. As they rode on, village folk turned from their last chores of the day in garden and field to wave and shout greetings of welcome when the carriage passed.

With conversation now possible, Catherine said, "People certainly seem eager to see us."

"We are arriving in my aunt's carriage. It is the custom that it be greeted warmly. All of the village has felt my aunt's kindness at one time or another. They love the Duchess — and the Lady Hilary. This little settlement thrives because of them and they, in turn, are most loyal to Briarcrest Hall."

"I think your aunt and the Lady Hilary must be remarkable people, Lydia. I should like to get to know them better."

"You shall, Catherine. These next few days will be a wonderful opportunity for you, and for them, as well. But, look! We approach the gate."

Someone had been watching for the carriage to arrive and the thick wooden gates swung open wide just as the horses reached them. The coach rolled into the enclosure without the animals' hooves missing a beat. As they slowed to a halt in the outer courtyard, they heard excited shouts and feet hurrying from many different directions.

The footman opened the door and offered his hand to help the women out of the carriage. Catherine stepped down first and was glad for the walk from the outer courtyard to the impressive front entrance, for it gave her a chance to get her stiff legs working properly again. Catherine followed Lydia through the great oak doorway, anticipating the adventure that awaited her within Briarcrest's walls.

Chapter
Sixteen

CATHERINE WAS NOT unfamiliar with places the likes of Briarcrest. On two separate occasions when she was an adolescent, she had accompanied her father on his travels. They had stayed at the residences of her father's friends and business acquaintances, some of whom were nobles. In adulthood, Catherine often went to the homes of the titled in and around Willowglen to tend their ills or deliver herbs and spices.

Upon entering Briarcrest Hall, though, Catherine saw the uniqueness of it immediately. Although it could have been a cold, dank place with its high walls of stone, it was not. Rather, it was a charming mixture of castle and manor house with a hall that exuded warmth and hospitality. Catherine felt welcomed.

The room was elaborately decorated for the May feast. Banners of bright colored fabric lined the walls, some with crests and symbols on them, others undecorated. Looking up, Catherine saw, suspended high above them, flowing folds of green and gold fabric interlaced with pine bough swags that reached out in all directions to the edges of the great hall. Catherine felt as if giant enfolding arms, perfumed with spicy forest aroma, were holding her in an embrace. In the center of the room stood a long dining table. It sparkled with tall, glowing tapers in silver holders. Arrangements of brightly colored spring flowers accented the table. Goblets and bowls were in place, ready for a meal.

As Catherine followed Lydia, several people bid them welcome. One young woman approached and took their cloaks and bags. Then she headed for the opposite end of the hall and disappeared up a long stairway that bordered a massive fireplace.

Lydia opened her arms in an encompassing gesture and

beamed. "Welcome to Briarcrest, Catherine. What do you think of it?"

"It is most extraordinary, Lydia, just as you said. So vast, yet so comfortable and inviting — and everyone is so friendly. The workers all seem so at home here."

"Beatrice and Hilary subscribe to a very different philosophy from that of my own father to those in his service. They believe that everyone at Briarcrest deserves to be treated well. In turn, they are rewarded with loyal, good-tempered workers. You would be hard pressed to find someone who was not completely faithful to the ladies of this house —"

A voice interrupted Lydia from the direction of the staircase. Marian stood on the landing above them, talking excitedly. "Welcome, Mistress Catherine. And Lydia, dear. I am so happy you were able to reach us before dark."

Marian met them at the bottom of the steps looking flushed and sounding out of breath. *The excitement of Lydia's return, no doubt,* Catherine thought, unable to hide her smile.

Marian embraced Lydia. When she turned to give Catherine a welcoming hug, an intuitive warning sounded within the young healer. Something was wrong. Catherine could not be certain of the exact nature of the problem, but she knew from experience that her feelings were always to be trusted. Marian's face, though red, had a pallor beneath her blush. Her panting was not from rushing to greet them, but from the strain of trying to get sufficient air to breathe.

Lydia interrupted Catherine's thoughts. "Marian, how are you feeling? Are you better?"

Marian nodded, a look of embarrassment on her face.

Lydia turned and explained, "I left for Willowglen so early yesterday that I did not get a chance to inquire if Marian had recovered from our journey. She does not take to long carriage rides very well these days."

Marian brushed away Lydia's remark. "Oh, Lydia, I am much better now. You worry about me far too much — but enough of me. How was your journey? I hope it was not too difficult."

Lydia laughed. Her voice rang with music. "We were quite jostled for a while, but we managed to hold our bones together. I was certainly glad that the road was not impassable. It would have been a shame if Catherine had missed this May feast."

"That is very true. There is none to compare with the May feast at Briarcrest," Marian pronounced. Then she added, turning her attention to Catherine, "And how are you, my dear? Did you survive the trip?"

"Oh, yes, Marian, I survived as you can see. Our journey was quite bumpy, as Lydia said, but the approach to Briarcrest smoothed out, and it gave us a chance to catch our breath and enjoy the scenery."

Catherine scrutinized Marian with a trained healer's eye as the conversation continued. The flush in Marian's cheeks did not disappear. If it were merely caused by the initial excitement of Lydia's return, her color should have been normal by now. Catherine also noticed that the older woman breathed with more difficulty than she should have from her short descent down the stairs. She looked at the hand that clasped hers as Marian spoke. Her fingernails had a slight blue tinge to them. But Catherine had to set her evaluation aside, for another figure had appeared out of the dimness on the landing above them.

"Aunt Beatrice," Lydia called. "Good evening to you."

Beatrice started down the stairway, beaming at her niece. "I am glad you arrived safely, children. How was your trip?"

"Happily uneventful," Lydia answered.

"And Mistress Hawkins, I am so delighted that you could join us to celebrate the May."

"Thank you for your invitation, Your Ladyship."

As Beatrice reached the bottom of the stairway, she gave Catherine a look of feigned horror. "Please, Catherine, we do not stand on such formality at Briarcrest. You must call me Beatrice."

It took Catherine by surprise. The Duchess commanded great respect. To be invited to this familiarity astounded the young herbalist. She stammered, "Yes, B-Beatrice. I would be honored."

"Good," Beatrice said matter-of-factly. "We have little use for titles in this house. We all know our duties. Therefore, it is not necessary to address one another as superior or subordinate. Whether we are related by birth or not, we are all one family here."

Catherine found Beatrice's viewpoint remarkable. In all of her experiences, she had never met anyone quite like this woman. This visit was going to be interesting and delightful, indeed.

Beatrice opened her arms and embraced Lydia. Then she turned to Catherine, giving her a warm, affectionate squeeze.

"Where is Hilary, Aunt Beatrice?" Lydia asked.

"She went with the grounds steward to see to some last minute details for the celebration. She will be along shortly. Oh, yes, be sure to see the new foal that was born while you were gone to Greencastle, dear. It is a lovely little one with a beautiful chestnut coat. Hilary does make over the young thing so. Make sure you ask about her, will you? You would think it was her child the way she carries on."

Lydia laughed. Catherine thought she heard music again.

Then Lydia explained, "Hilary is responsible for the running of Briarcrest's exterior. Everyone must account to her regarding the animals, the grounds, the forest and all such things. Aunt Beatrice takes care of the inner workings of Briarcrest."

"That sounds like an excellent arrangement," remarked Catherine.

Beatrice agreed that it had worked very well over the years. It afforded Hilary a reason to spend her days outside, which she loved, and it allowed Beatrice more time to devote to the duties of her position and to household affairs.

"By the way, dears, after dinner this evening, Hilary and I shall be having a bath for the four of us — if you are not too tired from your journey. We will be glad for your company and it will give us a chance to spend some time together."

Catherine said nothing. Communal bathing was customary, but it had not been her habit to do so. She was not sure she would be comfortable with it now.

Lydia responded, "Oh, Aunt Beatrice, it will be relaxing after the long journey and it will be wonderful to be able to spend some time with you and Hilary." Then she turned to Catherine, with a look full of anticipation and said, "Shall we, Catherine?"

Catherine surprised herself by saying that she would be delighted to join them. She even half-believed it.

"Lovely," replied Beatrice. "Lydia, perhaps you should let Catherine settle in, now, and after dinner I am sure you will show her the way to our chambers to join us. I am leaving Catherine's care to you, child."

"Aunt Beatrice," Lydia chided, "you know I will take excellent care of Catherine."

Lydia stole a look at Catherine. Her dancing eyes evoked the same response they always did in the young herbalist. Catherine glanced away quickly, afraid that Beatrice might see her reaction — and understand. She did not seem to notice, though.

Beatrice continued, teasing, "You had better, my dear, for I hear she took very good care of you while you were in Willowglen. It is the least we can do for her during her stay at Briarcrest."

Lydia smiled. Then, without warning, she bolted for the stairway, laughing with abandon. She stopped on the staircase, looked at Catherine disarmingly and called Catherine to follow.

Like a flying ember, passion jumped from Lydia to Catherine. She, too laughed from sheer happiness as she gathered up her long skirt. She excused herself quickly and ran after Lydia up the stairway. Catherine's heart soared. She caught up and stayed close behind her. At the top of the stairs, Lydia turned the corner. Catherine followed and stopped short. A long hallway stretched before them. Several large wooden doors loomed along one side of the corridor. She had heard that portals much like exterior doors had started to replace the tapestries on inner passages in the homes of the nobility, but the size and the ornateness of the massive carved doors astonished Catherine.

Lydia pushed open the one closest to them to reveal a large bedchamber. The bed had a huge canopy top with side curtains tied back exposing lavish bed covers. On the far side of the room, by a large window, a table held a pot of some steaming beverage, two goblets, and a small plate of pastries. The table was covered with a white linen tablecloth. Two chairs awaited their guests.

Lydia beckoned Catherine in from the passageway and closed the door. Catherine stood in the middle of the room, watching Lydia as she strolled toward the table.

As Catherine approached, Lydia handed her a cup and poured the steaming drink. A spicy mead aroma reached Catherine's nostrils as she looked into Lydia's eyes. She felt intoxicated. She had no desire to check her feelings. Lydia continued pouring the liquid into the cup, higher and higher. She looked down just as the cup was about to overflow and stopped pouring in time to prevent it from spilling over onto Catherine's hand. She threw back her head and laughed. Catherine thought she heard music again and it made her laugh, too.

The women sat at the table without a word. Lydia offered Catherine the tray of cakes. When Catherine bit into one, it tasted sweet and faintly nutty on her tongue. As she took a second bite, she captured Lydia's gaze again. Lydia blew gently on her drink, and held Catherine's eyes for a long time.

Bursting with emotion, Catherine felt like getting up and taking Lydia in her arms to kiss her with all the passion she felt. Instead, she wrenched herself away and looked out the window. She suspected that Lydia, too, was overcome when her voice cracked as she offered Catherine another cake. Catherine declined. She could eat or drink nothing at the moment. The two women sat in silence, staring out the window. Catherine traced the faint outline of tree tops visible below them in the light of a rising full moon. The glow mixed with the lamp light in the room and cast their shadows on the wall — two women seated at a small table, their heads tilted toward one another, moving closer, closer. *Might I act?* Catherine wondered. Would Lydia shy away if she kissed her? *I cannot. I mustn't.* Catherine looked back out the window.

The intensity of feeling softened and they struck up a conversation, pretending that nothing exceptional had taken place. Lydia concentrated on nibbling at a cake and Catherine followed her lead. A shadow on the wall behind Catherine mirrored the form of the seated woman, arms clasped around the knees closely listening to the conversation.

As they finished the last of the wine, a loud bell sounded. Lydia announced that dinner would be served momentarily. They had not eaten on their trip, and small cakes go only so far in quelling hunger. Still, they were reluctant to leave the room.

At the bottom of the stairs in the great hall, Hilary greeted both women affectionately. Other guests had joined Beatrice, Hilary and Marian at the long table. Catherine noticed additional places had not yet been occupied.

Hilary invited them to sit down and introduced Catherine to those she did not know. There was a baron from the northern part of Wales and several dukes from various parts of England. Some titled ladies had come from London as well. They all seemed to be long-time friends of the Ladies of Briarcrest. More guests, Beatrice said, would arrive early the next morning.

The guests engaged in lively conversation as dinner was served. When the food was set out, Catherine found another surprise awaited her. Those who had served the meal took their places at the table. The kitchen help also joined them.

Catherine had eaten at the homes of nobles before, but she had never seen those who served be allowed at the same table as their mistresses and masters.

Beatrice noticed Catherine staring down the table as the workers took their seats. "Are you surprised that we do not banish our help to some cold, dark room off the kitchen to eat, Catherine?"

Catherine started, hoping she had not offended her hostesses. "Yes, Beatrice. I must say, I do find it unusual," she said shyly.

"Good. Then we are as unconventional as we profess to be — now let me introduce you to those who have just joined us." Beatrice presented each person by name. As she did, they nodded with a smile toward Catherine. She acknowledged them in like manner.

With the introductions finished, dinner resumed. Catherine contented herself with listening to the diverse topics for most of the meal. The kitchen help discussed their activities for the preparation of the feast. The guests talked about their travels and of some of their mutual acquaintances.

There was a remarkable ease in the exchanges as discussions overlapped among the guests, their hostesses and the workers of Briarcrest. Everyone seemed to know one another from previous gatherings and no one seemed to notice class differences.

Between the wine Catherine had at dinner and the beverage she had earlier, Catherine felt bold and carefree. With no concern about what others might think, she looked long into Lydia's beautiful eyes. All through the meal, she and Lydia exchanged looks of passion. Oddly, no one seemed to notice.

When the meal ended, the help cleared the leftovers. The other guests excused themselves, saying their journeys had worn them out and they looked forward to a good night's rest. Marian begged her leave, too. She said she needed to attend to some matter for the children's party the next day.

"Marian still loves being around the young ones for the May feast," Beatrice explained to Catherine, forcing her to tear herself away from Lydia's gaze.

After Marian left, Lydia suggested that she and Catherine go upstairs to prepare for the bath. On those occasions when Catherine did not use her pitcher and basin, she preferred to bathe alone, using a small copper tub placed in the kitchen before the fire. She was not opposed to communal bathing, but her family had always preferred to be more solitary about their cleansing ritual. Although Catherine still struggled with uncertainty, she did not want to offend Beatrice and Hilary, nor did she want to disappoint Lydia. So she followed her companion upstairs to the large bedchamber without voicing her reservations.

In the women's absence, thick robes had been laid out on the bed for them. Catherine ran her hand over the garments. They were made of a soft, felted material. She turned to comment about the fabric in time to see Lydia removing her dress. She turned away quickly, feeling shy.

"Catherine, are you uneasy? Would you rather that I not share my bedchamber with you?" Lydia questioned.

"No, Lydia," Catherine answered quickly. "You just took me by surprise. I am...a little nervous about this communal bathing."

Unspoken emotion was beginning to take its toll on Lydia.

The next words slipped out of her mouth before she could stop herself. "If you would rather not stay here, I will arrange for another room for you, but you must tell me honestly."

Lydia regretted the sentence before she finished it. *I want you to stay, Catherine. How I long to be with you, even if only for a little while.*

Catherine stood in silence, bewildered. She did not want to leave. In an instant she decided it was time to stop holding back. "If you do not mind sharing your room with me, Lydia, I would like to stay. The house is full anyway, I imagine. Perhaps there is no other room available."

I do not want to go. I would like to share your bed, as you shared mine last evening. Even though we kept our distance, it was wonderful just being near you and holding your hand.

Lydia, still unsure of Catherine, said sharply, "There are other rooms, Catherine. You do not have to stay just because you think there is no other place for you to go." She caught herself. She did not want ill-humor to spoil this time. This was supposed to be a holiday, a time for them to enjoy each other. Still, she had to know something of what Catherine felt. "Tell me truthfully: Would you would really like to stay or not?"

Catherine looked deeply into Lydia's eyes. They looked to her as if they were on fire, and she felt her body burning in response. She became lost in a myriad of emotions.

"Catherine," Lydia repeated, "do you want to stay?" *Why am I always trying to pull your true feelings from you? I am afraid to be totally honest with you until I know how you feel. Please, Catherine, be truthful. I must know.*

Catherine's response was barely more than a whisper, but her eyes were bold and penetrating. "I want to stay, Lydia. With all my heart, I want to stay."

A deep sigh echoed from within Lydia. It was as if she had been holding her breath since the two women had parted months before on the feast of St. Andrew. Finally, Lydia felt as if she could breathe again. "And I want you to stay, Catherine."

As Catherine looked on, Lydia slipped off the rest of her clothes and put on one of the robes. Then, in a voice as soft as velvet, she said, "Let me help you, Catherine. Beatrice and Hilary are waiting."

Catherine blushed. Lydia smiled and put her hand on Catherine's shoulder. She crooned soothingly, "The bath is a very private affair for the ladies of this house, Catherine. Normally, they do not ask anyone to join them. It will just be the four of us. Remember, this is to be a time of enjoyment and respite."

Catherine tried to relax. "Yes, Lady Lydia, I shall try to keep that in mind."

Lydia helped Catherine undress and held out the other soft robe for her to put on. As Catherine slipped her arms into it, wrapping it around her body, she felt her apprehension fade. Lydia rubbed her hands reassuringly across Catherine's back. Catherine tried, unsuccessfully, to suppress a shiver at Lydia's touch.

The Bath

CATHERINE HUGGED THE soft robe tightly around her and followed Lydia down the hall. They padded past several large wooden doors and came to one standing ajar at the end of the hall. The glow of candlelight, visible through the opening, gave the room an inviting look. Lydia reached up and knocked on the door jam.

Beatrice responded from a distance. "Come in, dears."

Slipping into the room behind Lydia, Catherine felt as if she had entered a sacred place. *Peculiar. I do not ever recall having quite this feeling about any church or chapel I have been in, yet here is a holy place.*

She tried not to be too obvious as she looked around. Elegant tapestries hung on the walls. The bedcover of brocade and lace shone warmly in the candle glow. The carvings on the thick, dark posts and headboard were even more elaborate than the bed in Lydia's room.

They crossed the threshold to the suite's next room. Warm, moist air met them at the doorway. Beatrice and Hilary were submerged up to their necks, their eyes closed, in a large wooden tub. Although the steam that rose from the surface of the water made them look almost transparent, the contentment on their faces was still visible. A fire roaring in the fireplace provided the only other light for the room. Next to the tub, within arm's reach, a small wooden table held a pitcher, four metal cups, and a bowl of fruit.

Lydia's tone suggested that she felt the same reverence in these chambers as Catherine did. When she spoke, it was almost in a whisper of awe. "We're honored that you have invited us here tonight."

Hilary responded without opening her eyes. "Please, ladies, do come and join us. There is a chill in the air tonight. The sooner you get into the water, the better off you will be."

From a dark corner of the room, an older woman appeared

as if she had materialized out of thin air. Catherine recognized her as one of those to whom she had been introduced at dinner. Her name was Joanna and she had been in the service of Briarcrest for many years, since long before Beatrice had arrived.

Joanna invited the young women to remove their robes. Lydia slipped hers from her shoulders, then stepped onto a stool beside the tub and climbed in. As she sank down into the water, she gave Catherine a reassuring smile.

Catherine let Joanna help her out of her robe and she followed Lydia into the tub. As she lowered herself into the water, she discovered a low bench at the bottom and she sat down.

Herbs and dried flower petals floated on the surface of the warm water. The heated liquid penetrated Catherine's cool skin and soothed her. Beside her, Lydia heaved a deep sigh.

Beatrice welcomed them, asking if the water was warm enough for them. Both women moaned their approval.

Joanna filled four cups with wine and handed them to the women.

Beatrice opened one eye and took her drink. Then she glanced at Catherine and questioned, "Tell us, Catherine, has Lydia enticed you to stay with us for more than a day or two?"

"I hope to stay for a few days, with your permission, Beatrice. But then I must get back to Willowglen. I am expecting a shipment of spices to arrive and I must be there to receive them. This is also the first time I have left the shop in Sarah's care, so I am anxious to see how she will fare in my absence."

Hilary added, "You must think her capable or you would not have left her in charge."

"I think she is more capable than she knows, but I do need to return by the end of the week. I hope you understand."

"Of course we do, dear," Beatrice said.

Hilary added, "It is just that we want you to be able to rest and enjoy your stay. We are so delighted to have you here, but of course, you must look after your business. We understand perfectly well that a trade, like this household and its lands, must be properly managed."

Beatrice said, "Nevertheless, Catherine, while you are here, we hope you will not think of any of that. Just enjoy yourself."

"Thank you both," Catherine answered. "I am sure I shall. My visit has been wonderful thus far. I am looking forward to the rest of it, to be sure."

Beatrice motioned to Joanna, who had retreated into the shadows in a corner of the room. When the older woman came close, Beatrice said, gently, "You do not need to stay, Joanna.

We will be fine. I am sure you are tired. It has been a long day with all the May preparations taking place. Go off to bed now, dear."

"Thank you, mum, I shall," the woman replied. She took a final pot of water from the hearth and poured it slowly into the tub. Then she left, closing the big, wooden door in the outer room after her.

The four women chatted for a while. Catherine found the plans for the next day's celebration fascinating. She had never participated in so elaborate a May Day. She was more familiar with the Church's feast of the Virgin, celebrated at Wooster Abbey and in Willowglen, though she was well aware that the goddess rituals were still observed throughout the countryside. Briarcrest's holiday, with its woodland goddess theme, intrigued Catherine. Higher up the heirarchy, Church officials forbade participation in these pagan celebrations. Local officials frowned upon it, for the most part. In the countryside, however, they still remembered and relished the old ways. Catherine, although never having participated, knew the origins and meaning of the May celebration. May Day celebrated love, courtship and mating. The Queen of the May, with origins in the fertility goddess, dominated the celebration. In some cases, she was accompanied by a King. Symbols of life were everywhere. No matter a person's station in life, she or he spent May Day gathering flowers and reveling in the forest. Catherine listened as they spoke of the ancient foundations of the day. The guests, Beatrice said, looked forward to a romp in Briarcrest Forest throwing off inhibitions and acting on their most intimate desires.

Catherine wondered if she could abandon her own reserve. She glanced over at Lydia and discovered that unsettling gaze waiting to meet her own. Catherine smiled self-consciously. She realized she was surrounded by a sea of grey-green again. It must have been for a longer time than she thought, for Hilary was asking Catherine a question and Catherine had no idea what the topic was.

"I apologize, Hilary. My mind wandered. I didn't hear your question. What was it that you asked?"

Hilary studied Catherine. Then she smiled and said, "It was of no importance, dear."

Conversation picked up again. It surprised Catherine how easy it was to sit, talking casually, in a tub of water with these women. She sat back and took a sip of the spiced drink. The liquid slid down her throat without effort. The aroma from the warm bath water wafted over Catherine. Without thinking, she identified a mixture of chamomile and rose hips with a little lavender added—a mixture to promote relaxation and well being. It was working.

Catherine melted into the warm water. It felt so good to be here and to have Lydia beside her. Conversation trailed off. Only an occasional sigh broke the comfortable silence.

"I think if I do not get out of this tub soon, I shall fall asleep right here and drown," Hilary said.

They all chuckled their agreement. Lydia and Catherine climbed out of the tub and found a large piece of felted drying cloth by each of their garments. They dried off quickly, donned their robes, thanked the ladies, and bid them good night.

As the two young women stepped out into the hall, the cool air made their skin tingle. They hurried down the hall to Lydia's bedchamber and dove under the covers of the large canopy bed as quickly as they could. Lydia found and held Catherine's hand as they had done the night before in Willowglen. The room was pitch black. Both women smiled contentedly.

After a while, Lydia whispered, "Catherine? Are you asleep?"

"No," Catherine replied. "I am enjoying the soothing aftereffects of the bath. The herbs in it were very good for relaxation."

"Yes, I know."

"How do you know?"

"I had an excellent teacher in the art of herbs and herbal blending."

"And who might that have been?" Catherine inquired, teasing.

"Perhaps you have heard of her. Her name is Mistress Catherine Hawkins."

"I believe I may have heard the name before, but how did you come to know of her?"

"I met her once, in a town called Willowglen. She caught my eye when I attended the fair there." Feeling very brave in the darkness of the room, Lydia added, "Soon after, she captured my heart."

Silence.

"Lydia?"

"Yes, Catherine."

"I have the feeling that you already knew a great deal about herbs when you came to me. Am I correct?"

Silence.

"Well?"

"Yes, Catherine. As you probably realize by now, Beatrice and Hilary are well versed in herbology. They have taught me a great deal over the years."

"Lydia?"

"Yes, Catherine."

"Why?"

"Do you not know?"

"Tell me."

"Because from the moment I first saw you, I knew...I was...in love with you."

Catherine was afraid to move, afraid of the desire welling up within her.

Lydia, too, was fearful, having spoken what she had not dared to say for so long. She too was still.

More thick silence followed before Catherine dared to speak again. "Lydia?"

"Yes, Catherine."

"I'm glad you came to me."

"So am I, Catherine."

Lydia moved closer to Catherine. Catherine could feel the warmth of her body now. Lydia propped herself up on her elbow and brought her face close to Catherine's. Catherine felt Lydia's breath on her cheek. Lydia found the cord around Catherine's neck and traced its path with a finger until she reached the medallion just above the space between Catherine's breasts. Lydia felt Catherine's chest rise and fall beneath her fingertips and heard Catherine's breath quicken. Catherine did not protest Lydia's touch.

Lydia picked up the pendant and caressed it between her fingers. The polished metal felt smooth. It still held the warmth of Catherine's body. "It makes me happy to know that you wear the medallion I gave you."

Catherine opened her mouth to speak. At first, no sound emerged. She tried a second time. "It...makes me happy to wear it."

"Why?" asked Lydia.

"Because it reminds me of you. It makes me feel close to you."

"Your cloak does the same for me. I am saddened that soon I shall have less occasion to wear it. It will be too warm even for evenings in the garden."

"I must think of something else to give you, then. Something you can keep with you no matter the season."

"I would like that very much, Catherine."

Lydia wanted to caress Catherine's skin, to feel its

smoothness beneath her hand, but she dared not. *If she became ill at ease, I could not bear it. For now, I shall savor the sweetness of this moment and be content.*

Lydia carefully replaced the medallion on Catherine's skin. She leaned back onto the bed and wondered what Catherine was thinking, but she dared not ask.

Perhaps it was just as well. For Catherine, again, struggled with confusion, wanting Lydia to touch her, wanting even more to take Lydia in her arms and caress her. Yet how could it ever happen? She experienced a goodness, a wholeness with Lydia. She did not want to jeopardize that. She could not risk frightening her away.

Catherine reached for Lydia's hand this time. Both women lay in the dark without speaking. After a time, their desire quieted and they finally drifted off to sleep.

BEATRICE AND HILARY, still sitting in the warm, fragrant water, speculated that if the two young women had not already engaged in lovemaking, it would not be long before they did. They talked of their sadness at the fact that Lydia's father would not allow her to follow a path different from that which he had ordained for her.

Beatrice sighed. "It is difficult enough to be a woman in these times without the likes of my brother for a guardian. Would that things could be different, but I am afraid it is too much to ask. It makes my heart heavy, Hilary. He will only choose for Lydia that which will take her spirit away. She could be so happy and she deserves no less."

Hilary caressed Beatrice's greying hair with dampened fingers. All she could offer was an empathetic, "I know, love. I know."

Then they, too, fell silent for a while.

Chapter
Seventeen

May Day
Briarcrest

IN SPITE OF her struggles the night before, Catherine awoke refreshed and feeling content. When she reached over to find Lydia's hand, she discovered that the other woman had already gotten up. Catherine threw back the covers and swung her legs over the side of the bed. As she stood, she tightened her muscles into a stretch, then felt them relax. The spring sun that streamed though the window at her back warmed her. While she dressed, Catherine's thoughts were of Lydia. *She is so lovely. She makes my heart sing. I wonder, does she want what I want? Do I know what I want? I am beginning to think so, and is this not May Day? Is this not the day — what was is that Beatrice said last night? — when we should abandon all our inhibitions and seek our heart's desire?*

The door swung open and Lydia entered the room looking as if she had blown in on a soft spring breeze. She was radiant. Catherine smiled.

"Good morning, Mistress Catherine. Are you ready for this grand celebration of May Day?" sang Lydia.

"I am not sure that I know how to join in these festivities, Lydia. Remember, the only May celebration in which I have taken part is the May procession at the Abbey to honor the Virgin."

Lydia laughed. "Well, I do not think it is a virgin we honor today. We celebrate the goddess of the May rather than the Church's Virgin Lady."

Catherine seemed deep in thought. Lydia waited, accustomed to Catherine's reflective moods. Finally, Catherine spoke. "Lydia?"

"Yes, Catherine."

"Is this not the day to throw off our inhibitions and act without restraint?"

"Why, yes, Catherine." Lydia's eyes danced. "Why do you ask?"

Catherine felt unnerved. "I was just wondering..."

Lydia teased, "Why, Catherine, what wild, raucous thing would you like to do this May Day?"

Catherine blushed and struggled for words. "I was...that is, I thought...I mean, we..." Her eyes pleaded for rescue from her embarrassment.

Lydia threw back her head and laughed a deep, unfettered laugh. Such an expression might have seemed unbecoming of a lady in some circles, but Catherine found it attractive.

Lydia offered, "Perhaps we all have our inner longings that we would like to act on this day, Mistress. I would encourage you to act upon yours. I, for one, intend to look for an opportunity to carry out mine."

As Lydia looked away, suddenly shy, Catherine tried to guess what Lydia meant. Was her interpretation pure folly?

A knock on the door prevented her from questioning Lydia any further. One of the kitchen maids waited outside with a tray of food. Lydia thanked the girl and took the tray, depositing it on the table.

"I had a light meal prepared for us before we join the celebration in the forest. I hope you don't mind, I thought we could eat here instead of going down to the main hall."

"I can't think of anything I would rather do than enjoy the morning meal here alone with you, Lydia, except..." Catherine's thought alarmed her.

Lydia turned, surprised by Catherine's half-finished sentence. *Perhaps bringing Catherine to this May celebration was an even better idea than I imagined. Maybe she will reveal her heart to me before this day ends. How I want to tell her mine. Oh, how very much I want to tell her mine.*

Wrestling with embarrassment, Catherine changed the subject. "I find I am quite hungry this morning, Lady Lydia. What have you there?"

"Some bread and spiced potatoes, and a large pot of your favorite mint tea."

Catherine picked up the pot and poured a steaming cup for each of them. Then they sat and ate in shy silence.

Glancing out the window, Catherine followed the carpet of trees below. Briarcrest Forest, vast and plush, spread out before her. A stream wound its way around the edge of the wood, glinting in the sun like a thin silver ribbon. Several small bridges spanned the stream. There was a great deal of activity on them. People carried large baskets and bundles into the forest. Others returned empty-handed.

"Briarcrest Forest looks beautiful from up here," remarked

Catherine.

Lydia agreed.

They lingered over their meal until they heard another knock at the door: The kitchen maid, come to retrieve the tray, and to let the women know the festivities had begun. Lydia excused herself for a moment, saying she had something to attend to, asking Catherine to wait for her in the courtyard. Catherine made her way downstairs wondering just what had put the light in those dancing grey-green eyes.

BRIARCREST HALL WAS quiet when Catherine entered it. Everyone had left for the forest. Catherine found the large double doors that led to the garden. Through the paned windows, she saw a pond at the center of the enclosure with several benches surrounding it. More seats were nearly hidden here and there among flowering bushes and tall plants climbing arched trellises. She walked outside to wait for Lydia.

Catherine chose a stone seat by the clear pool in the well tended garden so that Lydia would find her easily. She studied the reflection of the water blossoms in the mirror-smooth surface of the pond and sighed. *I think it could be very difficult to leave this place.*

A moment later, Lydia arrived carrying a small, covered basket and inquired, "Are you ready to be my companion to search for the Queen of the May, the Green Lady? You shall need an escort through the forest. Every new guest to Briarcrest Wood must have a guide. I shall be yours, M'lady." Lydia bowed low in the manner of a nobleman.

Catherine blushed and murmured, "Why, thank you, Lady Lydia."

As the two women wound their way through Briarcrest Hall, Catherine admired the festive decorations once again.

When they reached the outer courtyard, Catherine marveled at its transformation. It had changed from an active work area to an enclosure for a fair. When their carriage had pulled into the courtyard the day before, it had been bustling with workers. Now the stables, located at the far north end, the kennels, and the aviary to the east were all quiet. The area had been brightly decorated for the children's version of the May celebration. A small feast, set out in a tent made of netting, awaited the arrival of the guests, and various games had been set up on the grounds. Catherine tried to envision the area filled with youngsters running about, squealing with delight, and Marian in the midst of them all.

Lydia watched with pleasure as Catherine scanned the courtyard and smiled. Lydia stretched out her hand. When Catherine reached for it, her whole body shivered with delight. A stolen look at her companion told Catherine that Lydia had felt it, too.

Catherine quickly examined her feet. Boots. She noticed her boots and tried to recall getting dressed that morning, but it was difficult to remember much of anything at the moment. She was not able to move. A tumult of emotion washed over her once again. She wanted to flee but her feet would not accommodate her. She had to force herself to remember that this was the May celebration and that she was there to enter into the spirit of the feast with Lydia.

She looked into Lydia's eyes and grasped her hand firmly. Lydia squeezed Catherine's hand in return. Oh, how Catherine wanted to take Lydia in her arms right there and kiss her fully on her lips. To keep from doing just that, she broke into a run with Lydia in tow. They sped toward Briarcrest Forest, laughing as they plunged into the observance of the day. Their skirts whipped around them in the breeze as they ran. Briarcrest's great gated entrance had been thrown wide open and festooned with colorful fabric. Banners and flags suspended from poles marked a path to a stone bridge that took them into the forest.

When they reached the wood, Catherine dropped onto a fallen log to catch her breath. Lydia slowed to an amble and wandered amid nearby trees. The aroma of rich earth and pine sap met Catherine's nostrils as she breathed deeply to recover from her sprint. Forest shadows caressed her face and neck in welcome coolness. In the distance, birds chirped the message that their home was being invaded. Deeper in the forest, she heard laughter and shouts as people called to one another playfully. Their faint muffled footsteps padded on the pine-strewn ground as they moved about.

The woods, like Briarcrest, had been decorated for the May celebration. Long streamers of colored cloth hung from tree limbs and banners adorned trunks here and there. Lydia approached a branch and removed several ribbons. She started back toward her companion with them in her hand.

Catherine drank Lydia in as she approached. *I can never seem to get enough of her. I wonder why that is?*

With her eyes twinkling mischievously, Lydia crooned, "You must be properly dressed for the celebration, M'lady. I fear if you are not, I shall have to call the Lord Forester to banish you from these woods."

Catherine, catching Lydia's playfulness, replied, "Oh,

please, Lady Lydia, I am new to the way in which the May is celebrated at Briarcrest. I didn't know that I wasn't dressed properly. Please don't send the Forester after me."

"Well, then, you must let me dress you with these emblems of the celebration."

Lydia put her basket down and removed Catherine's net bonnet. Her thick dark brown hair fell and lingered on her shoulders before cascading to her waist under its own weight. Lydia ran her hand through the silky strands. Catherine thrilled at her touch. Lydia could barely continue, such was the burning in her own breast. Only with great effort did she will her hands to move. She tied the ribbons into Catherine's tresses, wondering if Catherine felt the message of love she tried to convey with each touch.

Suddenly, Catherine caught Lydia's hand and took the last ribbon from her. With as stern a look as Catherine could summon, she spoke with pretended sharpness. "How dare you tell me you would give me over to Sir Forester, when you yourself have not come into the forest with the proper streamers in your own hair. You shall have to submit to my decorations, M'lady, or I shall be forced to give you over to the dreaded Forester myself."

With feigned resignation, Lydia replied, "Yes, Mistress Catherine. I shall submit." *I wonder if you would like me to submit to more than putting ribbons in my hair? I should certainly like to, but you are so restrained. Will you allow yourself to follow your heart's desire today?*

The women changed places. Catherine, following Lydia's earlier lead, removed the young woman's cap and let her hair fall down her back. A sweet pain rushed through Catherine as she watched the long, sleek auburn hair drop down her back. Small sparkles of sunlight filtered through the trees and played on the reddish-brown strands. Catherine fumbled with the strip of cloth in her hand. Time seemed to stand still as Catherine struggled with her feelings. She wanted to scoop Lydia's soft hair into her hands and nuzzle it. She wanted to bury her head in her neck — and kiss her.

Lydia turned to see if something was wrong.

To conceal her thoughts, Catherine pronounced, "Now, I think M'lady may not be festive enough with just one of these ribbons, but it will have to do for now." She tied Lydia's hair into an intricate lacing of cloth and tresses, working slowly. It felt good to touch Lydia.

As Catherine finished tying the ribbon, she sighed, "I suppose we will never find the Queen of the May if we don't start looking."

Lydia laughed, "My dear Catherine, we are in no hurry to find the Queen. We shall all find her by the end of the day. Who shall be first and who shall be last matters little. What matters is taking delight in the day, the beauty of the wood, and being able to act upon the desire in your heart."

Bashfully, Catherine replied, "I thought the sport was to find the Queen — but then, I have never taken part in this game before."

"Allow me to enlighten you in the celebration of the May Queen as it is done here at Briarcrest, Mistress Hawkins." Lydia scooped up the basket and took Catherine's arm. She led her through the trees, speaking as they strolled along.

"The Queen of the May shall be found in Briarcrest Wood by one and all who enter into her feast there. She is Mother of All and Lady of All Living Things. It is she who bestows new life, which we honor during May Day. It does not matter who arrives at her hiding place first or last. The conquest is in the joining. Success is in the celebration of life to its fullest. The object is to be carefree and have your fondest wishes granted all during this day."

As Lydia continued, Catherine thought, *If you only knew my fondest desire, Lady Lydia, perhaps you might not be so willing to have me here with you now.* After a time, she ventured, "What is your heart's desire, Lydia?"

Lydia did not answer. She longed to reveal her heart to Catherine, but she had hesitated for so long, afraid that they were not of the same mind, that she found it difficult to do so now. *If I reveal my heart to you, Catherine, will you flee? I wish I knew for certain how you truly feel.*

"Will you tell me? Will you tell me your heart's desire?" Catherine pressed.

"Perhaps before this May Day is finished, I shall, Catherine. Perhaps I shall. But for now, I am your guide. Follow me if you dare. However, we must beware the old Hag of the Wood. If she sees us and gives us a dry branch, the Queen may not look kindly upon us when you come into her presence. We must avoid the Hag at all costs."

Catherine, taken by this tale, questioned, "Why does she haunt this wood? Can we tell of her approach? Can we hide? Can she be fooled into not giving us her branch?"

Lydia smiled softly. "She is one who did not reach for her heart's desire, so now she tries to keep others from achieving theirs." She looked around, then put her mouth close to Catherine's ear and whispered, "She wears a bell. So listen for it. If we see her and she has not yet seen us, we may flee her and hide. But once she says our names, we must accept the twig she gives us."

Just then, they heard the faint clanging of a bell. Lydia squealed, turned on her heel, and darted off. Catherine bounded after her.

As they ran along the edge of the wood, Lydia pointed beyond the forest. "Quick — into the meadow — I know a place we can hide there. The old Hag never leaves the forest."

They pounded toward the field. The grass was knee-high, thick and green. Bursts of color from spring wildflowers surrounded them as they ran. The bell resounded behind them. Catherine's heart pounded. How would they conceal themselves in the open meadow? She stopped, studying her surroundings.

Lydia called to her, "Quickly, Catherine. Follow me."

Catherine still did not move.

Lydia retraced her steps, seized Catherine's hand, and pulled her along. As they ran, the grass became taller. It came to their hips, then to their waists. When it was almost up to their shoulders, Lydia pulled Catherine to the ground, shouting, "Down!"

Gasping to catch their breath, the two women lay surrounded by a soft, green wall of blooming grasses. The scent of spring enveloped them.

Catherine strained to hear the bell. The clanging sound did not seem to change. She listened again. Yes, she was sure it was not changing. How would they ever get back into the woods if the old Hag never left her spot where the forest and meadow met? Finally, Catherine could bear it no longer. "Lydia, she is not leaving. How will we get back to the celebration?"

Lydia stared at her, blinking in disbelief. Finally, a hint of a smile showed at the corners of her mouth. She struggled to hold back her laughter, but she could contain it no longer. Her giggle swelled until Lydia was howling with merriment, while Catherine watched her in dismay.

When it seemed Lydia would never stop, Catherine cried, "Why are you laughing at me, Lydia?"

Lydia wiped tears from her eyes as she confessed, "Oh, Catherine, it is a game! There is no old Hag. There is no dry twig. There are only bells, hung throughout the forest for our amusement. Don't be perturbed with me. Can you forgive me? I could not bear it if you were angry with me!"

A smile stole across Catherine's face as she realized the humor of the prank. Then she, too, began to laugh, more at herself than anything. Lydia joined her. They held their sides, roaring wildly. They rolled in the tall grass, kicked their feet and howled some more. When their laughter died, their eyes met.

Catherine felt submerged in the grey-green depths, encompassed by their beauty. Lydia looked long into the eyes of the woman who had first beguiled her long months ago in Willowglen. Her soul sang a wordless refrain, filled with love. Lydia moved closer. Catherine felt Lydia's breath on her face. They drew together and, lips meeting, they kissed softly.

When it was over, Lydia thought, *If I am to be rejected, it will be now.*

She waited, her eyes trained on Catherine's. Instead of rebuffing her, Catherine leaned forward and kissed her again, this time stronger, harder, feeling as if she never wanted to stop.

Lydia's breathing grew more labored. Catherine's breath quickened. She felt Lydia's lips part slightly, and Catherine opened her own. Like thirsty soil that had endured years of drought, they drank each other in.

Thoughts raced through Catherine's mind now. Thoughts she questioned if she dare act upon. She had no time to decide, though, for Lydia's hand was on her vest, pulling at the laces. Catherine did not protest.

Moments later, Catherine felt the warm sun on her bare shoulders and breasts. Looking into Lydia's eyes, she recognized her own emotion. Feeling as if she were standing on the edge of a cliff, she took a deep breath and jumped, headlong, into a deep grey-green abyss. A long shadow followed her into the depths.

She peeled away Lydia's clothing to reveal her smooth, white skin. Catherine drank in the beauty of Lydia's body, marveling at her firm, small breasts. Their breathing became more labored still as they reached out and touched one another tentatively.

Catherine paused for a moment, concerned. Looking around, she asked, "Can anyone see us?"

Lydia's response was thick and heavy with emotion. "The grass is over our heads and everyone is deep in the forest by now."

All was forgotten then. They relished each other's beauty as they had yearned to do for so long. They kissed. They embraced, feeling the softness of breast against breast. Finally, they lay down surrounded by the sweet cocoon of grasses, the women's shadows a dark blanket that spread and gently writhed.

Catherine exclaimed to Lydia, "You feel so good against my

skin. I have wanted to feel you this way longer than I have known."

"And I, you, Catherine," whispered Lydia.

Lydia caressed Catherine's breast and felt the firmness of her nipple as it rose up to meet her palm. She felt her own desire expressed in the wetness between her legs. They kissed again. As they stroked each other, they felt their passion rise to an all-consuming fire.

Heedless of nothing now, only wanting more of Lydia, Catherine grasped her by the shoulders, pressing against her body. Kissing her again, she found the softness inside Lydia's mouth. Catherine thrilled at the feel of Lydia's skin against her own hand and, remembering her vow to celebrate the May with abandon, Catherine followed her heart's desire. Lydia responded fully, surrendering to Catherine completely. Lydia followed with her own longings for Catherine. That May Day, they expressed their love for one another as completely as ever was possible. Feeling the sweetness of their ecstasy, they held one another close. There were no words now. There was only a feeling of deep joy — and love.

CATHERINE AWOKE TO the sound of a bell. She smiled to herself when she thought of the Forest Hag and Lydia's prank. When she looked at the woman asleep beside her, she was overcome with feelings of deep love. Quickly, though, they were replaced by feelings of concern. *Surely two women have never before fallen in love this way. I fear it will never be understood. I cannot see how we can continue together. Yet I cannot bear the thought of giving her up.*

Lydia stirred. She stretched sensuously and looked into Catherine's eyes with longing. Catherine fought against her rising passion. It was replaced with doubt that moved like a fast-paced storm cloud. *Perhaps this is just a May Day lark for her. Perhaps she has done this merely for the thrill of the day.*

Yet, deep down inside, Catherine knew that was not the truth. Her doubt dissipated. *Or is it more than the wild abandon of May Day to her? I must believe, with all my heart, that she has expressed true feelings. If this is so, then we must find a way to be together. Somehow. We must.*

"Why do you look at me thus?" Lydia asked bashfully.

"I wonder what you think of, of what has happened between us?"

Lydia began, "I think..."

Catherine held her breath.

"I think I love you as I could love no other. I think that I have known this since the first day I saw you at Willowglen. I think I have wanted this day to come for a very long time, but I was not sure you wanted it, too. I could not act unless I knew you were of like mind. When we kissed, at last, I knew it was true. I was not wrong, was I, Catherine?"

Overcome by emotion, Catherine did not answer.

Lydia pressed her, repeating, "Catherine? Was I wrong?"

Catherine's voice was difficult to hear at first, but it strengthened as she expressed what was in her heart. "No, Lydia. You were not wrong. I have felt deep emotion for you from the first day I laid eyes upon you. At first I did not understand it. I have never felt thus for anyone before in my life. I was unsure of how to act—or even if I should take action. I was fearful that you might disapprove. I was afraid that I might lose the friendship that we had. And now? Now, I am still unsure, not of how I feel, rather, I wonder where will this take us? Having expressed my love for you so completely, I am not sure I can let you go. Yet how can we be together? You are someone else's ward. You must do as your father bids you. Perhaps, it might have been better had this day never come."

Lydia silenced Catherine by putting a finger on her lips. Moving closer, she kissed her. It was a long, loving kiss. When she moved away, Lydia looked Catherine in the eye and said matter-of-factly, "We shall find a way, Catherine, for I want to be with you. And, Catherine?"

"Yes, Lydia?"

"I love you."

Catherine tried to swallow her tears. With a tremor in her voice, she said, "I love you, too, Lydia. You are truly my heart's desire."

They kissed and embraced again. In the distance, a bell rang.

IT WAS MID-AFTERNOON by the time they ate the small lunch from Lydia's basket.

As they left the meadow, Catherine asked, "Do you think anyone has been looking for us?"

Lydia replied, "I am sure that everyone has been about their own observance of the Green Lady's feast. They have all been far too busy to miss us. However, on this day, one does not ask where others might be or what they might be doing. One does not attend to anything but one's own desires."

They walked on a little further and Catherine stopped.

"Is something wrong, Catherine?"

"Lydia, you have been to the May feast at Briarcrest before, is that not true?"

"Yes. Why do you ask, Catherine?"

"I just wondered if you had ever done anything like this..."

Lydia understood. "Catherine, I have not been with anyone other than you — not anyone. Do you understand?"

Catherine nodded assent.

Lydia moved close to Catherine and gazed into her eyes. "Now, I desire to be with none other."

A smile crept into the corners of Catherine's mouth.

Lydia continued, "As for coming to Briarcrest for the May celebration, it is true. I have been here often during May Day. However, I have always stayed inside the confines of Briarcrest's walls. When I was younger, I attended the parties in Briarcrest courtyard. The May celebration brings many children to Briarcrest, including the children of the staff and those from the village. Beatrice wanted me to have other children to play with when I was a child. She did not think it mattered that they were not the children of nobles, as my father would have insisted upon. Beatrice and Hilary always made sure that, as youngsters, we received our heart's desire on May Day.

"When I grew older, I was still not invited into the forest. Rather, I stayed behind and helped Marian with the parties given for the young ones. I was invited to participate in the banquet and the entertainment in the evening, but I have never been into Briarcrest Wood to look for the Queen. Until now, seeking my heart's desire on May Day consisted of enjoying sweet cakes and spiced wine and playing at children's games."

Catherine asked, skeptically, "How did you know about the bells and the old Hag, then?"

Lydia chuckled. "Even as a child, one hears the stories of the grownups' antics in the forest. Sometimes adults do not realize that children are listening. Then, too, whenever I had a question, I knew I could get a truthful answer from either Beatrice or Hilary. A few years ago, I asked them about the old Hag. After they explained the prank, they told me that someday, I, too, might have a special guest to play this trick on when we heard the bells."

Catherine grunted, finding it hard to believe that she had been so gullible.

They walked on quietly until they reached the edge of the forest again.

"This may seem a curious question, Lydia, but I wonder how is it that Hilary has been with your aunt all these years?"

Lydia smiled the smile of one who knew a secret. "Beatrice and Hilary are like us, Catherine."

"Like us? What do you mean?"

"I mean, they love each other. I mean, they have dedicated their lives to one other, similarly as do a man and woman in marriage."

Catherine was astonished. She squinted at Lydia, pondering her answer. At first, she had trouble believing it, but the more she mulled it over, the more she began to understand. Finally, when she spoke, it was with excitement in her voice. "This is amazing. Yet how could I not have realized? How could I have thought that Hilary lived here merely because of Beatrice's generosity to someone who needed a haven?"

Catherine began to pace as she spoke, trying to catch up to the thoughts that rushed through her mind. "How could I not have seen what becomes so apparent to me now? They are more than companions. And this is not just Beatrice's home. This is Hilary's home as well. This is incredible! Like us, you say? You mean there are others? And they have managed to find happiness together? Do you think we could find such happiness together?"

Catherine did not wait for an answer. Even as she uttered the words, doubt crept in until she found the whole idea absurd. How could Lydia know such a thing about Beatrice and Hilary?

"But you cannot be serious, Lydia."

"I most certainly am, Catherine."

Lydia's confidence took Catherine by surprise. "How do you know?"

"When I was a small child, I use to steal into their bedchamber early in the morning. Marian would try to stop me, but Beatrice always insisted that she be allowed to enjoy my childhood. *'Before we know it, she will be grown up and gone. Perhaps we shall not see her again. Let us enjoy her while we can, Marian.'* After that, I would climb into bed and snuggle up to the two of them, and feel so warm and secure. Sometimes Beatrice would tell me stories while I lay there—stories of strong, brave women who ruled kingdoms and did great deeds that some thought only men could do. There were times when, listening to her, I thought myself capable of anything. I cherish the memories of those mornings, Catherine.

"One day, as I was about to enter womanhood, I had been thinking about those times. A measure of sadness came over me, knowing that those comforting morning visits with the Ladies of Briarcrest were over. Hilary took me out riding that day in an effort to chase the dark clouds of my brooding away. During our ride, I asked her why it was that she and Beatrice slept in the same room when there were so many bedchambers at Briarcrest. Marian and I each had our own rooms when we visited and there were still others that sat unused until visitors came. Hilary responded that it was a private affair between herself and Beatrice, but that if Beatrice would be willing to talk to me about it, she, too, would agree.

"That evening, Beatrice and Hilary called me to their chambers. We sat at their little table in front of the fire and ate honeyed cakes together. They told me of their care for one another and they explained to me that some women had no desire to be wed. This was the first time that I had heard that others felt as I did. Until then, I had thought I must be the only young woman in creation who did not want a husband. However, when I told them this, they pointed out that not everyone was as fortunate as they were. Not everyone could live as they were able due to Beatrice's high station and treasury. Of course, Lady Hilary is a woman of some means herself, you know."

Catherine listened to Lydia, wide-eyed, as she continued.

"Then they explained that not everyone understood their association and they told me that, mostly, others chose to think that they were companions and nothing more. They asked me not to speak of it without discernment. I understood that it was important to do so, although it was not until recently that I realized just why. Oh, Catherine, I have had ample opportunity to observe these two Ladies over the years. No other pair is more devoted to one another. They care very much for one another. They love one another as we now know we love each other.

"Once, back in Willowglen, you told me you had not found any couple respectful enough or caring enough to cause you to admire their union. During that conversation, I said I felt the same way. I knew I had an excellent example in Hilary and Beatrice. However, since we had only recently met, it did not seem prudent to discuss these details of the lives of the Ladies of Briarcrest."

"I see," Catherine said thoughtfully.

They walked deeper into the forest. As they passed a tall fir tree, a tiny bell pinged its song. They looked up into the branches and laughed, then clasped hands and walked on. Following the strains of song and peals of laughter, they reached a clearing and met an extraordinary sight.

The trees opened to form a giant, vaulted area. Overhead, densely intertwined branches kept the vicinity cool and dark as night. A fire burned in a large pit, illuminating the blackness. Beyond it, they saw a long table, festooned with green and gold decorations. Most incredible of all was the huge figure of the Green Lady that loomed before them. Catherine's mouth fell open as she stared at the magnificent towering image. Made entirely from branches, vines and leaves, she sat on a twig throne raised up on a large platform. Flower garlands decorated her head. More blossoms adorned her leafy torso, forming a rich regal robe. She was the guest of honor at the feast, the Queen of the May herself.

Below the Green Lady, a group of people played instruments and sang rousing songs. They drank large tankards of ale and merrymaking abounded. A circle of people surrounded Lydia and Catherine and greeted them with joyful dancing. Each person was decorated with flowers and streamers. They placed flower wreaths on Lydia's and Catherine's head and laid garlands on their shoulders, welcoming them to the Lady's throne room. Goblets of a frothy, amber drink were thrust into their hands and they were drawn into the merrymaking. They danced and sang and drank until they felt lightheaded. Then Lydia and Catherine walked to a quiet corner at the edge the clearing.

As they sat and caught their breath, Lydia mused, "I wonder how Marian is getting on at the children's celebration? This is the first May feast that we have not been together. I hope she is feeling well enough to contend with all those spirited youngsters."

"Why do you say that, Lydia?"

"Her old body is giving her a great deal of trouble these days, Catherine. Even more than she lets on. I know she takes herbs—for a digestive malady, she says—but I wonder if they help her much."

Catherine asked, "Have you heard her speak of any particular difficulties, Lydia?"

"Oh, Marian never complains about anything, Catherine, so it's difficult to tell what might be ailing her. Now that I think of it, though, she had some trouble when we were at Greencastle. One day, I found her in her room looking very pale and holding her chest. She had not met me after the noon meal as she had said she would. I became concerned and went to look for her. When I found her, the sight of her frightened me. I didn't know what to do. She was pallid and weak, but she assured me it was nothing but poor digestion and that it would pass. She asked me to stay with her, which I did. I could not have left her alone in her state. I remember wishing that I had some measure of your skill at healing.

"After a time, the difficulty seemed to pass, and color returned to her face. She slept then, and when she awoke, she seemed almost her old self, so I thought she was correct in saying it was some bit of food that had upset her. She never seemed to get her old vigor back after that, though. Still, she will not admit that she is ailing."

Catherine recalled Marian's flushed cheeks when they arrived the previous day. The same warning sounded within her again, but she hesitated to speak of her concern. She did not want to frighten Lydia with her suspicion that Marian might well have a heart ailment. The skilled healer knew it might be treatable with foxglove, but she wondered if it would be possible to intervene discreetly. Catherine consoled herself with her newly gained knowledge that the ladies of Briarcrest were well versed in the art of using herbs—assuming, of course, that Marian had not tried to hide her affliction from them.

To soothe Lydia's concern, Catherine pretended indifference. "Marian is no longer a young woman, Lydia. She will probably lose more of her vitality as the years go by. Perhaps what she experienced that day at Greencastle was only as she said—a bit of bad food."

"I hope you are right, Catherine." Lydia smiled timidly.

Catherine knew that she wanted to believe the incident to be insignificant, but she was sure that the event was not as trivial as Marian had made it out to be. Yet nothing could be done about it at the moment, so Catherine took Lydia's hand and whirled her back into the festivities. "Come, Lydia," she said. "Let us join in the dance, for this is a day to celebrate."

In the center of the music-filled clearing, Catherine bowed from her waist. Lydia returned the bow. They held hands and leapt together to the music, joining a group dancing a jig.

THE FESTIVITIES CONTINUED until late afternoon. When a large gong sounded, the crowd fell into an eager silence. From between two large oaks, a pair of figures appeared. They were dressed in matching robes with pine boughs and golden streamers woven into their greying hair. Each robe was made from a fine white linen, embellished with rich embroidery over its entire surface. Beatrice carried a large golden headpiece with which she would crown the Queen of the May. Hilary walked at her side. They climbed the stairway and placed the diadem on the leafy head of the Green Lady.

Once done, they turned to the gathering and Hilary

announced, "The Queen of the May is among us."

With great ceremony, Beatrice added, "Long live the Lady of the Green."

The crowd intoned, "Huzzah! Huzzah!" and the Ladies of Briarcrest descended the stairs.

Beatrice and Hilary took their places at the head of the table. Their guests joined them and began passing trays of nuts, fruit and honey cakes for the enjoyment of all. Wine and ale continued to flow freely.

Later, as Lydia and Catherine sat talking to those around them, Beatrice and Hilary arose from their seats and lifted two beautifully embellished silver goblets in a toast.

Beatrice said, "My dear friends, Hilary and I hope you are enjoying the feast of the Green Lady. We encourage you to continue to celebrate your heart's desire for the rest of the day and beyond. Hilary and I especially welcome my niece, Lydia Wellington, to the forest festivities for the first time."

Everyone raised their cups and uttered their good wishes.

"We also welcome her dear friend, Catherine Hawkins. We are most pleased that she could join us."

Again, enthusiastic greetings. When the hails died down, Beatrice continued. "My friends, enjoy the feast. This evening, we shall be graced with the presence of Madame Toussants, the great troubadour from France, to sing for us. We have received word that her entourage will reach Briarcrest shortly."

A rousing cheer rose from the group. Madame Toussants was well known for her stories in song. She traveled many lands singing for royalty. Her talents were much in demand. That she would grace the halls of Briarcrest was a testament to the regard she had for the Duchess and the Lady Hilary.

THE LADIES OF Briarcrest spent the remainder of the afternoon circulating among their guests. When they approached Catherine, she remarked at the beauty of the workmanship of the goblets each one carried.

"They are the work of your own Willowglen silversmiths," Beatrice replied. "Edward's son, John, designed them and Edward fashioned them especially for Hilary. They were her gift to me for the feast. You can see the image of the Green Lady beautifully done on each one."

Beatrice held her goblet out to Catherine. The detail was exquisite. As she continued admiring it, Hilary inquired about her day in Briarcrest Wood.

"It has possibly been the most wonderful day of my life, My

Ladies," Catherine replied breathlessly. "I am ever in your debt for your invitation."

Hilary and Beatrice exchanged glances, silently affirming their speculation of the previous night. Catherine's enthusiasm and the glow of her cheeks led them to believe that she and Lydia had, indeed, followed their hearts.

In a teasing tone, Beatrice asked, "Have you found your heart's desire this day, then, Catherine?"

Catherine blushed. Trying to avoid eye contact, she looked past the older women. She exhaled in relief when she saw Lydia approaching. Trying to speed up her arrival, Catherine waved and called out to her. When Lydia reached the group, Beatrice repeated the question to her niece.

"Greetings, dear. I just inquired of Catherine, but she had not yet told us, if she had found her heart's desire this day. Perhaps you could tell us if you have found yours."

Lydia looked from the pair to Catherine and back again. She flushed visibly, but quickly composed herself. Giving her aunt a look of feigned scorn, she scolded, "I always understood that one was not to inquire about the activities of another during the May celebration. Why do you ask us such questions?"

Beatrice and Hilary looked at each other and burst out laughing.

Hilary answered, "You are quite right, dear. Forgive us. We are fanciful old fools."

Beatrice elbowed Lydia and added, "We are not, however, blind old fools, my dear." She winked. "But you are right. We have no excuse for asking such a question. Your activities are yours alone. Be on your way, you two. Enjoy the remainder of the feast. The afternoon is almost over and we shall be forced to move indoors soon."

Catherine returned the goblet to Beatrice. Their hostesses moved off into the gathering. The younger women heard them laughing as they walked away.

Lydia asked, "What brought *that* on?"

"I am not sure. I felt as if they knew about...this afternoon."

Lydia blushed again. "They probably do, Catherine. As my aunt said, they are not blind old fools."

The two women stared at each other, then Catherine caught Lydia's hand and reeled her into a group dancing to a melody played on flutes and drums. Lydia gathered up the hem of her dress and the two women plunged into the dance with abandon.

When the song ended, the gong sounded again. Someone doused the fire and the forest clearing darkened. Out of the blackness, two torches appeared, the light illuminating Beatrice and Hilary's faces. They led the guests in procession back to Briarcrest. As they walked, more torches lit up. A lone pipe struck a merry tune. A drum joined in, followed by other instruments, as the entire gathering journeyed back to Briarcrest at dusk.

They entered the large hall to a prepared feast. Briarcrest's workers had come back from their own celebration in the forest earlier. The long table had been pushed to one side of the room and set with all manner of meats, fowl, fruits and cakes, spiced wine, and other rich things to eat and drink. Benches and chairs had been placed on the opposite side of the room, ready for the performance.

Beatrice and Hilary briefly disappeared and changed from their robes into brocade and satin dresses. On their return, they sat in stately wooden chairs and watched as their guests mingled.

Wine and ale flowed from large pitchers. Visitors gradually took their seats. Hilary beckoned Lydia and Catherine to seats beside her and informed them that Madame Toussants had arrived and would be singing shortly.

When the singer entered the hall carrying a lute, a hush fell over the crowd. Several other musicians followed her, carrying string and reed instruments. The troupe bowed to their hostesses and settled themselves to begin. Catherine was surprised to find that Madame Toussants was not a young woman, but when the troubadour from France opened her mouth to sing, her voice rang clear and true.

Her first songs were full of fantastic voyages and exotic places. She mesmerized the crowd. Next came comical songs. The audience laughed uproariously. She sang a rather bawdy song after that. Most people chortled and wisecracked, but Lydia and Catherine were both somewhat embarrassed. Beatrice noted their reaction and laughed even more, making a coarse comment herself. The vulgarity of it, coming from Beatrice, shocked Catherine.

Finally, Madame Toussants and her company changed the mood of the hall by singing ballads of love lost and love triumphant. During one love song, Lydia got up and sat on the floor at Catherine's feet and took her hand. Beatrice pretended not to notice, but she lifted one eyebrow and smiled, looking at Hilary out of the corner of her eye while Madame Toussants' song continued:

Come, my love, and search your heart
Can you not see that I love you?

Come my fair one; tell of your heart's
Desire this night, for I love you.
I would give you gifts so fair.
I would tell you such secrets rare.
I would delight in your love, undaunted.
Do you not see that my soul you have haunted?
Come, my love, and search your heart —
Let me possess your treasure.
Come; engage in your Heart's
Desire — without restraint or measure.

Catherine glanced around the room. Many of the revelers
had paired off. To Catherine's amazement, many of the couples
were woman with woman and man with man. *This is, indeed, an
extraordinary celebration of the May.* A shadow on the wall behind
Catherine almost seemed to heave a sigh of contentment.

The troubadour and her ensemble ended their performance
with a rousing round. The audience joined in enthusiastically,
each section trying to out sing the other. When it was over, the
room rang with applause and cheers.

The musicians dispersed to circulate among the party-goers.
Madame Toussants stood where she had performed, her
admirers rushing to her with praises. Beatrice and Hilary
watched over the event like mother foxes watch their young kits
play from a distance. Finally, Madame Toussants tore herself
away from the group surrounding her and approached the
Ladies of Briarcrest. Beatrice embraced the woman warmly.

"Madame Toussants, you were wonderful, as always. Thank
you for gracing our May feast."

Madame Toussants feigned humility. "Please, Duchess, you
flatter me." With much more sincerity, she added, "I am 'appee
to be invited to this great 'all once again. I am only sorry that I
missed the earlier celebration in the wood. My carriage had a
wheel come loose on the road this morning and it took forever to
fix it. I was afraid that I might 'af to disappoint you, but I am
'appee that we could be here in the end."

Beatrice motioned Lydia and Catherine toward her. As they
approached, they heard Beatrice say, "You remember my niece,
Lydia — and this is her friend, Catherine Hawkins, who joined us
for the first time this year for the crowning of the May Queen."

The Lady Troubadour cocked her head and squinted one
eye. She looked from Lydia to Catherine and back again.
Breaking into a grin, she said, "It is a pleasure to see such
youthful beauty in these halls once again," and, glancing at her
hostesses, she continued, "We are getting too old, ladies. Ah,

but your niece and her friend bring youth and comeliness to Briarcrest."

The troubadour turned back to the young women and held out her hand to each of them in turn, adding, "I am very pleased to meet you, Mademoiselle Catherine, and to see you again, Lady Lydia."

When Madame Toussants shook their hands, she gave a warm, strong handshake, like a man would give another man.

Beatrice invited, "Please, Madame, join us in leading the line for the banquet. I am sure everyone is more than ready to dine by now." Beatrice gestured for Madame Toussants to lead the way. Lydia followed Beatrice and Hilary with Catherine at her side. As the younger women walked behind the trio, they heard Madame Toussants say to Beatrice, "So, zee niece, she is cut from zee same cloth, no?"

The singer winked at the duchess, who made no reply.

THE REVELRY WENT ON long into the night. At some late hour, Beatrice and Hilary invited the participants to continue the celebration as long as they liked. Then they bid them all goodnight. Catherine and Lydia stayed to enjoy the music and entertainment a while longer.

Finally, Lydia asked, "Are you tired, Catherine? Would you like to retire soon?"

Catherine replied that she was ready to retreat to a quiet place after the evening of song and celebration. The two women made their way across the hall, stopping here and there to speak to some of the guests before going upstairs.

Once they were behind the closed door of Lydia's bedchamber, Catherine surprised Lydia by boldly taking her in her arms and kissing her. Catherine noted her companion's reaction. "Am I too brash for you tonight, Lydia?"

"No, not at all Catherine. I just thought you might be tired and want to go to bed."

"I am not very tired...but I would like to go to bed."

Catherine looked into Lydia's eyes, penetrating to the depths of her soul. Lydia blushed and turned away as she started to unfasten her dress. Catherine approached her, astonished at her own daring. She took over loosening the shawl that Lydia had tied around her waist and continued helping Lydia disrobe. Lydia did the same for Catherine and they walked hand in hand to the large tapestry-curtained bed.

When Lydia went to extinguish the lamp, Catherine put her hand out to stop her. "Leave the light on for a while, Lydia. I want to be able to look at you. You are so beautiful."

Lydia began to protest Catherine's flattery, but stopped herself, shyly saying, "If you wish, Catherine."

They embraced each other. They talked. They kissed. They admired each other's bodies aloud to one another. When they kissed again, passion rose. They made love to each other, in turn, until each was fulfilled.

The last thing Lydia heard Catherine say to her that night as she drifted into a soft, sleepy mist, was, "Goodnight my sweet May Queen, my goddess, my own Green Lady. You have blest me with the ultimate blessing this day."

Then with more kisses and deep sighs of contentment, they fell asleep in each other's arms.

Chapter
Eighteen

The Morning after the May Day Feast
Briarcrest

THE SUN SLIPPED though a small opening in the tapestry window coverings waking Lydia. She turned over and studied Catherine's face. Although her features were not as refined as Lydia's, Catherine was still an attractive woman.

Catherine's eyes remained closed, but a smile stole across her lips. Playfulness filled her voice when she spoke. "Will you be staring at me every morning when I awaken, Lady Lydia?"

Lydia giggled and plunged toward Catherine. Catherine, her eyes open now, seized Lydia by the waist and drew her down against her naked body. She responded immediately to Lydia's warm, soft skin against hers. As they kissed and caressed one other, their breathing quickened.

A sharp rap on the door startled them from their desire. Lydia fell back onto the mattress before acknowledging the knock. When the door opened, Beatrice bustled in looking fresh and rested. "Oh, I am sorry, dears. Did I wake you? I thought you would have been up by now."

As she reached the bed, she saw the two women were visibly flushed and panting. For the first time in Lydia's life, she saw her aunt come close to loosing composure. The older woman stumbled over her words. "Oh, you poor dears, I interrupted. That is, I should have, that is..."

Lydia forced herself to come to her aunt's rescue. Still somewhat breathless, she offered, "Do not be concerned, Aunt Beatrice, we were just startled out of our sleep by your knocking."

Beatrice was relieved by this pretext. "I am sorry if I woke you. What I have to say can wait. I shall come back later." She turned to leave.

"Please, Auntie, stay. We want to hear what you have to say."

Beatrice hesitated, then offered, "Hilary has suggested that we go hawking later today. Would you like to accompany us?"

Lydia looked at Catherine, who had been lying very still next to her, trying desperately to overcome the passion she felt for Lydia. "Would you like to go, Catherine?"

Catherine took a deep breath and tried to speak without betraying her emotion. "I have never been hawking. I would be happy to go as an observer."

Beatrice inquired, "Do you know how to ride, Catherine?"

"Yes, I do. I rode often with my father. I do not own a horse of my own, but I hire one when I have need."

"Good. We shall go out after the noon meal. I think that will give you enough time to take care of your...needs." Beatrice smiled broadly. She had apparently overcome her embarrassment. As she left, she poked her head back inside the door and said, "Do not stay in bed too long, dears. You shall get a headache, or perhaps an ache elsewhere."

The door slammed behind her, but they heard her snickering as she walked down the hall.

Catherine turned to Lydia, wide-eyed. "She knows, you know."

Lydia broke into a wide grin. "Does it matter?" Then, imitating the French troubadour, she said mockingly, "We are cut from zee same cloth, you know."

"I know," Catherine replied dreamily, "and a fine fabric it is, too."

Both women chuckled. Catherine caressed Lydia again. "It is an extremely beautiful cloth."

Lydia moved closer and they took up where they had left off before Beatrice knocked on the door.

Hawking

AS THE WOMEN walked through the stables and kennels of Briarcrest, Catherine still found herself distracted by the garb Hilary wore. The older woman's appearance at the noon meal had yielded another in a long line of surprises for Catherine.

With everyone already seated at the long wooden table in the main hall, Hilary had appeared on the upper landing dressed in brown leggings and a tunic, much like men wore, though made to fit her perfectly. Catherine recognized the linen from which the tunic had been made. It was the fabric Hilary had purchased from Catherine during the fair.

The older woman wore high leather boots that stopped just

above her knees. Her hair was pulled up on top of her head and she had replaced her usual net cap with a forester's felt hat. A single long, graceful pheasant feather decorated the cap.

All conversation stopped. The staff, who were in the process of serving the meal, halted. Everyone except Beatrice looked toward the landing and stared, mouths opened. Hilary stood with her hands on her hips, looking somewhat like a woodland sprite, defying someone to mock her appearance. As if an enchanted spell had been cast by Lady Hilary appearing in men's clothes, no one spoke or moved.

Beatrice decided to take matters into her own hands. Without turning around, she said, "Hilary, I told you that outfit was going to shock everyone if you wore it at table. Could you not have waited until our guests had departed?"

Hilary bounded down the stairs like a gazelle. She spoke in a teasing voice as she skipped down the steps. "But, Beatrice, this is my heart's desire: to dress comfortably. I could not dress this way yesterday, because it did not fit the occasion. But this afternoon, we are going hawking. It will be the perfect time for such a costume. So, I thought, since it is still so close to May Day, I would try it out. Just to see if it is truly as functional as it seems, you know." She came to rest at Beatrice's elbow just as she finished her explanation. She wore a sheepish grin.

Beatrice sighed deeply, then announced, "Ladies and gentlemen, Lady Hilary means to dress in this attire when she attends to her duties outside. If anyone finds it humorous, please, share the humor with all of us now, for laughter is good for the soul. If anyone finds fault in it, I suggest that we hear your views before we proceed any further. We shall have no ill talk behind our backs."

The silent stares continued. Finally, Matilda, the young kitchen maid, broke the silence by speaking directly to Hilary. "It looks very practical, mum. It looks good, too, I think. Might not mind havin' one o'them outfits m'self."

All attention turned to the young woman as she spoke. Everyone seemed in awe of the fact that she was so forthcoming with her opinion. For her part, Matilda was enjoying center stage. She added, "Although I do not think I would like the looks of it on the Duchess quite as well as I do on you."

Beatrice looked at the young girl with feigned dismay. "What?" she said, as if deeply hurt. "You mean you would not have me wear the mate I have to these clothes?"

Another silence followed. Although some had been unsure of the sincerity of Beatrice's remark, others, after a brief consideration, realized that Beatrice had no intention of dressing in such attire.

First, there had been tenuous chuckles.   Soon the giggles turned into loud laughter.   Beatrice and Hilary had joined in.   By this time, the room was in an uproar.   Hilary, still laughing, took her place beside Beatrice.   The staff resumed their serving, some still chuckling and shaking their heads as they went.   The uncertain moment had passed.   Hilary's new attire was accepted.

Catherine shook off the recollection as she followed Hilary and Lydia into a small enclosure to see the new foal.   The newborn was indeed beautiful, a chestnut color with a large white diamond on her forehead.   The young animal looked back at the women in wide-eyed wonder as she stood at the mare's side.   The large horse nickered softly as if assuring her offspring that the visitors were friendly.

"Have you named her yet, Hilary?" Lydia inquired.

"Not yet, although I think I shall call her Queen of the May. She was born before May Day, but 'tis the season, and she is so full of life."

"It suits her, don't you agree, Catherine?" Lydia asked.

"Yes, it seems perfect. She is beautiful and lively."

Hilary patted the mother and baby affectionately.

The women headed back out to the main yard. Henry met them at the entrance.

Catherine recognized him immediately. "Henry, it is good to see you again. How are you?"

"Fine as can be, thank you, Mistress. I hope you have been well, mum."

"Yes, Henry, thank you."

Henry informed Hilary that four horses were ready for them. He would ride ahead to the hawking field and meet them there.

They found Beatrice waiting for them when they reached the horses. Catherine was assigned a large black mare. A stable hand appeared to assist the ladies onto their mounts. Hilary did not wait for help. After swinging herself onto the horse, she turned to Beatrice and said, "You see, my dear, it's so much simpler in this attire. No need for a man to mind your skirts, and no question of riding pillion at all."

Beatrice chided, "You never rode pillion a day in your life, Hilary. You're just thrilled there's no need to tuck all that skirt between your legs once you've straddled the saddle."

The women laughed. They had to agree that Hilary's new clothes did look more comfortable for riding than their own dresses. Catherine could not help but think that she would not mind being dressed thus for riding, herself.

They rode off to meet Henry and his apprentice-son, Tom, who sat, waiting on mounts, each with a large hawk on one arm. Soft leather hoods covered the hawks' heads and colored leather thongs dangled from their legs. The birds seemed content to wait patiently while Hilary and Henry discussed which bird would be hunted first. The decision having been made, Henry handed the big hawk over to Hilary, who removed the bird's hood. She spoke words of encouragement. The hawk seemed very interested in every word. Then, raising her arm quickly, Hilary propelled the bird skyward.

They watched the bird soar, reaching outward with its wings for the air. Finally, it began gliding in an ever-downward slow spiral, searching for prey as it went. Catherine marveled at the beauty and grace with which it moved through the ether.

Suddenly, the hawk dove toward the low brush a short distance from them, flushing out a hare. The second hawk, which had been released after the first one, spiraled behind it. It seized its catch in powerful talons as the animal darted from the underbrush.

It was over in an instant. The hunter waited patiently on the ground, the prize held tightly in its claws. Henry approached and fed the bird a piece of meat from a pouch on his belt. The hawk took it, and jumped off the carcass. Henry took the dead hare and tied its hind legs with a leather strip as the hawk consumed the meat it had been given. When he held out his arm, the bird jumped onto Henry's well-padded sleeve.

The scene was repeated several more times in the course of the afternoon. Each of the Ladies took a turn sending the hunters on their way. Eventually, the hawkers were satisfied with their catch and the group headed for home. Henry had half a dozen rabbits suspended from his saddle, dinner for the next evening. A large hooded hawk rode balanced on his arm. Tom had the other hawk perched on his shoulder. The two men led the party back toward Briarcrest's gates in the fading afternoon light.

When the group arrived back at Briarcrest Hall, Beatrice went off to attend to some household duties and Hilary excused herself to change into less controversial attire. Catherine and Lydia made their way to the inner courtyard off the main hall. They found a small wooden bench surrounded by rose bushes just beginning to bloom. Sheltered among the flowers, Catherine took Lydia's hand in hers and spoke.

"Lydia, you know that I must return to Willowglen. I think it better if I leave in the morning — and that I should go alone."

"I do not want you to go, Catherine. Can you not stay a day or two longer?"

"I need to get back, Lydia. My new spice delivery will be arriving and I do not want to leave Sarah too long."

"I could go with you. Who knows how long it will be before my father comes back from France. It could be days or weeks — perhaps longer — before he returns."

"If we prolong our farewell, Lydia, it will only be that much more difficult. As it is, when I think of it now, I feel as if my heart will break at the thought of leaving you."

Lydia looked away and tried not to yield to the tears welling up in her eyes.

Catherine plunged on. "I intend to asked Beatrice to give me passage back to Willowglen tomorrow after the morning meal. We must not make this any more difficult than it needs to be. However, if either of us can think of a way that we can be together, we must send word to the other immediately. For now, though, I am afraid I can see no alternative. I must leave. Therefore, I think I should leave quickly and with as little disruption as possible."

"I know you're right, Catherine, but my heart does not want to let you go."

They were silent. Catherine's thoughts wandered back to the previous All Saints' Day when Lydia had announced she would be leaving Willowglen. Feeling much the same way as they had that day when they sat in front of the fire, basking in each other's presence, they sat in the garden now, saying little, holding hands until the evening chill drove them inside.

"BEATRICE, I AM afraid it is time for me to return home. I am very grateful for your hospitality, but I must get back to Willowglen."

Beatrice stared as if she were trying to read Catherine's innermost thoughts before she spoke. She assured Catherine that a carriage and escort would be available to her the next morning. Catherine was grateful that she didn't try to talk her out of leaving.

Beatrice and Catherine found Hilary and Lydia in the main hall, talking in hushed tones. Lydia looked as if she had been crying, but when she saw Catherine, she put on a brave smile. She failed in an attempt to say something humorous and Hilary tried, without much more success, to rescue her from the tense moment. Just then, the kitchen help arrived with supper, so they took their places at the table, grateful for a diversion.

THE SMALL GROUP that dined at the table that evening ate quickly with little conversation. They decided that the day's activities had proven tiring and that they would all retire immediately after the meal. At one point, Catherine made an unsuccessful attempt to inquire about Marian's health. The older woman made it clear that she did not want to discuss her health with Catherine, or with anyone.

At the end of the meal, Catherine and Lydia excused themselves and went upstairs. Once the door was closed behind them, they made love recklessly. When it was over, they both felt lonely and sad. Since neither woman could sleep, they held one another long into the night, sometimes drying each other's tears.

Catherine awoke at dawn with heavy eyelids and a tightness in her throat. She tried to shake off her gloom, more for Lydia's sake than her own, but she could not. She leaned over and kissed Lydia on the brow. When Lydia opened her eyes slowly, they looked red and puffy. The women held each other, desperately, for a long time.

At last, Lydia said, "Catherine, we shall think of something. We must. For I cannot bear to be separated from you again. Knowing our true feelings for one another now, I will not let my father stand in the way of our happiness. There must be a way. We shall find it, Catherine. I know we will."

"You are right, Lydia. There must be something..."

But Catherine did not hold out much hope. Lydia kept her hopeless thoughts to herself also.

Departure

MARIAN DID NOT come down to the hall that morning. She requested some tea and biscuits be brought to her room. Catherine was concerned about her, but her grief clouded her mind and she could not see a way to try to help.

Before the morning meal was over, Henry came into the hall to tell Beatrice that the carriage was ready. He offered to escort Mistress Catherine back to Willowglen himself and Beatrice agreed. Catherine excused herself to go upstairs and Lydia followed behind her. In the bedchamber, they held on to each other one final time and struggled to choke back tears.

Finally, Catherine said firmly, "Lydia, I must go. Stay here. It will be better for both of us if you do not come to the carriage."

Lydia heaved herself onto the bed. Desolately, she looked

up at Catherine and muttered agreement. Catherine put her hand on the large wooden door to leave. With desperation, Lydia called to her. "I love you, Catherine Hawkins."

Catherine stopped, waiting for the pain in her heart to subside before responding. "And I love you, Lydia Wellington."

Catherine looked away quickly, hiding her tears. She opened the big wooden door a crack and slipped out, not knowing if she would ever see Lydia again.

Lydia knew that it was better for both of them if she did not go downstairs. That did not stop her from wanting to run after Catherine. She struggled against the confused feelings washing over her until, finally, she flung herself onto the bed and wept inconsolably.

Catherine arrived downstairs to find Beatrice and Hilary waiting for her. Together, they walked to the outer court in silence. Before boarding the carriage, Catherine asked Beatrice to say good-bye to Marian for her. The older women bid Catherine a safe journey with a fond embrace, and she climbed into the carriage before anyone inquired about Lydia.

Henry was at the reins with his son beside him. Hilary secured the door and waved him on. As the carriage moved out onto the road, Catherine clenched her fists and refused to cry. She choked back her tears for several hours, but finally, as the carriage jolted her repeatedly on its approach to Willowglen, she could no longer hold in her sorrow.

From his seat atop the carriage, Henry thought he heard something that sounded like wailing. He considered stopping, but then he decided it might be wiser to get his passenger home—the faster the better—so he sped up the horses. After a time, the only sound he could hear was the noise of the carriage and the pounding of the horses' hooves accompanied by their jangling traces, so Henry relaxed his grip on the reins a little. By the time they reached town, dusk had given way to night.

Henry escorted Catherine to the shop, and she went straight to the box of shop receipts. She removed two coins and gave them to Henry. He tipped his cap, mumbled *"Thank you, mum,"* and left without another word.

Sarah heard the shop door open and came in from the kitchen just as Henry left. She knew that something was wrong immediately. "Are you all right, Mistress?"

"Yes, Sarah, I'm fine. I'm just tired from my journey. The trip is long and the road outside of Willowglen is rough. Do not trouble yourself. All I need is a good night's sleep and I will be myself again."

Sarah doubted it, but she didn't question her mistress.

Instead she offered her some supper. Catherine refused, saying that she only wanted to go to bed.

Picking up her bag, she bid Sarah goodnight. She started for the stairs then stopped. She looked around the shop and remarked that it looked neat and tidy. "You have done well in my absence, Sarah."

Sarah was pleased.

Catherine then inquired about Sarah's brother. The young girl said he was using his arm quite well. Earlier that day, he had gone to talk to one of the market merchants about working for him.

"Fine, just fine, Sarah," Catherine said in a distracted tone. She turned and started back toward the stairs. Before she reached the top, tears were streaming silently down her cheeks.

Chapter
Nineteen

The Eve of the Feast of St. John the Baptist
June 23, 1459
The Shoppe of Hawkins & Hawkins

THE DAY BEFORE the feast of the Baptist dawned warm and sunny. Catherine busied herself in the garden for most of the morning. When the summer heat became too intense, she moved into the stone drying shed to lay out her harvested herbs. She was happy to be so busy because, that way, she paid little attention to the dull ache in her heart.

Correspondence had gone back and forth between Briarcrest and Willowglen since Catherine's return from the May celebration. There had been no word from Lydia's father, and Catherine questioned her decision to keep Lydia from coming back to Willowglen over and over again. Lydia's notes lamented the pain of their separation. Catherine found these portions difficult to read but she would not consider asking that the letters stop. She treasured their exchanges.

Lydia sometimes enclosed flowers from the courtyard at Briarcrest. She would pick them and press them, sending them to Catherine between the folds of her notes. As each new bloom arrived, Catherine tried to envision the changing garden. She could not help but see Lydia walking the grounds, gathering up the petals to send to her. The image increased Catherine's longing for Lydia even more.

Catherine tried to keep her responses to Lydia's letters light and cheery, but she did not usually succeed. Often after she had penned a few sentences, she would end up telling Lydia how much she missed her, too.

Catherine shared the changing garden behind the shop with Lydia in exchange for the flowers from Briarcrest. Whenever Lydia opened a note from Catherine, herbs and blooms came tumbling out onto her lap. Somehow, these expressions bridged the distance between them.

Most recently, Catherine had received a letter that troubled her deeply. It had contained the tragic news that Marian had died. Lydia wrote that the older woman had missed morning meals more and more frequently, sometimes taking to her bed for days at a time. One day when Beatrice went to check on her, she found Marian's cold and lifeless body. Apparently, her weak heart had finally failed her. Lydia's anguish came through clearly in her letter. Her grief clouded her thinking. She wrote erratically, making little sense at times. This alarmed Catherine.

The young healer longed to hold and comfort Lydia. She wanted to soothe her sadness away, to give her back her innocence and joy, but she knew that, even if she were to go to her, she could not.

Catherine fretted over what she should do about Lydia as she hung the fresh herbs to dry. Asking her to come to Willowglen was not a good idea, she decided. Once Lydia's father sent for her, the pain of their separation would begin all over again and Catherine feared what another parting might do to her.

She contemplated sending word of her concern to Beatrice, but that, too, seemed futile. What could she hope to accomplish by pointing out to Beatrice what she probably already knew? Catherine dismissed the idea.

It had been several weeks since Lydia's last letter. Catherine grew more and more uneasy about the silence. To quell her fear, she tried to tell herself that Lydia was surmounting her grief by keeping busy, and therefore had little time to write. The more she tried to convince herself, the more her anxiety grew.

CATHERINE FINISHED LAYING the herbs out to dry and returned to the shop. Her agitation built as she tried to occupy herself by tidying her workbench. When Sarah came in from church with Will, they were laughing and enjoying themselves as young lovers will. Resentment welled up within Catherine. Fiercely, she blurted out, "Will, why are you here instead of at the Grouse and Pheasant? I cannot be responsible for your bad work habits, you know."

Catherine realized what she had said only after the words had escaped from her mouth and she could not take them back. Sarah and Will stared at Catherine. Surely she knew that Sunday was their day of rest. Beyond the minimal chores necessary at the Inn, Will was free for the day, as was Sarah.

The strain was more than Catherine could bear. She muttered an apology and ran to the kitchen to hide her tears.

She sat at the table with her head in her hands.

Sarah came in and put the kettle on the fire.

Catherine dried her eyes and watched the young girl's movements until she felt composed enough to speak. "Sarah, where is Will?"

With her back to Catherine, Sarah said, "I sent him off."

"Why did you do that, Sarah? This is your day to be together. I am sorry I spoke out of turn. Go and be with him."

Sarah turned around. Her face was ablaze with anger. Her look alarmed Catherine, for she had never seen Sarah like this. Catherine had become so fond of this young woman, it made her feel even worse to know that she was the cause of her rage. But when Sarah opened her mouth to speak, Catherine found that her fury came from a much different source than Catherine had imagined.

"Mistress Catherine, you are one of the kindest, most caring people I have ever known. Your temperament is usually as steady as a rock. There is only one thing that can turn you from your customary nature and upset you like this. Do you know what that one thing is, Mistress?"

Yes, Catherine knew, but she was taken aback, again, to think that Sarah might know.

Sarah demanded a second time, "Do you know, Mistress, what that one thing is — or not?"

Catherine put her head back in her hands as she released the cause of her distress in a word. "Lydia," she cried as she allowed the pain to surface.

"Yes, Mistress, Lydia. Always Lydia. But only Lydia when she is gone. Why do you torture yourself by making her stay away?"

Catherine looked up and stared into Sarah's eyes. *It's almost laughable how transparent I am to her.*

When Catherine spoke again, her voice quivered. "You are doing it again, Sarah."

"Doing what again?" asked Sarah, annoyed.

"Being a wise woman."

"Oh, Mistress." Sarah's anger dissipated. She spoke with concern, now. "Why do you not tell her to come and stay, Mistress?"

Thoughts Catherine had struggled to keep at bay flooded in. *It would be so easy — I could write today and take the note to the Governor's Hall. It could probably be in Lydia's hands by the day after tomorrow...*

Catherine pushed the thought aside. "She has her own life to lead, Sarah. A life that her father has more control over than either she or I have. He wants her to go to France and marry a nobleman."

Sarah weighed her next thought carefully before she spoke. "If it were me, Will would fight for me."

"What?"

"I said, 'if it were me, Will would—'"

"I heard you. I just cannot believe that you see things so clearly. You are right, of course. I should not give up, not without a fight."

"Good," pronounced Sarah.

Both women were silent again until Catherine repeated the question she had asked earlier. "Sarah, where is Will?"

Sarah broke into a wry little smile. She cocked her head in the direction of the Inn down the street. "He is waiting for me at the Grouse and Pheasant."

"Go to him, Sarah. Someone in this house should have her heart's desire."

"Yes, Mistress." Sarah lowered her eyes, embarrassed at knowing too much. She started to move toward the door without looking at Catherine.

"Wait, Sarah, I have more to say."

"Yes, Mistress?"

"First, when you see Will again, please tell him I am very sorry."

"Will is not one to hold a grudge, Mistress. He will be fine."

"But you will tell him, will you not?"

Sarah looked directly at Catherine. "Yes, Mistress, I shall tell him. Is there anything else?"

Catherine had given what she was about to say a great deal of thought. Before this, she hadn't known how to broach the subject with Sarah. Now, she decided the time was right.

"Yes, Sarah. During my short stay at Briarcrest, I learned a great deal. In particular, I came to realize that titles are for naught. No one is above or below another. You and I work closely together every day. Why should I be Mistress to you? It is not necessary. I would be honored if you would call me Catherine."

Sarah grew quiet.

"Will you do that, Sarah?"

"Yes, Mis—Catherine."

Now it was Catherine's turn to pronounce, "Good, then. Now go to Will. And Sarah?"

"Yes, Mis...Catherine?"

"Thank you."

"You are welcome. Catherine."

Sarah did not move.

"Is there something else, Sarah?"

"Will you be all right, Catherine? If I go, I mean."

"Yes, Sarah. I think it would be good for me to be alone right now. I have a great deal of thinking to do."

Sarah smiled. She walked over to Catherine and embraced her.

STEAM ROSE FROM the kettle and demanded Catherine's attention. She got up from her seat to prepare her mint tea. Just before she added the leaves to the pot, she changed her mind. *Perhaps some comfrey instead — to calm my concern and help me to think more clearly. It is true what Sarah says, it is always Lydia, and only Lydia. Oh, Lydia, I miss you so much.*

Catherine took her tea to her upstairs room and did something most peculiar. She sat on her bed in the middle of the day, drinking slowly and waiting for inspiration. None came. Still, she felt untroubled. She attributed it to the soothing herb, but it was really the calm before the storm.

Chapter
Twenty

The Feast of St. John the Baptist
June 24, 1459 – Before dawn
The Shoppe of Hawkins & Hawkins

CATHERINE FELT EXHAUSTED. She wanted to stop running, but her sense of urgency pushed her on. She was caught in some unfamiliar plaza surrounded by a maze of stairs with halls in every direction. She searched in a frenzy with no clear idea of who it was that she was supposed to find. Over and over, she took a turn that ended nowhere and had to retrace her steps. Running down an alley, she found it blocked by a huge door. She tried to force it open, but it would not yield. Catherine gave up and took a stairway. As she climbed, each step became narrower and narrower until passage was completely impossible. She turned back once more, frantic. She tried another flight of stairs. It ended abruptly at a solid wall. Turning back, she found the way from which she had just come was now blocked by a heavy wooden railing. Overcome with frustration, she thrust her clenched fists hard against the barricade. Pounding on the thick beam again and again, she felt the vibrations reverberate all the way up her arms.

Catherine emerged from the thick fog of her fitful sleep bathed in perspiration. Realization came slowly. The pounding had not stopped. It came from somewhere below. Someone was beating on the shop door downstairs, demanding entry.

Catherine bounded out of bed and threw on her dress. Running down the stairs, she met Sarah crossing the shop with a lit candle in her hand. In the glow, the young girl looked as if she had seen a ghost.

The pair approached the door together. The determined banging continued. Catherine pushed the wooden bolt back and tentatively pulled the door open a crack.

Peering into the night, her mind struggled to identify the

murky figures. One had a fist raised, ready to beat on the door once more. A smaller form stood beside a larger one. Both had the hoods of their riding cloaks pulled over their heads. Catherine blinked, trying to focus on the faces of the dark forms.

Was it two men? No. A man and a boy? Then, recognition: The man was Henry. She squinted at the boy. It was not Henry's son, yet the frame was familiar. Realization struck. Hilary! Hilary, dressed in tights and tunic with leather boots that came past her knees. Catherine swung the door open wide, anxiously beckoning them inside.

As they stepped across the threshold, Henry and Hilary pulled back their hoods. Catherine led them into the kitchen. Sarah followed, wide-eyed at the sight of Lady Hilary in men's clothes. Catherine bid them sit down, adding that she would make some tea, but Hilary interrupted.

"There is no time, Catherine. We have come to take you back to Briarcrest. Lydia has been gravely injured."

Catherine gasped and grabbed the edge of the table to steady herself. Sarah jammed the candle into a holder quickly and sprang to Catherine's side. She steered her toward a bench by the shoulders and sat her down.

Catherine tried, in vain, to compose herself. With a tremor in her voice, she asked, "H-How?"

Hilary answered, "Lydia received word that her father had settled the arrangement for her betrothal. As you probably already know, she was grief-stricken over Marian's death, not to mention her distress at not being able to have your companionship.

"When she heard that her father wanted her to return to Greencastle to set sail for France, she became distraught. Beatrice and I tried to calm her, but she would not be comforted. Finally, exhausted, she went to her room to rest. However, later that evening, unknown to us, she packed her bag and slipped away.

"Very early the next morning, Isadore, the priest, showed up with some of Greencastle's knights. He said he had come to claim Lydia and bring her back to Greencastle for her father.

"It was only then that we discovered that Lydia was gone. When Joanna went to call her, she returned looking as if she had seen a specter and she had a note that said that Lydia was on her way to the Abbey of St. Nicholas. We believe that she went there to seek sanctuary. The foolish child was traveling alone and on foot. Unfortunately, when Joanna brought the news that Lydia was gone, Isadore was still with us.

"He set off after her immediately. I followed, after enlisting the help of Briarcrest's best men. Isadore and his henchmen caught up with Lydia on the road before we got there. Apparently there was a struggle. Perhaps she became unreasonable; she can be willful, as we all know. At any rate, Isadore had her b-beaten..."

Thus far, Hilary had spoken calmly. Now anger and sadness welled up and her voice trembled. She swallowed hard in order to continue. "Beaten within an inch of her life. Then, it seems that when he realized how badly injured she was, he abandoned her at the Abbey doorstep. Left her for dead. Then he and his pack ran like the cowardly dogs they are.

"The Abbey of St. Nicholas is isolated and the nuns very austere. They cared for Lydia's wounds as best they could since we dared not move her. She did not wake from the sleep of injury all the time we were at the Abbey.

"After a few days, we decided it would be better to risk taking her back to Briarcrest. We feared for her safety, and at Briarcrest she would be better protected. We tried to move her carefully, but the journey was difficult. She awoke only briefly, but she could not speak. I was very relieved when we got her home.

"As soon as we settled Lydia at Briarcrest, Henry and I left to fetch you. Beatrice is caring for her, but she is most anxious to have you return with us. Lydia's life may well depend on your healing skills alone, Catherine."

Hilary paused for a breath. "We brought a horse with us for you, Catherine. You had better get ready. We must go quickly."

Catherine sat motionless, stunned by this news. Sarah leaned close to Catherine and spoke into her ear. "Catherine, you must go upstairs and get ready to travel. Do you want me to help you?"

Catherine looked from the pair from Briarcrest to Sarah, then back to Henry and Hilary again. As if waking from her earlier dream once more, Catherine shook her head. She spoke as if her assistant had just entered the room, and knew nothing of what had happened. "Sarah, I must go to Briarcrest. It is urgent. Will you attend to the shop while I am gone?"

"Yes, Catherine. Do not trouble yourself about the shop. I will take care of it and I will get Will or my brother to help. I do not want you to concern yourself with anything here."

"Sarah, you are too good to me. You deserve a rich reward, which you shall have upon my return."

"Never mind that, now," said Sarah. "Just prepare for your journey—and hurry. Lady Lydia needs you." Sarah lit a lamp and handed it to Catherine.

Upstairs in her bedchamber, Catherine ran methodically through a mental list of medicinal herbs she would bring with her. She checked the contents of her herb bag. Everything she needed was there. She tried to hurry, but her movements felt thick and slow. Hilary's tale echoed in her mind as she dressed. Anxiety welled up as she heard Hilary's words again. *"Beaten within an inch of her life..."* She almost knocked the lamp over as she reached for it. Her hand trembled as she picked up her bundle.

Hilary and Sarah were talking in hushed tones when Catherine returned to the kitchen. Henry had gone back outside to attend to the horses. When Catherine appeared in the doorway, Sarah jumped up from her seat and went to her. She embraced her mentor and said, "Do not trouble yourself about anything here, Catherine. Stay at Briarcrest until you are able to bring Lady Lydia back home with you."

Catherine could only manage to whisper, "Th-thank you, Sarah." She feared if she tried to say more, tears would flow. She did not want anything to delay the start of their journey to Briarcrest.

Hilary, also concerned about Catherine, looked her in the eye and said firmly, "Catherine, you must have your wits about you to ride. It will not be light for several hours and the road is not easy. If we could wait until after sunrise, it would be better for us, but we do not have a moment to waste."

Catherine's reply sounded more confident than she felt. "I'm fine, Hilary, really. We must not delay." She accepted a farewell embrace from Sarah, donned her own hooded cloak, and followed Hilary out the door.

Outside, Henry had joined his son, Tom. The two stood between four saddled horses. When Hilary and Catherine approached, Tom, looking very somber, greeted Catherine politely. He handed her the reins to one of the horses. She mounted, swinging her leg over the animal, straddling the saddle and tucking her dress under her. Hilary watched from atop her own mount and nodded her approval. She turned to her stable master, nodded again, and the hollow clapping of hooves sounded as the group broke into a canter down the cobblestone street.

At the end of town, they turned toward Briarcrest, urging their mounts to greater speed. When they reached the more treacherous stretch of road outside of Willowglen, they slowed their pace and strained to see the path ahead. The horses grew uneasy. The riders could feel their muscles tense as they carefully picked their way along. Several hours later, with the dawn of morning over the distant hills, each horse and rider relaxed a bit. Now that they could see more clearly, the horses would be more sure-footed, but they would still not be able to break into a gallop until the road smoothed out, several miles outside of Briarcrest.

They moved along the smoother edge of the road, single file. Henry headed the column with Hilary behind him. Catherine and Tom brought up the rear. As they plodded along, Catherine's thoughts focused on Lydia. It would be late afternoon by the time they arrived at their destination. Another day would have passed during which Lydia would be lying, battered and bruised, without Catherine at her side. Tears stung her eyes. She wiped them away quickly with her cloak and steeled herself against her feelings. This journey was difficult enough. Catherine could not break down now.

By mid-morning, horses and riders were exhausted from their strenuous ride. Henry was concerned for Hilary and Catherine. Hilary had not slept in days, first tending to Lydia at the Abbey, then riding all night to reach Catherine. He glanced back at Catherine and saw that she, too, looked tired and drawn. Knowing that neither woman would consent to stop for themselves, he insisted that the horses needed the rest. Hilary deferred to his wishes regarding the animals.

They turned off the road and trudged up a grassy hill. At the crest, a wide meadow, ablaze with colorful summer wildflowers, came into view. Catherine winced at the memory of the field outside of Briarcrest wood and the May Day celebration. They made their way toward a grove of willows bordering a pond in the distance. When they dismounted, Henry passed a water bag around. Then he and Tom led the horses to the pond to drink.

The two women sat on the soft ground with their backs against a rock, watching the horses and their caretakers in the distance.

Hilary, concern in her voice, inquired, "Are you enduring the ride, Catherine?"

"Do not trouble yourself about me, Hilary. I only want to get to Briarcrest and be with Lydia."

"I understand. We should be there by early afternoon."

"I know Beatrice is taking good care of her. I only hope I can do something more for her when we arrive."

"Beatrice will be relieved to have you there. She needs you as much as Lydia does, Catherine. She knows you understand how much it hurts to see someone you love..." Hilary stopped. She did not want to risk upsetting Catherine any more than she knew she already was. The remainder of the journey would require all of their concentration. But Catherine had only half-heard Hilary. Her thoughts were a confused jumble, filled with too many emotions and questions.

"Hilary, what will happen now? What will Lydia's father do?"

"We cannot be sure, Catherine. He may try to come after her, but he will see that she cannot be taken all the way back to Greencastle in her present state. Beatrice sent word to him that Lydia is gravely ill and that he should dismiss any plans to sail for France indefinitely. We can only hope that he will honor his sister's request."

"Is he aware of the source of her injuries?"

"Not likely. I imagine Isadore has fled somewhere far away from both Briarcrest and Greencastle. I would be very surprised if we heard from him any time soon. Some of our men are pursuing him, but I do not know if they will be successful."

Catherine was pensive. Her thoughts wandered to the Hallow's Eve night incident in the alley. She told Hilary the story, relating her feelings of rage toward the monster that tried to hurt and violate Lydia. "I was shocked to find that I had such violent emotions within me that night. Now I find that I have the same contempt for this cleric who ordered my, my..."

Catherine's eyes filled with pain. Anguish prevented her from continuing.

Hilary knew that Catherine needed to speak of her fears and concerns, so she pressed her. "Say it, Catherine. You must."

Catherine looked at Hilary through a cloud of agony and confusion. *Say it? Say it out loud so that someone other than Lydia might know? I cannot say it.*

"Catherine?"

"Hilary —"

Tears welled up in Catherine's eyes now. They seemed to wash away her bewilderment. Remembering just who this companion of hers was, that Hilary and Beatrice... *What was it that Lydia said? 'They are like us, Catherine.'*

"Hilary," Catherine started again, "I feel as if I could kill this fiend who has hurt my beloved Lydia."

Hilary cooed, "Catherine, you must not hold it in any longer. Tears will cleanse you so that you can continue this journey."

Catherine buried her face in her hands. Allowing herself to open to all of the emotion she felt, she shuddered and tears gushed forth as if a floodgate had been opened. Hilary put her arm around Catherine's shoulders and sat with her in silence.

When the tears finally stopped flowing, Catherine felt stronger. She sat up and looked Hilary in the eye. "I love her, you know."

"I know you do. And she loves you. I hope you know that, too."

"I do."

"I do not know what we can do to help you, Catherine, but know that Beatrice and I shall do all that we can. At the moment, though, I am afraid all we can do is help Lydia get well again. Her condition warrants your expertise in the healing arts, to be sure. It may take a long time for her to recover. Are you prepared for that?"

"I will do whatever it takes, Hilary. I could never turn my back on her. Not now, not ever. When I told her not to come to Willowglen, I only wanted to make it easier for her to keep peace with her father. I only wanted her to come to no harm, especially at my doing."

Catherine stared straight ahead and continued, "When I left Briarcrest after the May celebration, I wanted so much for Lydia to return to Willowglen with me. After I arrived home, I used to imagine her just outside in the garden, tending one of the herb patches. I would think, 'soon she will come though the door into the shop and say something to me at which we will both laugh.' I wanted her with me so much it hurt."

"I don't know if you can believe this, Catherine, but I do understand."

"I believe you, Hilary. I've seen you with Beatrice, and I hope you will not mind, but, well, Lydia told me about you two."

"Lydia told us, Catherine. We have no need to hide from one another."

Catherine continued, "Seeing you and Beatrice — your love for each other — it is apparent that it has matured over the years. It has a richness about it that I can only hope Lydia and I can find in the future."

"You will have it, Catherine. I feel sure of it."

They sat in silence again. Catherine absently reached for the pendant around her neck and caressed it between her thumb and forefinger.

After a time, Henry and Tom rounded up the grazing horses and led them toward the women. As they approached, Hilary said, "The time has come, Catherine. We must get you to Briarcrest. Are you ready to ride?"

Catherine's "yes" was strong, emphatic. The women mounted their horses, and the group started back toward the

main road. After going a short distance, they reached the fork in
the road that would take them to Briarcrest. Their spirits lifted
just a little, for soon the road would smooth out.

Once it did, Henry looked back at Hilary, who ordered, "Let
us make haste, Henry — to Briarcrest, as quickly as we can."

Henry squeezed his horse's flanks with his thighs and took
off at a gallop. Hilary followed suit. Catherine stayed at her
side. Young Tom quickened his horse right behind them. They
made better time now and, by early afternoon, a large cloud of
dust could be seen on the road approaching Briarcrest. Beatrice
had sent a man to the tower to watch for their approach. When
he saw the shadow billowing up from the road in the distance,
he knew it must be the riders from Willowglen.

The watchman climbed down from his lookout post and
returned to Briarcrest Hall. He found Beatrice as he had left
her — seated beside a small, battered-looking figure lying on a cot
in front of a blazing fire. He bent down to Beatrice's ear and
whispered his message.

"Thank God," Beatrice sighed.   Then she turned her
attention back to the ghostly shape lying in front of her.

Chapter
Twenty-one

The Feast of St. John the Baptist
June 24, 1459
Briarcrest Hall

FOUR RIDERS DISMOUNTED and handed over their horses to a stable hand. Hilary insisted that Henry and Tom go home to rest. The two women shook the dust from their cloaks. Passing several guards, they entered the great hall of Briarcrest.

Catherine glanced around the expanse of the main room. It felt desolate and cold compared to the first time she had been there, in spite of the huge fire burning in the fireplace at the far end of the room. Catherine breathed a sigh of relief when she saw the blaze. They were keeping Lydia warm. That was important.

Beatrice turned when she heard them come in, but she did not leave her post. As the pair approached, she got up and greeted Catherine with a silent embrace. When she let go, Catherine saw the Duchess' eyes were filled with tears.

Catherine went to Lydia's side and knelt down. Behind her, she heard Hilary ask about the young woman's condition. Beatrice whispered that there had been no change.

Catherine took Lydia's delicate hand in her own. She choked back her own tears as she whispered softly, "Lydia, it's Catherine. I'm here. I have come to help you get well."

Silence.

Catherine had ministered to many sick and injured people over the years. Once, she had to attend to someone who had been badly mauled by a wild animal. Another had been thrown from a horse. She had treated still more with fevers and other mysterious maladies. She had felt compassion for them all. She was angered, too, by the injustice of the human condition. Still, she was not prepared for the gamut of emotion she experienced when she surveyed the battered Lydia.

The only color on the young woman's face was the blue

discoloration turning to yellow and green around her eyes and a large, raw scrape on her cheek. Her once-smooth shoulders had red, angry gashes on them from the lashes of a whip. Catherine was at once terrified, saddened, and enraged. She bit her lip as hard as she could. She had to remain in control for Lydia's sake.

She searched deep within herself for one small, glowing ember of strength and confidence. Finding it, she fanned the spark until it burst forth into a bright flame. When she was sure the fire would not die, she stood up and turned to Beatrice and Hilary.

With confidence, she said, "I have probably had more sleep than both of you together in the past few days. Go and get some rest. Leave me with Lydia. I shall attend to her. I have some herbs in my bag with which to soothe her wounds. All I require is some hot water and a few soft pieces of cloth."

Beatrice started to protest, but Hilary took her by the arm and led her to the stairway. She half-whispered, "Beatrice, she is right. We both need to get some rest. Catherine will need to be relieved later and we should be ready to do so. For now, leave her alone with the child. It will be good for both of them."

Catherine had already set to work, removing several small bundles of herbs from her bag. She looked up from her preparations and encouraged them with a nod. They looked exhausted.

Beatrice sighed in resignation, "You are right, Hilary." Then she turned and spoke to Catherine. "I know you will take good care of her, Catherine. I shall send Joanna down to help you. She will get you anything you need."

Beatrice started up the stairs slowly, heavily weighted down by concern and fatigue. Hilary walked at her side, her arm around Beatrice.

A SHORT TIME later, Joanna came downstairs. She had dark circles under her eyes, undoubtedly from worrying about Beatrice and Hilary as much as from her concern for Lydia. She greeted Catherine eagerly. "Oh, Catherine, I am so glad you have come. Beatrice said you require some water and cloths. I will get them for you."

"Thank you, Joanna."

The older woman padded off toward the kitchen.

As she waited for Joanna to return, Catherine let her eyes drift down the length of the great hall. By the dim glow of candlelight, she could just make out the antechamber at the opposite end of the room. Two guards, in helmets and full mail and armor, and with large swords sheathed at their sides, stood watch.

Catherine turned back to the small cot. Her sad sigh echoed through the hall. She shook off the heaviness and reached for the flame deep within her being. She folded back Lydia's covers carefully and swallowed hard when she saw the full extent of Lydia's wounds.

Catherine lifted Lydia to one side gently to examine her back. Lydia moaned. Catherine's rage welled up again. The Hallow's Eve monster's face materialized before her. She saw herself chasing him through the streets. When she caught up with him, she wrapped her hands around his flabby neck, clamping tighter and tighter as she watched him gasp for air. This time, the ghoul wore the robes of a cleric.

Catherine shook off the ghostly vision and refocused her attention on Lydia. She carefully laid the young woman back onto the cot and gently covered her frail-looking body.

Joanna returned bearing a basin and a pitcher of steaming water. Several soft, felted towels hung over her arm, a smaller version of the kind Catherine remembered using during the May celebration. *The May celebration—it seems like an eternity ago. Everything is so different now. But it will return to happier times. It must. And it will be even better than before, for Lydia and I will be together. Now I know that I cannot keep her from my life. First, though, I must get her well.*

"Shall I help you, mum?" Joanna asked softly.

"Yes, please, Joanna. I shall need you to hold her while I bathe and dress the wounds on her back."

Joanna brightened. "Yes, mum," she replied enthusiastically.

Catherine took a cloth from the older woman's arm. "Can you tell me what has been done for her thus far, Joanna?"

"Beatrice cleaned her wounds and bathed her with comfrey."

"Good," pronounced Catherine, "but there is more I can do. I shall require a small, clean bowl."

"Yes, mum."

While Joanna went off toward the kitchen again, Catherine poured hot water over one of the cloths and washed the grit and grime of the road from her hands and forearms. Then she removed a small mortar and pestle from her bag. She placed a few dried plantain leaves in the cup and began grinding skillfully.

By the time Joanna returned with a small pottery bowl, Catherine had the leaves reduced to a powder. She poured the fine particles into the bowl and took another herb, white willow bark, from a container. It, too, would be added after she ground it down. When the mixture was prepared, Catherine poured a small amount of water into the dish and blended it into a thick paste. Once applied, the compound would ease Lydia's pain and help soothe the infection that Catherine saw had already started. She motioned to Joanna and the older woman turned Lydia gently. Catherine applied the poultice to the open gashes across Lydia's back, touching the injured woman as lightly as she could during the process. Once the application was finished, Catherine took another soft cloth and dipped it into the warm water. She laid it across Lydia's back to keep the herb mixture soft, allowing it to penetrate deeply. When she was done, they rolled Lydia back onto the cot.

Catherine continued medicating Lydia's injured shoulders, neck, chest and abdomen with skilled proficiency. Finally, she applied the poultice to her arms, her legs, and the wound on her face. Had Catherine not been concentrating on her ministrations, she probably would have had to fight off her rage again.

The two women placed the cover over Lydia's body again. She did not stir. Catherine watched her shallow breathing and decided that she had been through enough for the moment. "She should rest, now, Joanna. We will not need to change the cloths for some time."

"I shall be back after a while, then, mum," Joanna said. She picked up the water vessel and moved off toward the kitchen.

Catherine took up Beatrice's vacant post. The house grew quiet. Fatigue from the ride and the toll of the emotion at seeing Lydia's condition overtook her like a heavy mist. She nodded off. Her rest was brief, though, for a few moments later she was awakened by Lydia's moaning.

Catherine sprang to the injured woman's side. She spoke to her in soothing tones, telling Lydia about the treatment she had just given her. She asked her to forgive her for the pain she had caused her and assured her that she would try to limit her discomfort by doing only what was necessary to make her well. Then she added that, when Lydia was better, they would be together—always.

Catherine was not sure if it was what she said or merely the sound of her voice, but Lydia became calmer and breathed a little easier, so Catherine decided to continue. She told Lydia about being awakened in the early morning hours to find Hilary and Henry at the door of her shop. She even laughed briefly as she related the look on Sarah's face at seeing Lady Hilary in men's clothes. She recounted the journey from Willowglen including her conversation with Hilary by the watering pond.

Lydia seemed to rest more comfortably. When she looked as if she were sleeping peacefully, Catherine sat in silence, holding Lydia's hand.

BEATRICE RETURNED TO the hall later that evening looking somewhat refreshed. Catherine informed her of her course of treatment. Beatrice nodded and smiled. "Catherine," she said haltingly, "I am so grateful that you have come. Lydia needs you here. I need you. I thought, if she knew you had come, she might not give up. I thought, with your skilled care, she might have a chance. I hope you do not mind that I sent for you."

"Oh, Beatrice, do you think I could stay away knowing that something had happened to Lydia? Nothing could keep me in Willowglen when I heard. We both want the same thing for her. We both...love her."

There was sadness in Beatrice's smile, and tears welled up in her eyes. She tried to choke them back, unsuccessfully. Patting Catherine's arm, she tried to convince the young woman to go upstairs and rest, but was not surprised to be refused. She knew Catherine would not be willing to leave Lydia's side just yet. They sat together, trying to will Lydia back to them.

Chapter
Twenty-two

The Feast of St. John the Baptist
Nightfall
On the sailing ship Stella Maris

COLD SPRAY PUMMELED Isadore's face. He had never liked the sea. He did not trust it. After all, there was always the chance of falling off the edge of the world. People said it was not possible, that the earth was round, not flat at all, but Isadore did not believe it.

All his life, the cleric had made every effort to stay away from sailing vessels of any kind, to keep his feet firmly planted on the ground. It was ironic that he should end up on a ship now, fleeing for his life.

He had known immediately that there would be no place to hide in all of England. The men of Greencastle had abandoned him immediately after depositing Lydia's limp body at the Abbey. They had scattered in different directions to save their own hides, wanting nothing more to do with him.

After running for several days, he made his way to the coast. In desperation, he struggled to overcome his contempt for the sea when he realized that fleeing by ship seemed his only alternative. At first, the captain of the vessel bound for Spain would not allow him passage. Saying that he looked like a man on the run, he added that a man on the run usually brought trouble. The captain did not want trouble.

In an uncharacteristic stroke of genius, Isadore concocted a story about being sent to Spain on an urgent errand for the local Inquisitor. Since the last thing the captain wanted was problems with the Inquisition, he asked no more questions. Instead he waved Isadore onto the deck, grumbling under his breath as he did. The captain then barked orders to the crew who scurried around heaving the last of the heavy cargo on board from the dock. When everything was loaded, they hoisted the sails—

hours before they were scheduled to leave port.

Up on the ship's deck Isadore sat contemplating his fate. He had not meant his life to come to this pitiful hour. He had once entertained noble and pious ambitions. When he became a priest, he thought himself bound for greatness. He dreamed of becoming a university teacher, but he was never to realize his dream. He found the world much too distracting to apply himself to his studies. Frustration deepened with the passing years and he was not able to obtain the recognition that was so important to him.

His studies had made him a marginal teacher, at best. To his discredit, he had little patience with people. He fought constantly to control his temper, as well as his passions. Once he secured the meager scrap of a position he had as the tutor of a nobleman's woman-child, he found that his hostility only increased. He knew full well that he had been granted the commission by Lord Wellington only because of pressure from the man's sister. It seemed she believed the girl should be given an education. He didn't really understand why, but it presented him an opportunity unlike any other. His deception secured his place. He had told the Earl that he had, in fact, been a university teacher. Fortunately for the clergyman, there was no one in the vicinity to dispute his claim.

It didn't take Isadore long to figure out that the nobleman was not very noble at all. Anger heaped upon a lifetime of anger made the fire of resentment fester in Isadore's belly. He regarded the Earl as arrogant and self-important, always demanding his own way.

Lord Wellington cared nothing for the piety that Isadore had hoped to instill in him and his household. The final indignity was that, once he was in the service of the Earl of Greencastle, the man adopted a dismissive attitude toward him. Even the woman-child's nurse got more recognition than he did, and her wishes were always honored. It seemed to Isadore that her wish to take the child to Briarcrest was always granted a little too willingly. It was all very hard for Isadore to swallow.

Then there was her newest protector — the herbalist. He felt an ache between his shoulder blades and he felt a shortness of breath when he thought of her. What did she think she was doing — fighting like a man in the dark of night? He had arrived in town the day before Hallow's Eve and waited for his chance. He was wild with anticipation when he realized what good fortune was his when the two women attended the gathering in the square and then left alone, but it hadn't worked. No it hadn't worked at all. Because he didn't deserve it? Or because it was his fate to be a tormented, miserable wretch for the rest of his life?

He shook his fleshy fist into the damp night air and cried, "I shall show them all the error of their ways one day."

A plume of salt water splashed over the deck as the boat started to pitch again. For the fourth time in an hour, Isadore charged to the side of the ship and heaved the meager contents of his stomach over the railing. He spat and muttered a curse into the night.

Returning to the crate he used for a seat, thoughts rushed madly through Isadore's head. His mood changed when Lydia came to mind. "Such a sweet child," he whined.

The fire in the pit of his stomach flared up again. Every time he thought of her, his skin tingled. It was a sweet pain and he liked the feeling. But that infernal nursemaid had never allowed him a moment that was not filled with lessons.

"Lessons, lessons, lessons. Always lessons," he chanted bitterly.

Well, he'd taught them all a lesson, now, hadn't he? He had shown them. The child had grown far too willful. Imagine, refusing to acquiesce to his—that is, her father's—orders to return to Greencastle with him. If it was not his responsibility to teach her a lesson, then whose was it? Perhaps in the future she would remember her place. After all, she was only a woman.

The old crone who guarded her night and day was finally dead and gone. Good riddance, too. As soon as he heard the news, he seized the opportunity to act, but he had failed, miserably. He plunged his head into his hands and rocked back and forth. "Such a lovely child," Isadore crooned.

His painful fantasy made him wince. He had wrestled with thoughts of Lydia for most of his years at Greencastle, from the time she was but a child. As she matured, his torment grew with her. Unable to overcome his wicked thoughts, he fluctuated between despondency and self-righteousness.

A sinister laugh emerged from his fleshy lips. If he could not have her, no one would. Perhaps she was dead by now. A fate she surely deserved.

"And look at me in my miserable situation," he seethed. "Abandoned and fleeing from everything I have ever wanted— forced onto a ship, for heaven's sake! I shall show them. I shall show them all—if I survive."

Isadore ran for the side of the ship again. As he retched, he hurled his curse into the dark, turbulent sea.

He had no idea where he would go once he reached Spain. At the moment, he cared little. His only prayer was that he be able to plant his feet on firm ground again. Perhaps he could find a monastery willing to extend him their hospitality. He knew he would not stay long, though, for the austerity of the monastic life held no attraction for him.

He shuddered, thinking of the alternative. He could end up a poor, homeless beggar. Even worse, he still might not survive this wretched voyage at all.

Overcome with cynicism, he hissed to himself, "This is your downfall, Isadore. You would not be in this predicament if you had only been able to control your passions. You are depraved — a sinner — deserving of death — and this journey might well be your undoing."

The battle continued to rage within him as the ship tossed about on the sea. He was right; he was wrong. He was pious; he was profane. He was pure; he was obscene. He was honorable; he was contemptible. In his misery, he began to think dying on the high seas might be a preferred alternative, but cowardice overcame him. Trapped, ill, his mind by turns racing and stuttering, he at last found comfort of a sort in assigning blame. Seasickness faded before the thought of revenge.

Raising a fist again, he cried out to the blackness, "They can't kill me. I will not allow it. By the God above, they will pay for this. I vow, here and now, that they will all pay."

He barely got his oath out before he was back at the rail of the ship, vomiting.

Chapter
Twenty-three

Lydia's Healing
June 1459
Briarcrest Hall

CATHERINE SUPPLEMENTED HER original mixture of herbs to fight the fever and to ease the pain with a fomentation of comfrey to soothe Lydia's wounds and aid their healing. The sun rose and set again. Still, Catherine would not leave Lydia's side. Having discovered that speaking to Lydia in quiet tones soothed her, Catherine kept it up.

She told stories of events in Willowglen, keeping her narratives light, hoping they would buoy Lydia's spirits — if, indeed, she heard them. When Beatrice came to Lydia's side now, Catherine encouraged her to follow her lead. Beatrice held Lydia's hand and talked to her softly, recounting tales of Lydia's childhood experiences at Briarcrest, hoping these, too, would help revive her.

Hilary also came and sat by Lydia's side, but she said nothing. During one such visit, Catherine realized that Hilary said nothing because she silently shed tears. Only then did she understand how much affection Hilary held for Lydia.

AT THE END of the second day, when Catherine still refused all offers to allow anyone else to replace her, Beatrice had another cot set up beside Lydia's. Catherine used the cot only briefly during the night when she could no longer keep her eyes open. Most of the time, she sat in the chair watching over Lydia, willing her to live.

AS THE FIRST light of the third day crept into the hall through the windows overlooking the garden, Lydia moaned. Catherine leaped to her side and laid a hand on her forehead. It felt cool for the first time since Catherine had arrived. Her fever had broken. The poultices were working. Catherine took Lydia's hand in her own and examined her bruised fingers. A single tear ran down Catherine's cheek. She wiped it away with her free hand and looked back at Lydia's battered face.

Lydia's eyelids seemed to move just a little. Catherine moved closer, inspecting the injured woman. She called to her soothingly and Lydia's eyelids fluttered open. With difficulty, she tried to focus on Catherine's face.

Catherine smiled at Lydia through tear-filled eyes. At first, she was so overcome, she could not speak, but she finally managed a whisper. "Everything is going to be all right, my love. You will get well now. I am here to take care of you. I will not leave you. I promise."

Lydia's lips were dry and cracked from her ordeal. She tried to speak but could not. Catherine offered her a small amount of liquid which she drank with some difficulty.

Catherine comforted, "Just lie still and rest, Lydia. There will be time enough to talk when you have regained some of your strength."

Lydia relaxed and nodded, and Catherine breathed a sigh of relief. Now there was hope that Lydia might well survive.

CATHERINE SAT WITH the chair pulled up to the cot, holding Lydia's hand and beaming. When Joanna came in from the kitchen to see if Catherine needed anything after her night-long vigil, the herbalist nodded toward the pale figure beside her. Joanna turned and realized that Lydia's eyes were open. The older woman gasped.

Catherine blinked back tears again and said, "Joanna, I think it would be a good idea if you would ask Beatrice and Hilary to come down." Then she turned to Lydia and said, "They have been very worried about you. They would have been here, except that I insisted they go upstairs and get some rest a few hours ago."

As Lydia nodded weakly, Joanna headed for the stairway with a new spring in her step.

BEATRICE APPEARED ON the landing in her stocking feet and wearing a felted robe. She looked uncharacteristically disheveled. Her hair was uncombed and she still had sleep in her eyes. Peering over the landing, she blinked a few times to focus on the small cot. She turned toward the darkened upper hallway and exclaimed, "Hilary, it is true!"

Beatrice headed down the stairs with Hilary close at her heels. The two women stood beside the cot, panting. It was true. Lydia's eyes were open. She was alive despite the wounds and bruises she still bore.

Beatrice dropped to her knees beside the cot and stroked her niece's hair. She spoke lovingly to Lydia, tears filling her eyes. "Lydia, Lydia, I am so happy to see your beautiful eyes again."

Catherine agreed wholeheartedly. "She has a long mending period ahead," the healer said, "but she will get stronger now, I am sure of it, Beatrice. She is having difficulty speaking after her ordeal but, hopefully, her voice will return soon. For the moment, some soothing tea would help. Then she must rest."

Joanna had followed Beatrice and Hilary back to the main hall and Catherine now requested some licorice tea to soothe Lydia's throat. When Joanna brought the drink, Lydia took a few small sips and mouthed "*thank you.*" Beatrice and Hilary, satisfied that Lydia truly had rallied, excused themselves to get dressed.

When Catherine was alone with Lydia again, she confessed, "As the days passed, I became concerned that you might never awaken. The thought frightened me so, Lydia. I am so relieved that you have opened your eyes at last." Shyly, Catherine added, "I cannot live without you, Lydia."

Lydia smiled — just a little. Then she mouthed, "How long?"

"How long have you been...ill?"

Lydia nodded.

Taking a moment to count, Catherine replied, "Ten days. Do you remember being at the Abbey?"

Lydia looked confused. Finally, she shook her head "no."

Catherine continued, "You were there for five days. Then Hilary brought you back here to Briarcrest and she and Henry came to fetch me — that was two more days. I arrived here three days ago. I have been tending your wounds ever since."

Lydia smiled again but the smile was replaced by a pained look. She mouthed her question in a single word. "Father?"

Catherine questioned, "Your father?"

Lydia nodded once.

"You want to know if we have heard from him?"

She nodded again.

"We've had no word. Beatrice sent a message that you were much too ill to travel and that your father should give up his plans, but he has sent no word back. It seems strange. We have no idea what he intends to do now, but do not be concerned. He will not be allowed into Briarcrest. Beatrice has seen to it that all is secure. No one will be allowed entry unless Beatrice permits it, I can tell you that. Look," Catherine pointed down the length of the main hall toward the guards at the other end. Lydia turned slowly. "Briarcrest's men are everywhere, standing ready. They are on guard outside, as well as inside the walls. You are safe. Do not be troubled, my Lydia. Only rest and get well."

But Lydia did look troubled. She wanted to speak but could not. Frustrated by the absence of her voice, she closed her eyes in weariness and sighed. Catherine understood.

"I want, with all my heart, to see you well again. Rest, Lydia. Do you think you can sleep for a while?"

Lydia nodded "yes" without opening her eyes. She moved with great effort and held out her hand to Catherine. Catherine took it tenderly in her own.

"Sleep, my dear. I shall be right here when you awaken."

Lydia smiled weakly. Catherine, too, smiled for she could see a faint hint of color returning to Lydia's pale skin. There was hope. Catherine felt it. Finally, as the sun rose higher in the morning sky, Lydia drifted off to sleep.

Chapter
Twenty-four

Feast of St. Mary Magdalene
July 22, 1459
Briarcrest Hall

LYDIA'S WOUNDS, WELTS and bruises made movement extremely painful. Catherine waged a vigilant battle against infection with her potions, teas and ointments. Several times a day, she massaged an herbal mixture into Lydia's scarring tissue to help keep her skin soft and pliable. Although it was painful, Lydia endured it. After a few days, her voice returned, at first only in a whisper, but it grew stronger as time passed. Catherine allowed Lydia a little solid food, along with the broths and teas that she prescribed as she regained her strength. In tending to Lydia, Catherine found yet another expression of her love for her in her healing art. It pleased her to see the progress Lydia was making.

Catherine now allowed herself brief intervals to get some much-needed rest each afternoon. However, she would not allow anyone else to stay with Lydia during the night, for the recovering woman was frequented by horrific dreams. Images she could not describe haunted her. In fitful sleep, she moaned and cried out. Sometimes, it was difficult to awaken her. She would be bathed in sweat and frightened beyond words. During those times, all Catherine could do was hold Lydia close and soothe her fears away gradually.

Each evening, as the rest of the household retired to their own chambers, Catherine took up her post in the chair or on the cot beside Lydia while she slept. During the day, Beatrice, Hilary or Joanna stayed with Lydia since the nightmares plagued her only at night.

One afternoon, Lydia looked at Beatrice, who sat by her side, and spoke in a hoarse whisper. "Auntie, I wish I were able to walk up the stairs to go to my own room. It would be more comfortable for Catherine since she will not let anyone else stay with me at night. And," she added shyly, "I wish we could be together."

Beatrice needed no further explanation. "Perhaps you will be well enough soon, dear," she replied, already formulating a plan to grant her niece's request. When Catherine returned later that afternoon, Beatrice excused herself, saying she had some business that needed her attention. She disappeared quickly, and was absent until just before the evening meal.

Beatrice and Hilary returned to the main hall leading two muscular young men carrying a chair suspended between two large poles. Catherine's curiosity was piqued.

Beatrice announced, "Lydia expressed a desire to be moved into her own room today, and this seems a good thing to me. Does it not seem so to you, Catherine?"

Surprised, Catherine responded, "Why, yes, Beatrice. It might be more comfortable for her in her own bed. She is recovering well enough to be away from the fire and the weather has been pleasant anyway."

The two lads waited patiently as Beatrice and Catherine slowly helped Lydia off the cot, wrapping her in the fur cover from the bed, and carefully settling her onto the chair. Hoisting the makeshift throne gently, the pair stepped up the stairway. Lydia sat suspended between them. By this time, a small crowd of household staff gathered to follow the group up the stairs, chirping their excitement and admonishing the young men to take care with the injured woman.

When they set the litter down, Beatrice and Catherine helped Lydia into the tapestry-curtained bed. The boys left without a word, the household staff chattering excitedly behind them as they departed. Before Joanna left, she encouraged Lydia to rest. It was apparent that the journey from the great hall to her bedchamber had taken its toll on her.

When Catherine and Lydia were alone, Catherine encouraged, "Sleep, now, Lydia. There is time before they bring the evening meal to you."

Lydia patted the bed beside her with some effort and said in a gravel-textured voice, "Come and lay beside me, Catherine. I will rest so much better if you do."

A look of concern crossed Catherine's face. "Lydia, I am not sure it is wise. It would be better if I had the cot brought upstairs. You are still in a great deal of pain."

Lydia's hoarse "no" was adamant. Then, with pleading in her eyes, she said, "I should rest with you beside me. That is how I will rest best, and I do not want you to endure that uncomfortable cot any longer."

Catherine thought about opposing Lydia, but decided against it. She did not want to agitate the young woman. *Besides, I want to be with Lydia, to lie beside her again. Perhaps it is the best thing we can do for her healing.*

Thus, they passed their nights side-by-side in the large tapestried bed. The days came and went with Lydia devoting herself to rest and recuperation. Catherine did everything she knew to assist Lydia's healing — and it seemed to be working.

DURING ONE OF Beatrice's afternoon visits, Lydia and Beatrice spoke of Marian.

Lydia admitted for the first time, with tears in her eyes, "I miss her so much."

"I know, child. I miss her, too," Beatrice replied, patting her niece's hand.

"What do you suppose she would say about all this, Auntie?"

Beatrice grew thoughtful. Finally, she replied, "Marian understood more of what went on in your life than you realize, Lydia. She sheltered you more than you know. However, she knew that you had come to a crossroads and she could not protect you any longer. You would have a difficult road ahead of you, especially if you chose to defy your father over your coming betrothal. She knew well that Catherine was important and special to you. She did not intend to stand in the way of your happiness, even if your father would."

"Do you think that's possible, Auntie?" Lydia's tone was full of hope. "Do you think that Catherine and I could ever find the happiness that you and Hilary have found here?"

"You must understand. Hilary and I came together by chance. What we made of our feelings happened only because fate chose to smile on us. If Hilary's father had not died, leaving her with no betrothal plans and no family who cared to interfere with her future, and if the Duke of Briarcrest had not met his untimely death, our lives might have been vastly different."

Lydia was quiet, hesitating before daring the question she had long wondered about. "Did you love him, Auntie?"

The question took Beatrice by surprise. She had not thought about it for many years — not really. Nevertheless, Beatrice had always been honest with her young niece, so she tried to answer her truthfully. "I did not choose the Duke as my husband, Lydia. He was chosen for me by my own father, your grandfather, who was Earl of Greencastle then. For my own part, I understood that I would marry someone of my father's choosing. I never questioned it.

"My father was not very different from yours in that he looked long and hard for a husband for me, but that is where the similarities end. His reasons for choosing carefully were different from your father's motivation, for my father was content with his title and fortune. He only wanted a good man of suitable title who would treat his daughter with decency. He thought he had found that man in the Duke of Briarcrest, and he thought correctly. In our short time together, I found the Duke to be a kind husband. He was quick to praise my virtues and tried, although he did not always succeed, to be attentive to my desires. He never mistreated me.

"When he went off chasing his own ideals, he was content to leave Briarcrest in my hands, for he knew I had his best interest at heart and that I was capable of managing his estate well. He went away — unknowingly to his death — leaving me in charge of his household, his lands, and his fortune, willingly.

"Did I love him? I respected him, as he respected me. Did I love him? I did not feel passion for him, no, not like the passion I found for the young Hilary when she came to Briarcrest those many years ago. Not like the passion I feel for her still. She makes these old bones feel alive, and she gives me strength and support. She is truly a helpmate, Lydia."

Beatrice paused, blushing a little at her own candor, before continuing. "I do not know if you and Catherine can find the same peace and happiness that Hilary and I have found. We gained the respect of those who served us over the years. Our own peers accepted us each for our station in life, for Hilary is a Lady of Court in her own right, as you know. Oh, we were not without trials, but we overcame them. They seem of little consequence to me now for we have found that, if people appreciate you, they will leave you in peace.

"Of course, having the treasury of Briarcrest at our disposal has not hurt, either. You, on the other hand, will not be as fortunate. The coffers of Greencastle are not available to you. Still, Catherine has her business, and you have never been afraid to roll up your sleeves and do a little work. I have always said that trait would stand you in good stead.

"I do not think it totally out of the question for you and Catherine to make your way together. However, we must think of a way to get around this will of your father's to marry you off to a French noble. Do not be troubled, though, child. When the time is right, we shall know what to do. I am sure of it."

Chapter
Twenty-five

The Feast of the Assumption of the Virgin
August 15, 1459
Briarcrest

THE DAY LYDIA left the upstairs bedchamber and made her way slowly down the stairs for the first time, Catherine breathed another sigh of relief. At last, she felt confident that the young noblewoman would recover completely.

In the beginning, Catherine and Beatrice would permit her to lean on no one but them. Lately, however, they allowed Joanna to accompany her, for she was able to negotiate the stairs alone. Oftentimes, now, she did not even need to stop and rest going up or down. During the warm summer afternoons, Lydia had taken to sitting in the little inner garden. This bright day, she sat by the pond watching some birds bathe and drink.

Catherine joined Lydia in the courtyard and wandered off to a corner bench to write Sarah a note. She sat with her back against a stone wall, its firm coolness pleasant on the warm summer day. A wooden lap desk, borrowed from Beatrice, rested on Catherine's knees. She dipped a quill into the ink bottle and carefully penned to her young assistant the news of Lydia's improvement. She expressed her secret desire to bring Lydia home to Willowglen when she was well enough to travel. Looking over at her beloved sitting by the pool's edge, Catherine thought, *Perhaps I should tell Lydia of my plan...*

Smiling to herself, Catherine returned to her note, anxious to finish. Beatrice had informed her that a man would be leaving on an errand that would take him close to Willowglen. If Catherine wanted to send Sarah a message, he could deliver it.

Catherine signed the note and joined Lydia. "I am going to give Beatrice my note for Sarah. Would you like me to help you upstairs first?"

"I thought I would stay downstairs for the evening meal

tonight, Catherine. I am tired of eating in my chamber. It will do me good to be among the household at table, don't you agree?"

"Why, yes, Lydia. If you feel up to it, that means you are progressing better than I had hoped."

"I think for now, though, I'll stay outside and enjoy the last bit of the afternoon warmth. You go ahead, Catherine. I shall join you later."

Catherine caressed the top of Lydia's head. She looked into the grey-green eyes and, for the first time since May time, their souls touched for a brief instant. It took Catherine by surprise. She blushed, touched Lydia's cheek affectionately, and quickly left the enclosure.

BEATRICE SAT IN her study behind her large, ornate writing table. A stack of papers was piled up in front of her. She looked up as Catherine knocked lightly on the open door. "Come in, Catherine," Beatrice said. "I was just about to send for you."

"My letter to Sarah is done, Beatrice. Here it is."

"Oh, yes, fine," Beatrice said distractedly. She pointed to one side of the desk where a stack of finished documents lay rolled and tied with red ribbons stamped with the wax seal of Briarcrest. "Put it there, dear. Those will be sent off in the morning, but that is not why I wanted to call you. I have news — of Lydia's father."

Catherine's heart sank. This was news that she didn't think she wanted to hear. Trying to sound indifferent, she inquired, "Oh, and what news is that, Beatrice?"

"News that confirms my suspicions, Catherine. News that Lydia's father had not returned from France when Isadore showed up here for Lydia. We were falsely informed. Some of my people have been able to gather enough information for us to piece together the patchwork of events.

"First, there was no message from Lydia's father. It was all Isadore's invention. Most likely it was all to serve his own, let us say, insidious end."

Catherine stood before Beatrice without blinking. Past conversations with Lydia went hurling through her mind. Those that included Isadore came to the forefront, and in a flash of insight, Catherine understood. Concern replaced comprehension instantly. When she looked into Beatrice's eyes, she knew that it was all true.

She thought out loud, "Marian never left Lydia alone with

Isadore when she was a child."

Beatrice, looking solemn, clarified, "She never left Lydia alone with Isadore at any time in her life. She never trusted him."

Alarm now replaced her concern. Catherine weighed her next question carefully before she asked it. "Then, Isadore wanted Lydia for himself?"

Beatrice studied Catherine. "I am afraid it is so, Catherine."

"How long have you known this?"

"Since Lydia was a child. You see, that is how she and Marian came to spend so much time at Briarcrest. Marian found that my brother would never deny her request to bring Lydia to visit. He was never certain if I might serve some purpose of his. Perhaps I might be manipulated into granting him something he desired. Marian used that selfishness on my brother's part to get Lydia away from Greencastle whenever she could, especially when Lord Wellington was gone.

"Isadore watched himself carefully when the Earl was there. He dared not act out of turn. However, whenever my brother left Greencastle for any length of time, Isadore would become brash, leering at Lydia. Marian feared what else he might do, given the chance. So she brought Lydia here as often as she could."

"Beatrice, did you know that Isadore himself gave Lydia that beating?"

Beatrice sat back in her chair and stared. "How do you know this, Catherine?"

"Lydia is starting to remember her nightmares. Fortunately, the more she remembers, the less they seem to trouble her. They contain the details of what happened to her, just as we suspected. She told me that when Isadore caught up to her she was only a short distance from the Abbey. When he ordered her to come with them, she refused and kept walking, trying to reach the Abbey gate. Because of her defiance, Isadore ordered the men with him to seize and beat her, but they hesitated. No doubt they weighed the consequences of harming their master's daughter against those from refusing Isadore's orders. When they did not take action fast enough, Isadore became enraged and took matters into his own hands. Lydia said that the last thing she can recall is her surprise that such a flaccid little man could have so much power as he lashed the whip."

Beatrice looked somber. She spoke slowly, deliberately. "And yet, I am not surprised. His anger was, no doubt, that of a man who has had his passion thwarted for years. He probably took all of it out on Lydia—his obstructed lust for her, his contempt of Marian, his loathing of Lydia's father, and especially for his plans to send Lydia away to be given to another man. No," Beatrice added bitterly, "I do not doubt for one moment that Isadore was directly responsible for Lydia's injuries."

It was distressing to Catherine to think that Isadore had been a threat to Lydia for most of her life. Marian, alone, had deflected that threat by her own cleverness for years. In the end, though, from her final resting place, Marian had not been able to protect Lydia.

Catherine thought, *And what about us? What of Beatrice and Hilary and I? Will we be able to protect Lydia now? Those of us who are left and who love Lydia still — can we continue to shield her from those who are after their own desires for her?*

Catherine had no answers. She only had more questions — questions she decided not to ask Beatrice at the moment. However, her anxiety, for some reason, made her wonder, *Who was it that had come out of the alley on Hallow's Eve night and tried to drag Lydia off?*

LYDIA CAME IN from the garden and sat by the fire in the main hall. She looked tired, but she would not hear of it when anyone suggested that she go upstairs and allow her meal to be brought up to her. She insisted that she wanted to prove to herself, as well as to everyone else, that she was truly on the mend.

At dinner, conversation at the long dining table in the great hall was buoyed by Lydia's presence. However, it came to an abrupt end when they heard a great commotion in the antechamber. The muffled exchange grew to a shouting match, causing the diners to fall into a hushed silence. In the distant shadows, a guard tried to prevent someone from entering the hall.

Lydia grew pale at the sound of the argument. Beatrice and the healer exchanged a whispered conversation. They decided that they would not draw attention to Lydia by ushering her from the room unless they had reason to believe she was in immediate danger. Catherine kept her eyes on her companion and her ear to the next room, ready for action.

The voices stopped. The guard stomped to the doorway, his anger visible on his face. He struggled to keep his tone pleasant when he spoke. "Forgive the intrusion, Beatrice. A messenger has come from Greencastle. He says he will give his message to none other than yourself. Will My Lady allow —"

The guard plunged forward, losing his footing. The intruder had come up behind him and shoved him out of the way. Not waiting for permission to speak, the uninvited caller bellowed, "You must listen to my message, for I have been sent by Lord Wellington, Earl of Greencastle."

The guard regained his footing and reeled toward the trespasser with his sword half drawn.

"Enough!" Beatrice roared.

Surprised, both men whirled back toward Beatrice and stared, wide-eyed. Beatrice drew in her breath. Speaking in a softer tone, her voice still betrayed her irritation. "Speak, sir, if you must. I would rather hear your unbidden words than see your blood spilled before my eyes for your insolence."

The guard riveted his eyes on the man and his hand tightened on his resheathed weapon.

The intruder shrugged at him in mocked innocence and continued, "My Lord Wellington sends you word that he is on his way here. He shall call for his daughter, the Lady Lydia Wellington, three days hence. She is to be ready to return to France with Lord Wellington upon his arrival."

Beatrice and the messenger glared at one another.

"And how am I to know this message to be truly from my brother? Others have come before you, making claims that have proven untrue."

Feigning politeness, he said, "I know nothing of other messages, good Lady. I know that I, myself, have come from France with Lord Wellington only days ago. As soon as we made our way to Greencastle and we found the Lady and her maid still gone, my Lord bid me come here with this message, straight away."

Beatrice inquired, "Tell me, sir, what do you know of Isadore, the cleric?"

"Nothing, Lady. There are those at Greencastle who say he has done some dastardly deed and fled the country. Perhaps the Lady of Briarcrest knows more of him than do we. For I have heard that some of Briarcrest's own men pursue him still."

"Do you know the reason for this pursuit?" Beatrice inquired.

"No, Lady. All we have heard is that the cleric is responsible for some abomination and would dare not return. We have heard nothing else."

"And has my brother no concern for this news?"

"Lord Wellington bid him good riddance if he cannot act according to his station in life. He said he cannot trouble himself with the man, for he has leeched from him for too many years as it is. As my Lord has said, he has more pressing concerns, for he must deliver the Lady Lydia back to France with haste."

"Does my brother not wonder what the cleric has done?"

"I did not hear him inquire. I only know that Lord Wellington wishes to have his daughter back."

Beatrice, impatient with the man's answers, still persisted. "Was my brother not given my message that his daughter was gravely ill and could not travel?"

"He was given the message, Lady, and he responded that surely she must be recovered from whatever silly woman's malady has befallen her. It was then that he decided he would come for her himself to make sure that his will is carried out."

The hall filled with an uneasy silence again. No one but Hilary noticed the vein that swelled and pulsed on the side of Beatrice's neck, a sign of her growing anger.

Beatrice boomed with indignation, "If it is his will, then who are we to interfere? Tell my brother, by all means, come to Briarcrest if he wishes. After all, we live and breathe to serve him. Heed my warning, however, sir. He may not find things as he would have them when he arrives."

Unsure of how to respond to Beatrice's message, the man opened his mouth to speak, but hesitated, then looked puzzled. Beatrice dismissed him. "You may rest in the outer courtyard until you have eaten, then you are to leave. Briarcrest's hospitality extends no further."

The man seemed to take no note of the fact that Beatrice was banishing him. He bowed low, turned on his heels, and smiled at the guard. Then, brushing him with his shoulder as he passed, the messenger strode off. A second guard had arrived and was waiting in the shadows. He now fell in behind the man to escort him out.

Beatrice spoke to the knight before her. "Have some food and drink brought to him from the kitchen, please, Guy. Then see that he is on his way quickly. He is not welcome to stay the night."

"Yes, My Lady."

Sir Guy stomped toward the kitchen.

DURING THE IMPASSIONED exchange between Beatrice and the man, Catherine watched Lydia turn ashen at his message and become unsteady in her seat. Catherine discreetly put a hand on Lydia's arm to steady her. When the stranger left the hall, Catherine turned toward Lydia just in time to catch her as she fainted.

A flurry of activity followed. Someone ran to get water from the kitchen. Catherine held a cool, wet towel to Lydia's forehead while she steadied her against her chest. Moisture trickled down Catherine's arm as she held the cloth in place. The small rivulet distracted her from her concern for a moment. But then, in the midst of tending to Lydia, Catherine stared at Beatrice. *What, I wonder, does the Duchess have up her sleeve?*

A collective sigh rose up in the hall, when Lydia finally opened her eyes. When she realized that everyone was staring, Lydia apologized for causing a fuss. Then she added, "Perhaps I must resign myself to going with my father. It would cause you—all of you—far too much turmoil if I were to refuse him."

Beatrice's jaw tensed. Then she boomed, "I will not hear of any of this, Lydia. The man has no idea of the grief and pain he causes by his selfish ignorance. I do not want to hear you talk like that any more, do you hear me?"

Lydia nodded meekly.

Relief washed over Catherine as she thought, *So, Beatrice has no intention of handing her over.* She spoke up now. "Beatrice, I think that Lydia should go upstairs and rest. This has been quite an ordeal for her and she has been up for the greater part of the day today. She is exhausted."

"Yes, yes, of course," Beatrice said apologetically.

Turning to Lydia, Catherine asked, "Are you able to walk, Lydia?"

"Yes, I think I can manage, Catherine. I'm just a little shaken, that's all. I'm so sorry to have caused a scene, Auntie."

Beatrice, also concerned for her niece's well-being said, comfortingly, "Lydia, do not worry about causing a scene. If that ruffian had been cooperative with Guy, I could have received his message in private and spared you this shock. However, perhaps this has happened for the best—but we shall speak of it later. For now, go upstairs and rest."

"Yes, Auntie," Lydia replied, pulling herself up slowly.

Catherine steadied her.

"I am rather tired," she sighed.

Joanna hurried to help Lydia by steadying her on the opposite side.

As they reached the top of the stairs, Catherine heard Beatrice say, "Hilary, this has gone far enough. It is time to act. Come with me to the study..."

JOANNA HELPED CATHERINE settle Lydia into bed. When Catherine asked Lydia how she felt, she replied in an exhausted whisper, "I shall be fine, Catherine. I'm just a little tired."

"Do you know that rogue, Lydia?"

"No. He must be new in my father's service. I've never seen him before tonight."

"As I suspected," Catherine replied, "since he did not acknowledge you. He had no idea that you were sitting right in front of him as he spoke..."

ONCE LYDIA FELL asleep, Catherine joined Beatrice and Hilary in the study. She found them pouring over an old map.

As Hilary motioned Catherine closer, Beatrice looked up and asked, "Is she going to be all right, Catherine?"

"She will recover, Beatrice. She is just tired, now. She was asleep before I left her."

The lines in Beatrice's face seemed to lessen a little.

"She told me she never saw that man before tonight. She does not know who he is. She said he is new to the Earl's service."

"It's not surprising," Beatrice said, "and it is to our advantage for my plan."

Catherine, full of curiosity, asked, "What do you have in mind, Beatrice?"

Beatrice answered, "Many years ago, the Duke of Briarcrest discovered an ideal hiding place. He called it his *'fortress.'* It is located in the foothills not far from here. Before he left on his last excursion, he gave me this map and told me to guard it well. *'The hidden stronghold is marked here,'* he told me, *'but it is obvious to no one. If danger should arise when I am not with you, go there,'* the Duke said. *'I shall come for you when it's safe.'*

"Fortunately, I have never had need of it. It has been a very long time since I have looked at this map. I have not even thought of it for many years."

Bewildered, Catherine asked, "Beatrice, do you intend to send Lydia into hiding?"

"Yes, my dear, that is exactly what I intend to do."

"But for how long?" Catherine asked incredulously. "She cannot hide for the rest of her life."

"It is true, she cannot. That is not my plan. Listen—"

The three women huddled closer together. As Beatrice revealed her idea, Catherine's mouth fell open.

Chapter
Twenty-six

August 16, 1459
Briarcrest

CATHERINE WANTED TO know about this Father Giles. He arrived at Briarcrest shortly after dawn and immediately accompanied Beatrice into her study. Catherine asked Joanna about him and was told that Giles and Beatrice had been friends for years.

"He is rather unconventional—for a priest. He even comes to the May feast, although this year his superior sent him on an errand, so he could not come. Beatrice thinks it was done to stop him from attending the May Day celebration."

Even though Catherine implored Lydia to stay in bed after the previous day's ordeal, she insisted that she wanted to get up. When Hilary found out that Lydia intended to be up and about, she intervened and ordered Lydia to remain out of sight. Catherine and her young companion spent the day in the upstairs bedchamber.

All morning long, Beatrice and Giles closed themselves up in the study with the door shut tight. Catherine, on her way to get some tea from the kitchen, saw the pair emerge later. She heard Beatrice invite Giles to stay for the noon meal, but he begged his leave, saying that he had to prepare for the next day's service.

After Father Giles left, the house grew very quiet—almost too quiet. It felt as if Briarcrest itself held its breath.

"Farewell"

IT HAD BEEN two days since the disruption brought about by the messenger from Greencastle, and the morning had dawned dark and dreary. Oppressive storm clouds gathered overhead, but no rain came. Catherine sat by the window overlooking Briarcrest Wood, watching the dismal clouds move closer. Sadness pressed in around her, but tears, like the rain, refused to come and bring relief.

Catherine did not respond to the knock on the door.

When no reply came, Beatrice reluctantly opened it. The older woman stood before Catherine looking pale and drawn. She urged gently, "Catherine, it's time. Giles is here and everything is ready."

Without a word, Catherine got up from her seat and followed Beatrice. When they entered the seldom-used chapel, a knot formed in Catherine's throat. In the sanctuary, surrounded by lit candles, was a plain wooden coffin. Beatrice and Catherine joined Hilary, who was already seated on a bench just outside the sanctuary. Most of the surrounding village was in attendance. Many of the women wept quietly.

As Catherine took her place in full view of the casket, she reeled with dizziness. Relief came in the form of a distraction when Father Giles emerged from the sacristy dressed in his priestly robes. A young man, acting as acolyte, preceded him. The lad carried a gold censer suspended from a heavy chain. Sweet-smelling smoke rose up from the burning incense and permeated the chapel. The odor made Catherine nauseous.

The men bowed low before the altar. Kneeling with his back to the congregation, Father Giles chanted the Prayers for the Dead. His young assistant responded.

"*...requiescat in pace...*"

"*Amen.*"

"*Domine exaudi orationem meam...*"

"**Et clamor meus ad te veniat.**"

"*Dominus vobisum...*"

"*Et cum Spiritu tuo.*"

"*Per Christum Dominum nostrum. Requiescat in pace...*"

Back and forth the prayers volleyed between the two until everything became a blur to Catherine. Finally, the priest took the incense from his assistant and walked slowly around the coffin, hurling smoke against its sides. When the ritual was complete, several men came forward and hoisted the heavy box onto their shoulders.

Catherine recognized one of the young men. He was one of the lads who had borne Lydia on the litter up to the bedchamber only weeks ago. The boy's eyes were rimmed red from crying. Catherine quickly lowered hers to keep her own tears from flowing. Although she would have welcomed the relief earlier, she would not allow herself to weep now.

Beatrice, Hilary and Catherine followed the young men as

they solemnly carried the casket. The women were followed by
Father Giles and his acolyte, with the rest of the congregation
behind them, as they walked to the burial site. Silently, the
procession gathered at the foot of a large oak tree. A dark hole,
dug deep into the earth, waited like the mouth of some giant
monster, open in anticipation of its prey. Catherine swayed as
dizziness overtook her again. Hilary caught her arm. More
prayers followed at the burial site. At their conclusion, Father
Giles nodded solemnly and the men lowered the box into the
ground on ropes.

Beatrice, looking as if she were a ghost herself, sprinkled the
first handful of dirt on the coffin. Others followed suit—except
Catherine. She could not bring herself to commit Lydia to dust
and ashes. She tried to imagine what it would be like to be
buried under so much crushing earth. Fear overwhelmed her. It
was more than she could bear. Finding it difficult to breathe, she
broke away from the crowd and hurried back to Briarcrest Hall.

LITTLE MORE THAN a subdued drone could be heard as
people gathered in the great hall. Catherine, for her part, sat by
a window, alone. She stared into the inner courtyard, not seeing
its beauty.

As the morning wore on, those who came to console the
household departed quietly. The staff returned to their duties.
Catherine continued to peer out the window, keeping no track of
her thoughts—although they were of Lydia.

Time passed in slow-motion. Hilary approached Catherine.
She whispered, "Catherine, go upstairs and lie down for awhile.
This has been hard on you."

Catherine forced herself to look in the direction of the voice
and asked, "Are you saying it has not been difficult for you and
for Beatrice, Hilary?"

"No, not at all," the older woman replied. "It has been more
distressing than we imagined it would be, I think, but it is you
that I am concerned about. You look pallid and you cannot deny
that you almost fainted this morning, more than once, I dare
say."

Catherine turned back to the garden. "It is foolish, I know."

"I do not think it so, Catherine. I think it is the reaction of
one who cares deeply."

"It is still difficult, Hilary."

Hilary put a consoling hand on Catherine's shoulder.
"Beatrice told me you are planning to leave soon, Catherine. I
wish you would allow me to convince you to stay for a few more

days so that you might rest a little before your journey home."

"My mind is made up, Hilary. I shall leave tomorrow. It may have been a mistake even to stay that long. Perhaps I should have left right after the burial. I don't know. I guess I'm a little frightened."

"I know. We all are, I think."

Surprised, Catherine asked, "Are you? Are you frightened, too, Hilary?"

"Yes," Hilary whispered. Her voice sounded as if it came from a great distance. She, too, stared somewhere beyond the garden now.

AS BEATRICE APPROACHED the two women, she recognized their far-off looks. She spoke apologetically when she reached them. "Ladies, I am afraid I have just received news that Lord Wellington will arrive earlier than we expected. He is only a short distance away and will be here momentarily. I shall receive him in my study. I suggest that both of you go upstairs and remain out of sight while he is here. There is no need for you to subject yourselves to the unpleasantness that will, no doubt, accompany his visit."

Hilary's response was quick and adamant. "No, Beatrice, I'll not let you do this alone."

Beatrice replied, "It is not necessary, Hilary."

"Perhaps it is not necessary to you, but it is essential for me. There will be no discussion, Beatrice. I shall not let you do this alone."

Beatrice's face softened. She smiled at Hilary.

"Nor shall I," said Catherine. "I will be there, also."

"You do not need to do this, Catherine."

"No, but like Hilary, I will not leave you to face Lydia's father alone. After all, I am, at least in part, the reason we have come to this meeting." As Catherine spoke, she felt the dark cloud lift from around her. With each word, strength and confidence replaced sadness and melancholy.

"So be it," pronounced Beatrice, her own expression visibly brightened, "but we must keep calm. I shall have some tea brought to us while we wait. Wait for me in the study."

Hilary and Catherine started across the great hall while Beatrice sent for the tea. The three women spent the remainder of the afternoon waiting for Lord Wellington to arrive. They exchanged little conversation.

THE CAPTAIN OF the guard informed Beatrice that Lord Wellington was outside Briarcrest's gates. She instructed him to allow the Earl and his men passage to the courtyard, but that Lord Wellington should be escorted into the house alone.

The armed men stood eye to eye, neither side willing to yield to the other. When the captain instructed Lord Wellington to give up his weapons before being allowed in, the Earl became furious. However, it did not take long for him to realize that he was not to be admitted unless he were unarmed. He grudgingly handed over his sword to one of his men.

The captain then demanded, "I would also have the dagger you have hidden, my Lord."

Incredulous, Lord Wellington protested, "I have no weapon hidden, sir."

With a stern look, the captain countered, "Perhaps you have forgotten..." Pausing for effect, he added, "We shall wait until your memory returns."

The two men stared at each other. The guards on both sides shifted nervously. Finally, Lord Wellington muttered a curse and produced a blade from within his tunic. His men raised their eyebrows, exchanging disbelieving glances.

The captain spoke again. "I am pleased to see that your memory has returned, my Lord. Is there anything else you have, uh, forgotten?"

"Nothing, to be sure," barked the Earl.

"You will follow me, then, alone."

The Earl started to object again, but the captain reminded him of the long wait over his dagger. He reconsidered and grudgingly motioned his men to wait and he followed the guard. When they reached the study, the captain stepped into the shadows, his hand resting on the hilt of his sword.

Seeing his sister did not thaw Lord Wellington's cold expression. "Beatrice," he snapped. He sniffed his disapproval of the presence of the other two women in the room.

Beatrice took the situation in hand. "We did not expect you until tomorrow, Hugo."

"I have an urgent task, Beatrice, and I would appreciate it if you did not interfere. I have no patience for it."

Beatrice, determined to maintain her composure, measured her words. "Urgent task, Hugo? I would think there is nothing of such urgency that you could not, at least, ask after the welfare of your own child. Have you no heart at all?"

"Heart? This has nothing to do with heart. I have a right to claim my daughter." He raised his voice, demanding, " —and I want her. Now!"

Beatrice lowered her gaze and shook her head solemnly. "It is not so much your heart as your soul that I am concerned about, Hugo. Although what ever motivation prompts you to be so unfeeling will have to wait. I am afraid that it is not within my power to hand Lydia over to you."

Hugo Wellington's expression became tortuous. From between clenched teeth he seethed, "Why not?"

Sorrowfully, Beatrice replied, "I truly regret giving you the news this way, but you leave me no alternative. I cannot hand Lydia over to you because your daughter is...dead."

"What?" screamed Hugo. "How can this be? How did you allow this to happen, Beatrice?"

Beatrice struggled to remain calm. She answered, "I am afraid that it is not I who allowed it, Hugo."

"Beatrice, what nonsense is this?"

"I shall try to explain, Hugo," Beatrice said, "but you must allow me to speak.

"Lydia received word from you many weeks ago. When Isadore arrived to collect her, we found that she had become so distressed at the thought of going to France for her betrothal that she had fled."

Confusion overtook him for a moment. "But, I sent no word until a few days ago."

"Do not interrupt, Hugo," Beatrice said sharply. "I shall come to that in time." She composed herself and continued calmly. "We did not know she had left the house until Isadore asked for her. When we found her missing, the priest and his band went after her.

"When he came upon her on the road, he gave her a severe beating, then left her for dead at the Abbey of St. Nicholas. When we found Lydia, she had little life left in her. We brought her back here and tried to treat her. At first, we thought she would recover, but she took an unexpected turn for the worse. In the end, she was just too weak to go on. We buried her only this morning. I am sorry..."

Hugo hung his head. He looked as if he might actually mourn the loss of his daughter. It didn't last more than a moment, though. His head shot up and he questioned, "How do I know you are not lying to me, woman?"

"If you would like, I shall show you the grave," Beatrice offered sadly.

"Show me the grave? You had better show me the body."

Beatrice stammered, "Hugo, would you desecrate your own child with such an act?"

Hugo considered for a moment. Then, he said quietly,

"Show me the burial site."

Beatrice turned to Hilary. "Hilary, will you go to the chapel? I believe Father Giles is still there, praying. Ask him to accompany us to the burial site."

"Certainly, Beatrice," Hilary answered. She turned and headed for the study door.

Hugo watched her go, a look of scorn on his face, until Beatrice demanded his attention again. "Hugo, this is Mistress Catherine Hawkins. She is an herbalist. We engaged her so that we could give Lydia the best care possible, but it was all to no avail."

Catherine nodded to the Earl. Her face was expressionless. He, in turn, glared at Catherine without acknowledging her. Silence surrounded the trio until Hilary returned with Giles.

Beatrice introduced the two men. Giles offered his condolences to the Earl. "It is unfortunate that you could not be here for the rites of the Church this morning, Lord Wellington. Perhaps it would have provided you with some measure of consolation."

Lord Wellington muttered, "Yes, well..."

Beatrice got up from her seat and walked to the door. Turning, she invited, "If you will follow me, Hugo, I will show you where your daughter rests."

As the group walked along the path toward the large oak tree, they saw someone kneeling by the freshly piled earth. They stopped some distance away and watched a young man in his private grief. Before departing, he placed a small bouquet of summer wildflowers on the dirt, then wiped his eyes with his sleeve. He walked away slumped over, looking very disheartened. It was the young man who had carried Lydia's coffin that morning. He was the same lad who had borne her on the chair to her bedchamber. Catherine wondered who he was and why he mourned Lydia so.

With the young man gone, the group drew closer. Hugo stood, staring at the earthen pile. Catherine bowed her head as if in silent prayer, but she watched Hugo out of the corner of her eye.

The Earl spoke to Beatrice, his voice quivering as he asked, "This is why Isadore fled?"

Beatrice nodded.

"I was so absorbed with trying to get here that I failed to listen to those at Greencastle who tried to tell me what he was up to. I never thought that it had anything to do with Lydia."

Doubts crept in on Catherine. She was beginning to feel sorry for him. If he truly mourned his daughter, how could she continue this deception? She had nothing to worry about, however, for his remorse was short-lived. The next words out of Lord Wellington's mouth exposed his true feelings.

With a look of sorrow on his face, he whimpered, "They were going to make me...a baron." Tears glistened in his eyes as he spoke.

Catherine understood now. He mourned, not the loss of his daughter, but the forfeiture of his promised elevation. His only regret was that he would not be able to redeem his prize in exchange for the one piece of property he no longer had—Lydia.

Catherine should have been filled with anger, but anger was more emotion than she could summon. She was drained. The ridiculousness of the situation overwhelmed her. She felt like laughing, but she knew that would be disastrous. An unbidden snicker formed in her throat. She struggled to keep it from emerging. Uncontrolled laughter pushed its way up through her chest. The sound caught in her throat as she struggled to stifle the sound. Finally, it emerged in the form of a choking cough.

Hilary came to her rescue, saying, "Catherine is worn out from caring for Lydia all these days and nights. There is a dampness in the evening air that does her no good. Let me take her back to the house. We'll meet you there."

Hilary and Catherine walked toward Briarcrest quickly. Catherine was visibly shaken. Once they were out of earshot, Hilary asked, "Catherine, are you all right? What happened?"

"I'm not sure. Lydia's father seemed to mourn the loss of his precious title more than his own daughter. I wanted to be angry, but I am so tired and the circumstances seemed so pointless—even comical. I felt as if I would burst out laughing. The more I tried to stop it, the worse it got."

"Do not trouble yourself too much about it, Catherine. Hugo is so full of himself that he will not think much of what happened to you back there."

Catherine breathed a sigh of relief at Hilary's words. She didn't want to cause any doubt about Lydia's death. Arriving back at Briarcrest Hall, Hilary and Catherine waited for the others to return. Beatrice and Giles came back shortly—alone.

Hilary inquired, "Beatrice, where's Hugo?"

"Gone," she sighed, "as quickly as he came. We did not have what he came for, therefore he had no need to stay. I imagine I have seen the last of my brother, Hilary."

"I am sorry," Hilary said quietly. "I know you would have liked Hugo to be different."

"Perhaps more like he was before Lydia's mother died, Hilary, but we cannot go back. Instead, we go forward. Our

biggest obstacle has been overcome. Hugo has come and gone—
without digging up that grave."

Chapter
Twenty-seven

The Village of Wickingham
August 17, 1459

THE OLD WORK cart creaked and shifted as Henry helped Lydia down. Dawn was just starting to break when he escorted the young woman into a twig-and-mud hut. They had left Briarcrest in the middle of the night. No one had seen them go except Beatrice, Hilary and Catherine. Inside the hut, Lydia was surprised to find the simple house was neat and comfortable. The room was lit by a single small lamp on a table. A stool was positioned on either side of the table. In a corner, by a lit stone fireplace, lay a straw cot. It was covered by a thickly woven covering that had been colored with green vegetable dyes. Some kitchen tools and tin dishes sat atop a crude wooden box under a tiny paneless, shuttered window. They were welcomed by Lucy, the grey-haired matriarch of the Wickingham clan. While Henry went to settle their things into another hut, Lucy and Lydia got acquainted.

"I knew your uncle," Lucy said with some pride.

"My aunt told me you saved his life," Lydia said.

"My mother was the one that healed him. I was just a girl then. I was the one that found him in the forest that day, though. I knew a little of herbs and potions, but my mother was the clan healer. A group of us went into the forest to pick mushrooms and wild herbs. I was the oldest. When I found him, he was in terrible condition. I shouted for the others and sent them to get help. When the men came and carried him back to Wickingham, my mother cared for him. Bandits had robbed him of his money, his horse, and the better part of his clothes. Left him for dead, they did, but my mother brought him 'round. Fine healer, she was."

Lydia thought of Catherine and smiled.

"Never thought we'd see the likes of you here again. No need to worry, though. You'll have to live a lot simpler than you are accustomed to, but if you can abide it, everything will be fine. Know all about your father and his nasty business. It's not right — forcing people to do something they have no desire for. Just not right at all. You stay here, though. Stay until that Duchess works it out. We will take good care of you."

"Thank you, Lucy. I am most grateful," Lydia replied politely.

OTHER THAN LUCY, no one in Wickingham knew the complete details of Lydia's story. She and Henry thought it better to discuss them as little as possible. There was some talk in the hamlet, at first — speculation regarding the nature of Lydia's situation — but Lucy, in her strong and direct way, put a stop to the gossip at once.

When the supplies they carried from Briarcrest had been unloaded, the men hid the wagon deep within the forest where it could not be found. They allowed the horses to roam and planned to claim no knowledge of their origin should they be questioned.

When Henry finally returned to Lucy's tiny house, Lydia accompanied him to another small hut at the edge of the village. The place looked old except for several newly patched areas, evidence that someone had prepared for their arrival. A tapestry curtain, brought from Briarcrest, had been hung from the low roof to divide the single room in two. Lydia peeked behind the curtain and found a small, crude cot set up. This, Henry informed her, would be her sleeping area. Henry would sleep on a mat in the front part of the room for the duration of their stay. He then proceeded to reveal the entire ruse.

When she heard the plan, Lydia chuckled, embarrassing him. Henry, already married with several nearly grown children, told Lydia that she was to be known as his new young bride. Together, they would live in Wickingham until her safety could somehow be assured. Not even Henry's wife knew what he was up to. He had told her he would be on an errand of great importance for the Duchess. That was all. In his absence, young Tom would be the man of the family.

LUCY, ONLY A few years Beatrice's junior, reminded Lydia of a combination of Beatrice and Catherine together. She couldn't help but like her. Lucy developed an immediate fondness for Lydia, too.

At Henry's request, the village healer took up the care of

Lydia's wounds where Catherine had left off. The first time she examined Lydia's scars, Lucy marveled that the injuries had mended so well. She acknowledged that they could only have done so at the hands of a skilled healer.

"Yes," Lydia replied shyly. "Her name is Catherine. She is very special to me."

"I'd like to meet this woman some day," Lucy said. "She's very gifted."

A smile stole across Lydia lips, but her eyes glistened with tears. Lucy observed her reaction, but said nothing.

Henry insisted that Lydia not lift a finger since she was still recuperating from her injuries. Lydia, however, knew she was capable of some activity. She begged him to allow her to work a little in the fall garden he had planted, but he would not hear of it. When Lydia felt as though she would go mad sitting idle, she asked Lucy to intercede with him and he finally allowed her to pick up a hoe.

Working their small crop, Lydia hummed to herself. She felt closer to Catherine in the garden and the burden of their separation was a little easier to bear.

Each evening, Lydia retired early, for she still needed extra rest. At times she missed Catherine so much that she considered finding one of the horses and riding back to Willowglen. Common sense won out, however, when she thought of what had happened the last time she tried to flee alone. To console herself, she tried to imagine what it would be like for her to be with Catherine without anything or anyone to stand in their way. She found it almost impossible to fathom.

Chapter
Twenty-eight

Catherine's Departure from Briarcrest
August 18, 1459

CATHERINE FOUND SAYING farewell to Beatrice and Hilary bittersweet. She hoped to see them at the next Willowglen fair, but she wondered if she would ever have the opportunity to visit the magnificent Briarcrest again. Then, too, she worried about Lydia. The evening before her departure for home, Catherine expressed her anxiety over how they would continue to hide the news from Lydia's father that she was alive. Catherine feared that Lydia would never be able to come out of hiding. Only because Beatrice's response seemed so full of confidence was Catherine's apprehension appeased.

"I know my brother better than he knows himself," Beatrice said. "I am convinced that all we needed to do was to get him to believe that Lydia was buried in that grave. When he gets back to Greencastle, I am certain he will not stay for long. He will set sail for France again and arrive at court with tears in his eyes. He will hope his friends see fit to console him over the loss of his daughter by bestowing his coveted title on him anyway. He will seek their pity and use it to his greatest advantage. If it works, he will come to think of this whole affair as the greater blessing.

"When enough time has passed, should he discover that Lydia lives, you can be sure he will deny it—to himself, as well as to others. To be certain, she will have no claim on any of Greencastle's wealth because, finally, just in case the rumor should prove true, her father will disown her to protect his precious fortune and his reputation. In the end, he shall have that which he most desires, and Lydia will be left in peace. The only thing that remains, now, is for you to be patient until it is safe for me to send Lydia to you. You must trust me, Catherine."

Of course Catherine trusted Beatrice. She did not even have to think about it. Without question, she was willing to wait for Lydia for as long as it took.

As the carriage bounced along the road toward Willowglen, her conversation with Beatrice repeated in Catherine's mind. Henry's son Tom drove. Henry had not been seen at Briarcrest since Lydia's 'death.' Fortunately, no one found his absence cause for suspicion since Beatrice often sent him off on one endeavor or another.

As the carriage rounded the final bend in the road, the rooftops of Willowglen appeared in the distance. Suddenly, Catherine longed for the fragrance of the herbs and spices in her shop. She yearned to touch the fabric piled on the old wooden shelves. She wanted to hear how things had gone with Sarah in her absence. Most of all, she wanted time to pass until Beatrice would allow Lydia to leave her hiding place.

The more Catherine thought about their deception, the more she could hardly believe that the scheme had worked. It was incredible that Lydia's father had accepted her death at all — but he had. The trick had worked, and now Lydia's whereabouts were a closely guarded secret. Catherine only had a vague notion of her location from an "X" placed on an old map years before by the Duke of Briarcrest. They had all agreed it would be safer for Lydia if few people knew her whereabouts.

The carriage wheels vibrated over the cobblestones of Market Street. Catherine was glad to be home. But a carriage such as one from Briarcrest could not come into town without drawing attention. Children ran behind it, calling out. Dogs barked. Chickens squawked as they fled from the horses' path. From inside the shop, Sarah heard the clamor. She opened the door just in time to see Tom helping Catherine down.

"Catherine!" cried Sarah. "Why did you not send word of your return? I could have had supper for you." Sarah ran to Catherine, embracing her. Catherine was, indeed, home. However, Sarah hung on just a little too long.

Captured in Sarah's grasp, Catherine asked, "What is it, Sarah?"

Sarah pulled back and said tearfully, "We heard about Lady Lydia only this morning." Then, with a surprised look, she added, "I thought you would be more distraught over her...death."

Now, here was a dilemma. Beatrice had been adamant that they keep up the guise of Lydia's death without exception. Beatrice alone would decide when the ruse should end. Until then, she was bound by her word and her concern for Lydia to carry on the deception.

Catherine found it difficult to speak her next sentence. "I have had time to adjust a little, Sarah. And, I am so very glad to be home, now. I shall keep busy and the time will pass."

Sarah thought she understood. "The saying goes: time heals the heart of its grief." She put her arm firmly around Catherine's shoulder and escorted her into the shop.

Inside the door, Catherine stopped and took a slow, deep breath, savoring the fragrant aroma of the various spices. It was good to be home. Turning to Sarah, she said, "The new shipment of nutmeg has come."

"Yes, it arrived two days ago. How did you know?"

"I can smell it."

Catherine smiled at Sarah. Her unexpected calm puzzled the young assistant. Yet, she had to admit Catherine seemed to be at peace. It was more than the young woman had hoped for when she had heard of Lydia's passing. Yet, to the ever-perceptive Sarah, something was not quite right.

When Tom finished bedding the horses for the night, he joined Catherine and Sarah for supper. Afterward, they set up a cot in the corner of the kitchen for him, so Catherine and Sarah had little time to talk privately. Catherine was grateful.

As soon as the pots had been cleaned, Catherine excused herself to go to bed. An exhausting fatigue overtook her as soon as she reached the upstairs room. As she drifted off to sleep that night, she thought she heard Lydia call her name. *I am here, Lydia, upstairs. Come and join me, my love.*

THE NEXT MORNING when Catherine came downstairs, Tom had already gone. Sarah said that he asked her to say good-bye for him and that he hoped they would see each other again.

Catherine merely smiled and said, "Tom is a good boy."

All that day, and in the days that followed, Sarah watched her mistress quietly. She looked for the old familiar signs of impatience and irritability, but none came. She had begun to resign herself to the fact that Catherine had, indeed, gotten over Lydia's death quite quickly. The realization caused Sarah great disappointment.

Chapter
Twenty-nine

Several weeks later
Willowglen

CATHERINE WAITED FOR an opportunity to reveal the surprise she had for Sarah and Will. It had taken her awhile to work out the details, but now she was ready to tell them her plan. One Sunday afternoon, she reminded Sarah of the conversation that had taken place between them months before. "Do you remember when I was about to leave for Briarcrest in the middle of the night, Sarah? Even though I was distraught at the time, I recall that, when you told me to go to Briarcrest and not to worry about anything here, I told you that I appreciated your help and that I would reward you for your kindness when I returned. During my long quiet days at Briarcrest, I had time to think of a way to compensate you properly. I had some details to resolve, but I think my plan is now ready."

Sarah blushed. "You do not need to do anything for me, Catherine. I am your helper. It is right that I should have taken over for you in your absence. I only hope that everything was done to your satisfaction."

"Sarah, you did everything just as I would have, perhaps better. Please, let me do this for you — and for Will."

Now they were both curious.

"What is this plan of yours, Catherine?" Sarah asked.

"I want to help you and Will...so that you can be married."

Will's eyes opened wide. He could hardly believe his ears.

Sarah turned red again, embarrassed and overwhelmed. She responded, with difficulty at first. "Oh, Catherine, we would like to marry, but Will says he cannot take me as his wife without a craft to earn his living."

"I think I may have the answer to that, Sarah — that is, if Will agrees to my idea."

"I shall listen gladly, Mistress," Will replied.

"Lord Pembroke has just returned from Germany. He is

most enthusiastic about the new device that puts writing on pages. He told me all about it a few days ago when he was in the shop. He purchased such a machine and it is being sent to him here. He would like to set up a shop for printing books. He will have need of an apprentice. He wants someone who will take an interest in this new endeavor and help to make it successful— someone who has a willingness to learn. I spoke to him about you, Will. He said he would like to engage you, if you are willing. It is a great opportunity. Books will be printed so that everyone will learn to read soon. They will not be just for those of privilege, hand-printed by monks in monasteries. I told him you would be perfect for the job since Sarah has been teaching you to read. What do you think, Will?"

"Think?" blurted Will. "Think? I think it is a miracle of God and his holy angels! I think, Mistress Catherine, that you are, in fact, one of those angels."

Catherine reddened and said, "Oh, Will, stop. I am not looking for your praise. Only tell me that you are willing to talk to Lord Pembroke."

"Of course I will. I shall sing to him if he requires it." The young man turned to Sarah and said, beaming, "Sarah, lovey, perhaps we will be able to marry after all."

Sarah looked away shyly and squeaked her thanks to Catherine. Tears of joy filled her eyes.

Catherine now revealed that there was more to her plan. "You know the drying shed is getting far too small for us these days, Sarah. I have inquired about having a new one built out back. I was thinking that, if you and Will do not mind, the old shed could be fixed up for the two of you to use for a while. Work begins on the new storehouse tomorrow."

Sarah wiped her eyes and stood up. Walking over behind Catherine, she wrapped her arms around the shopkeeper's shoulders. She pressed her cheek to the side of Catherine's face affectionately. "You are too good to us, Catherine. We do not deserve such kindness from you."

"You most certainly do, Sarah. You deserve the best that anyone can provide for you. You have become a very beautiful and discerning young woman since you came to work for me. You were such a weedy little thing, afraid to say anything much at all. And now, well, I knew you were growing up that first day you told me exactly what I should do about Lydia—"

Sarah and Will each sucked in their breath quickly at the sound of Lydia's name. Catherine noticed their eyes widen just a little. The couple exchanged a glance. Catherine understood the meaning, but she had to keep silent.

Ever since her return, she had tried not to speak of Lydia. That way, she did not have to deceive anyone. Sarah and Will had also refrained from bringing up the topic, afraid that they might upset Catherine, causing her pain. Now, Catherine turned the conversation to the couple's future again. "Why don't you two go and look at the shed. See what you think can be done with it. Then talk about when the wedding should take place."

Sarah replied tearfully, "Thank you—thank you again, Catherine."

Will chimed in. "Yes, Mistress Catherine, we are most grateful to you."

Catherine admonished, "Will, don't forget to see Lord Pembroke. You must not waste any time. Someone else may get wind of his plans and try to convince him that they would be better for the job."

Will called over his shoulder as he and Sarah headed for the back door. "I shall not forget, Mistress. I'll call on him as soon as we finish in the drying shed."

Life in Wickingham continues

AS THE FEAST of St. Remi approached, Lydia found it difficult to deal with the sadness that overcame her. Visions of Catherine in her shop, Catherine in her garden, and Catherine at the fair haunted her, day and night.

Lucy happened upon her one afternoon as she sat outside her hut wrapped in a shawl, her eyes filled with tears. Concerned, the older woman questioned her gently. "Lydia, dear, what is the matter? Do your injuries pain you?"

"No," Lydia sniffed. "It's my heart that pains me."

"Is there anything I can do?" Lucy asked.

"No," Lydia replied, wiping her eyes. "It's just that the coming feast of St. Remi brings thoughts of someone I miss very much."

"I see," Lucy said sympathetically. She sat with Lydia for awhile, hoping her presence would bring the young woman some measure of comfort. Although Lydia appreciated Lucy's care and concern, it could not quell the ache deep in her heart. Lydia wondered if this ordeal would ever come to an end.

Chapter
Thirty

The Michaelmas Feast
September 29, 1459
Willowglen

A FEW DAYS before Willowglen Fair was about to begin, Catherine received word from Beatrice. Sadly, she informed Catherine that she thought it best that she and Hilary not attend Willowglen Fair. It was the first word that Catherine had heard from Briarcrest since she left. She read one line in the letter over and over again—the one meant to tell her that Lydia was safe and well.

...your treasure is in good hands, and it shines as beautifully as ever it did...

The words made Catherine smile, but her joy was quickly replaced by the familiar underlying ache. Despite the activity of preparations for fair, despite the planning for Sarah's wedding, she missed Lydia terribly. How long would they have to endure this separation?

The Octave of the Feast of St. Remi
October 8, 1459

THE WHIRLWIND OF preparation was followed by another Willowglen fair. Catherine and Sarah feverishly prepared for, and survived, the onslaught of visitors. The fair was successful and prosperous, but exhausting. As soon as it was over, Will and Sarah busied themselves transferring everything out of the little drying shed into the newly built larger one. The couple made repairs to the old shed and Will worked every spare minute he had on simple furniture for their new home, sometimes laboring long into the night.

By day, he worked with Lord Pembroke to make the new book printing shop ready for the arrival of the printing machine. Sarah and Will continued their reading lessons as often as they could, so that Will would be skilled by the time the first book type was ready to be set.

The couple decided to wed before the start of Advent in the chapel in the Governor's Hall. Ordinarily, a couple of their stature would not have been allowed to do so, but Catherine made the request and it was granted without issue. As preparations continued for Sarah and Will's life together, Catherine thought of the many things that she wanted to share with Lydia and her heart ached with longing.

The master of the Grouse and Pheasant was not pleased with Will's departure, but he was a good man at heart. He could not deny that the young lad had been presented with a golden opportunity. He would be foolhardy to let it pass him by. In the end, he presented Will and Sarah with a fine pewter pitcher for a wedding gift. It was a gesture of good will, as well as one of good wishes.

A gift for the couple even arrived from Briarcrest. They received a set of fine bed linens from the Ladies, Beatrice and Hilary. Two notes accompanied the gift: one for Sarah and Will with fond wishes, and one for Catherine.

Another disguised message accompanied Catherine's note. Lydia was still well and still cared for in her place of hiding. *How long can we continue this separation? Lydia, my Lydia. I miss you so...*

Chapter
Thirty-one

October, 1459
Briarcrest

NEWS OF LORD Hugo Wellington's demise reached Briarcrest in mid-autumn. When Beatrice heard the news, she decided not to act hastily. Instead, she dispatched some of Briarcrest's men to investigate the matter. They came back with word that, as Beatrice had predicted, Lord Wellington had set sail for France. Soon after putting out to sea, it seemed, a rogue storm arose. The odd and inexplicable occurrence swept the ship with its occupants to the depths. There was one survivor to tell the tale. He had witnessed the deaths of all on board, including, as he put it, the arrogant and self-serving Hugo Wellington. Beatrice mourned the loss of her brother silently — and waited.

It did not take long for a battle over possession of Greencastle to break out. Two contenders came to the forefront. In the end, Lord Robert Wellington, a young distant cousin of Beatrice and Hugo, won the fight, banishing all who would not pledge fidelity to him. Most of Hugo's men were gone from Greencastle in a matter of days.

When news of these events reached Beatrice's ears, she decided that it was time to take action.

November 6, 1459
Greencastle

AS BEATRICE AND Hilary climbed down from their carriage, Lord Robert came out to greet them. The three embraced warmly and Robert offered an arm to each of the women to escort them into the main hall.

As they entered the room, Robert said, "Ladies, I must apologize for the dungeon-like atmosphere of Greencastle. You would have thought that Hugo was a penitent the way he lived, but it will become more livable in time."

"I'm sure you will make it very comfortable, Robert — but we have come on a most urgent matter. We must speak privately."

"Why certainly, Beatrice," Robert replied. "Follow me."

He led them to a room that had served as a kind of tactical chamber for Hugo. Beatrice could see that Robert had already made some changes. His extensive collection of hand-copied books, as well as some of the newer ones, printed on the new printing devices, were stacked on a table.

"I shall come to the point, Robert," began Beatrice. "We need to speak of Lydia."

Robert's face saddened. "Beatrice, I know how much you cared for her. I was so sorry to hear of her passing — "

"That is precisely what we must discuss, Robert. She is not dead. She is very much alive. She is being cared for in a place I would rather not reveal at the moment."

Robert blinked in disbelief. "I found the annals of Greencastle, Beatrice. Lydia's death was written in Hugo's own hand. He said she died during the Octave of St. Mary Magdalene."

"It was a ruse, Robert. Her father wanted to drag her off to France to marry. She did not want to go."

"Mmm, no doubt the marriage was to further his own cause," speculated Robert.

"Yes," replied Beatrice.

"I know he was your brother, Beatrice, but I never did like the man. He was a bit too calculating for my liking. When I received news of his death, I could not help but think it was a good riddance. I even thought I wanted no part of a claim to Greencastle, but Philip convinced me otherwise. He is tired of traveling, he says, and he wants a place to call home. I must admit that the older I get, the better that starts to sound to me, too. So here we are in this dark hole, trying to make it more habitable.

"By the way, Beatrice, Philip was very perturbed with me that we did not get to Briarcrest for the May feast this year. I thought I would never hear the end of that one. Nevertheless, I told him 'you cannot have everything, Philip, you have to make some choices.'"

Beatrice shook her head and stifled a smile. For all his pretensions, she liked Robert.

"But I digress, Beatrice. Come. Tell me all about this deception of yours. What would prompt you to chance so dangerous a thing as to defy Hugo by feigning Lydia's death?"

SOME TIME LATER, Robert emerged from the room with Beatrice and Hilary laughing and talking about old times. The two women stayed at Greencastle overnight, dining with Robert and Philip in their private rooms. The next morning, before they returned to Briarcrest, Robert handed Beatrice a rolled document with the Wellington seal affixed to it. As Philip closed the carriage door, he assured the women that he intended to see that he and Robert attended the next May feast at Briarcrest without fail. As the carriage started down the road, Beatrice held up the scroll and smiled triumphantly at Hilary.

THE JOURNEY FROM Greencastle to Briarcrest took several days longer than usual because of a storm.

As Beatrice and Hilary sat watching the rain from their room in a wayside inn, Hilary spoke. "Do you have everything you need now, Beatrice?"

"Yes," Beatrice replied. "My brother's death has been confirmed, and Robert has given me this." She patted the roll of parchment sitting next to her on the table. "With it, Lydia is free."

Hilary smiled.

When the storm finally let up, Beatrice and Hilary set out for Briarcrest again. Beatrice wasted no time when she arrived home — she went to her study immediately, sat down and penned two notes. When she was done, she called for two messengers. One she dispatched to Wickingham. The other, she sent to Willowglen.

Chapter
Thirty-two

The Feast of St. Martin, the Plowman
November 11, 1459
Willowglen

CATHERINE CLOSED THE shop in celebration of Sarah and Will's wedding day. The modest festivity was in progress at the Grouse and Pheasant when the messenger from Briarcrest arrived in Willowglen. Finding the shop of Hawkins and Hawkins closed, he went to the Inn to inquire about Mistress Hawkins' whereabouts and located her there. He gave her the note from Briarcrest and was invited to a glass of ale amidst the festivities.

Catherine sat in a quiet corner pouring over the message. Upon learning that Lydia would be able to come out of hiding, Catherine's hand flew to her mouth to stifle a cry.

Even in the midst of the merrymaking, the young bride kept an eye on her mentor. From her seat beside Will, Sarah watched the messenger deliver the note. Her eyes followed Catherine as she withdrew to a corner of the room. When Sarah saw Catherine's reaction, she feared that the news was not good. She jumped out of her seat and ran to Catherine's side. "Catherine, what is it?"

Catherine looked up. She had tears in her eyes, but through her tears, Catherine's face was beaming. Sarah knew then that the news could not be bad as she had feared. She breathed a sign of relief.

Catherine confessed, "I have kept something from you these past months, Sarah. I am sorry, but it was important for Lydia's safety that I not tell anyone that she is, indeed, alive. And now," the spice vendor added, trying to contain her excitement, "she is coming back to Willowglen. Her father is dead. Beatrice is her guardian now and she is sending her to me."

"I knew it!" Sarah cried. "I knew you were too much at peace. I know you too well, Catherine. You care for her too deeply not to be troubled at losing her."

Catherine blushed and looked down at the note, not seeing it. When she looked up again, Sarah was grinning from ear to ear.

"So, this is a double celebration today, Catherine."

"Indeed, it is, Sarah. Indeed, it is." Catherine wiped her eyes and arose from her seat. Putting her arm around Sarah, she said, "I think you should go back to your husband. He looks rather lost without you by his side."

The two women looked over at Will. He was standing with Sarah's aunt and uncle, looking very uncomfortable as the festivities went on all around him. Both women laughed.

"Do you think I should go and rescue him?"

"You should if you want him to survive his uneasiness."

They approached Will. His expression brightened when he saw Sarah.

Sarah turned to Catherine and said, "I am so happy Lydia is well, Catherine, and that she is coming home."

The remark jolted Catherine briefly, but she recovered quickly, breaking into a smile. *Yes, it is true. Lydia is coming 'home.'* On the wall of the Inn, a shadow could be seen to throw up its arms and whirl around in joyful celebration.

The festivities continued long into the late afternoon. As Catherine watched the young couple, she prayed that they would find delight in each other for the rest of their lives. Before the party sent the newlyweds off to their little bungalow, Catherine spoke to Lord Pembroke and got him to agree that Will could have a few days off to be with his bride. Catherine had already decided that she would grant Sarah the same leave. The herbalist then went to the couple and told them the news that the next few days were their own. When they set out, with a flurry of good wishes from the guests, Sarah and Will shouted their thanks back to Catherine. They then ran full speed down Market Street, anxious to be alone.

THAT EVENING, CATHERINE stood at the door of the Grouse and Pheasant and watched the last guests depart. It had been an emotional day, even before Beatrice's message had arrived. Catherine felt tired, but she was not ready to go back to the empty shop just yet.

When the Master of the Grouse and Pheasant came into the room, he found Catherine clearing tables of their dishes. He shouted excitedly, "Mistress Catherine, you have paid me well to give this feast for the young couple. It's not necessary for you to do this. It's our duty to tidy up here."

"I know, Master Elbert," replied Catherine, "but I need to work off a little of your fine feast before I go home to bed. You and your wife have outdone yourselves with the food you've served us. I'm very grateful to you both. I'm sure Will is thankful to you, too. You've been most gracious, especially after losing him as a worker."

Elbert scuffed a foot over the floor in front of him. "Oh, it was nothing. Will's a good lad, a hard worker. I was sorry to see him go, but I'm glad that things have turned out so well for him. We'll manage here.

"But what of you, Mistress? How goes business for you?"

This was Catherine's opportunity—with a word to Elbert, she could spread the word that she would be taking on a partner. "It goes very well, Master Elbert, I can hardly keep up. In fact, I may be getting someone else to join me soon. You remember Lady Lydia who stayed here at the Inn while she studied herbs with me?"

"Yes, I do. She was a lovely young thing."

"Yes, well, she will be coming to stay, I think."

"A lady of her position is going to work in a spice shop? Pardon me, I do not mean to make little of your work, Mistress. It's only that it seems such a one as Lady Lydia has no need to be thus engaged. Now that I think of it, I thought I had heard that she had died."

"I'm happy to say that's not true. She was quite ill for a time, but she has recovered. It's Lady Lydia's father that has met with his demise. His estate has fallen to someone who has no interest in the Lady's future. Beatrice, Duchess of Briarcrest, is her guardian now. It's with her blessing that Lady Lydia shall come to Hawkins and Hawkins."

Catherine knew the Master of the Grouse and Pheasant held the Duchess in great esteem. He would say nothing out of turn knowing that Lydia was her ward now and that she had given sanction to her niece's endeavor. Catherine also knew that, by giving this information to the Master of the Grouse and Pheasant, it would spread throughout Willowglen Township quickly, for Master Elbert had quite a reputation as the town gossip.

The Feast of St. Martin, the Plowman
Wickingham

THE SECOND MESSENGER dispatched from Briarcrest

approached the little hamlet of Wickingham. He did not come on horseback. Instead, he rode atop a carriage that bore the mark of Briarcrest on its doors. Tethered to the carriage, a riding horse followed dutifully behind.

A villager tending his garden left his plot to scrutinize the approaching coach. As the carriage drew closer, Henry recognized the driver. He waved to Sir Guy as he reined the horses to a halt.

As the two men talked, their breath suspended white in the chill fall air before disappearing. Guy held out a small, rolled piece of parchment tied with a red ribbon and sealed with the emblem of Briarcrest. Henry nodded and took the note into the hut. Inside, a delicate young woman sat working at some stitching. She looked out of place there, in spite of the plain brown peasant dress she wore.

Henry handed the message to Lydia. The two exchanged a wordless look. She broke the seal, untied the ribbon and unrolled the paper with her long, delicate fingers. Then she read aloud:

My dearest Lydia,

It is with a mixture of sadness and relief that I write this message. I have received word, and feel it is on good authority, that your father is no longer a threat. God has seen fit to take him to his eternal rest. I can only hope he finds some measure of peace reunited with your mother. Your cousin, Lord Robert, has taken possession of Greencastle and has turned your guardianship over to me. Because of this, you are free to leave. Henry may escort you to your chosen destination. It is not necessary for you to come to Briarcrest. I only hope that we shall see you again once you are settled. Inform the good people with whom you are staying that they have my sincere gratitude for their trustworthiness and hospitality. I shall send a shipment of supplies to thank them shortly. In addition, the horses and wagon in which you came is their first allotment. Henry may return to Briarcrest once he has seen you safely settled.

With my fondest greeting,
Your loving aunt,
Beatrice, Duchess of Briarcrest

At the bottom of the page, a note to Henry read:

Henry, my trusted friend,

I expect you will accompany Lydia and see her safely to her destination. I look forward to seeing you again, and to hearing about your stay these past months. Your family is well. I shall inform them of your imminent return. I am certain that they look forward to seeing you after your long absence.

With utmost gratitude,
Duchess of Briarcrest, Lady Beatrice

Henry said, "I am sorry to hear about your father's death, mum."

"I hardly knew him, Henry. He was only someone who occasionally lived in the same cold, dark citadel as did I. The one person who made Greencastle home for me was Marian. It is she whom I shall miss for a very long time, not father."

"Yes, mum," murmured Henry. He understood. He had not taken much to the Earl himself. As a matter of fact, he failed to see how anyone could mourn his loss. After a moment, he ventured, "Sir Guy brought us the carriage. He has his own horse with him for his return to Briarcrest."

Lydia said, "Tell him that he is welcome to stay the night with us, Henry."

"I shall, mum. Lucy and her people will be pleased with the horses and work cart. It was good of Beatrice to think of that."

"They will be a great aid to them," Lydia said.

Henry remarked, matter-of-factly, "It's a two-day trip to Willowglen if the weather holds."

A smile spread across Lydia's lips and she teased, "Henry, how did you know that would be our destination?"

He shrugged and winked. "Lucky guess, mum. I had better go and see how Guy is doing. He was bedding the horses in the lean-to. Then perhaps I should tell Lucy about the other horses and the cart."

"Lucy told me she saw the horses grazing nearby only yesterday. I am sure she will want them rounded up as soon as possible."

Henry nodded and turned to leave.

"Henry —" Lydia called.

He stopped and looked back at Lydia. "Yes, mum?"

"You have been a good 'husband.'"

Henry blushed. "Yes, mum," he murmured.

Lydia added, "If I desired a husband, I would want one as good and kind as you are, Henry. Your wife is a lucky woman."

"Yes, mum," he said, more embarrassed.

"What I am trying to say, Henry, is, well, thank you."

"I could do no less for you, M'lady, for you or for the Duchess and Lady Hilary. I owe them my life. You know that. Besides, I would do it for you alone."

Now, it was Lydia's turn to blush.

LYDIA SAT WITH her stitchery abandoned in her lap, re-reading Beatrice's letter. It was true. She was free to go to Willowglen — to Catherine. She could hardly believe it.

Outside, Henry found Guy where he'd expected to, bedding the horses in the small shelter. "You will need a place to stay tonight, Guy. My home here is no more than a shack, but you are welcome to what warmth you can get from my fire."

"Thank you, Henry. I am sure it will be better than sleeping here with the horses."

"I must find the clan leader. Beatrice sent a message for her. Will you finish up here while I do that?"

"Yes, go on, Henry. I still have my own horse to bed. I will be a while more."

Henry found Lucy and informed her that he and Lydia would be leaving. He told her that the work cart and horses were Wickingham's to keep, to which Lucy replied, "We have become very rich, indeed, Master Henry." She was visibly pleased by the gesture and wasted no time calling some young boys to round up the horses and retrieve the cart from its hiding place.

Henry returned to the lean-to and escorted Guy back to his hut. Guy knew that Henry had been on some mission of great importance for the Duchess, so he had been surprised to find him living a reclusive life in a distant hamlet. He had no idea of the true nature of Henry's assignment. When Guy entered Henry's hut that afternoon, he was stunned by what he saw.

"My Lady! I thought you were, uh..."

"Dead?" offered Lydia.

"Yes. Dead," replied the stunned man.

Henry said harshly, "I suppose you were mistaken, then."

Guy understood. No one knew the will of the Duchess as well as Henry. If Henry thought this must not be spoken of, then Sir Guy would comply. He was loyal to his Ladies.

Later that evening, the trio ate a simple meal together.

Lydia inquired about her father's death. "Do you know how it happened, Guy?"

"Drowned, they say. It happened weeks ago, but Beatrice wanted proof. She said she knew well that rumors of death are not always true. Now I better understand her remark."

Lydia tried to stifle a smile.

Henry asked warily, "What of that cleric?"

Lydia shivered at the mention of Isadore.

"He's nowhere to be found. It's rumored that he has fled England completely. Most likely it is true, since our pursuit ended at the port harbor to the south. I think it not likely we shall ever see the 'good' father again. Good riddance, I say."

Henry agreed. Then he turned to Lydia and said, "I suppose we should make our plans. Shall we leave in the morning, then, mum?"

Without concealing her excitement, Lydia replied, "If it were not that it was night, we could leave right now, Henry. But the morning will be fine. There's not much to prepare. I shall be ready."

With a wry smile, Henry quipped, "If you will allow me to say it, mum, you made a pretty fine peasant wife."

Guy puzzled over their banter until he realized the nature of their deception—Henry and Lydia married and living in Wickingham? It was quite comical—even absurd. He joined in their laughter.

EARLY THE NEXT morning, Sir Guy rode off toward Briarcrest. The inhabitants of the little hamlet of Wickingham came out to bid farewell to Lydia and Henry. Lydia thanked each villager in turn for the kindness she had received from them as they said their good-byes.

Lucy hung back until the last. Then she embraced Lydia for a long time. "You've become like my own daughter, Lydia. I wish you joy."

"Thank you," Lydia replied. "You have been so kind to me. I shall never forget you, Lucy."

They embraced again and Lucy found the softness of the fine purple cloak Lydia wore a new and pleasant experience.

Even once they were on the road, Lydia could not quite believe that she and Catherine would soon be together. She pinched herself to see if she was really awake. Having felt the sting of it, Lydia knew it was true. She was on her way to Willowglen at last.

The journey should have taken only two days, but a

rainstorm delayed them. They stayed at a small wayside inn waiting for the road to dry out before going on. To Lydia, the wait seemed unbearably long.

A misty rain started to fall again as they reached the outskirts of Willowglen. When the carriage finally rolled onto the cobblestone streets of town, they were quiet and quite deserted because of the rain. Within a matter of minutes, the mist had quickly become a steady downpour. Henry brought the horses to a halt in front of the shop and jumped down from the driver's seat. The pair ran for the shop, which was shuttered tightly against the storm. Henry tried the door latch, but it had been bolted for the night. As the storm picked up momentum, Henry shielded Lydia from the rain with his own traveling cloak, then raised his hand and pounded loudly on the shop door.

Chapter
Thirty-three

Inside The Shoppe of Hawkins & Hawkins
Willowglen Township

CATHERINE HAD JUST stoked the fire and put a kettle of water on for tea to warm herself against the storm. She was grateful that the weather had been warm and bright several days earlier for Sarah and Will's wedding.

The young couple had taken Catherine at her word. They had not so much as poked their heads out from the drying shed that was now their tiny cottage home for days. When Catherine finally saw them again, they looked content and happy. Now, both young people had returned to work and were adjusting to married life together. She smiled at the thought of the two of them cuddled up together by the small stone fireplace Will had built in one corner of their cottage.

Catherine brewed her tea and walked to the small kitchen window. Sipping the warm drink, she watched the grey smoke rising lazily from the cottage chimney.

The loud banging made Catherine jump. She put her cup down and hurried to the shop door thinking perhaps someone had taken ill and needed her help. She unlatched the door and pulled it open.

Spice odors wafted across the doorway to meet Lydia and Henry. Catherine stared at the two wet forms for an instant. Then, she reached out and pulled Lydia into the shop. Henry followed, closing the door behind him. By then, Catherine had Lydia in a wordless embrace. She held her gratefully, afraid to speak, concerned that she would cry, even though, if she did, the tears would be tears of joy.

Lydia protested that Catherine was getting as wet as she. Catherine cared nothing about her damp clothes, but then she remembered Henry standing there waiting quietly. She let go of Lydia and went to him. Catching him completely off guard, she embraced him, too.

Catherine looked back and forth to both of them and said breathlessly, "Oh, I am so glad you have finally come. But I didn't know when you would arrive. Let me prepare some supper for you both."

Henry cleared his throat, sheepishly, and said, "I need to get the horses inside, mum. I'll go to the blacksmith's behind the Grouse and Pheasant and stay the night there, so don't be concerned about me."

Lydia said, "You will come by in the morning to say goodbye — you must, Henry."

Henry smiled. "Yes, mum. I couldn't leave without saying goodbye to you and Mistress Catherine." He went back to the shop door and wrapped his cloak tightly around his body. Plunging into the storm, he went to the horses and led them toward the blacksmith's stalls.

Catherine bolted the door behind him and stood before Lydia. She untied the cord holding the purple cloak around Lydia's neck and let the cape fall to the floor. Lydia didn't move. She gazed into Catherine's eyes. Catherine took Lydia in her arms and kissed her. Desire coursed through them.

Catherine's voice quivered as she spoke. "I have missed you, Lydia."

Lydia returned, "There were so many nights when I couldn't sleep. I lay on my cot thinking about you — thinking how very much I missed you — and I wondered, at times, if I could survive the endless waiting."

"Beatrice would not allow anyone to know where you were. She felt it was safer that way."

"Beatrice is very wise. I trust her. It was difficult, but I was among caring people. There was a woman there named Lucy. She's a healer. She took up care for me where you had left off. She praised your skill in the healing arts. She said she would like to meet such a talented practitioner. Perhaps we could visit her one day."

"I would like that," Catherine said dreamily.

Standing amid the perfume of the herbs and spices, caressing each other, as if becoming reacquainted, they explored arms and shoulders, touched finger tips to cheeks, traced lips...

Catherine stopped abruptly. "I have forgotten my manners. Please forgive me, Lydia. Would you like something to eat?"

Lydia pulled Catherine toward her again. "My hunger is for you, and you alone."

Catherine met Lydia's gaze. The glowing sparks in her grey-green eyes flared into a wild inferno. Catherine took Lydia's hand and led her up the stairs. In the bedchamber above the shop, they helped each other undress. When Lydia's garment fell from her shoulders and her scars were laid bare, Catherine winced.

Uneasily, Lydia offered, "I healed skillfully at your hands, Catherine. They give me no trouble at all."

Catherine examined Lydia's back. She pressed her fingertips lightly against two of the deepest scars. "Are you sure these do not hurt?"

"Not at all." Lydia turned to face Catherine. Her face had no scars. Even if she had them, she would still be as beautiful as ever. Her eyes were burning, deep green wells. "You are not afraid to... touch me, are you, Catherine?"

"No, my love. Never. I could never be fearful of you."

"I could not bear it, were it so."

Catherine drew Lydia against her. Then, together, in the simple room above the spice shop, they were reunited in their love.

IT WAS NOT until early the next morning that Lydia learned of Sarah and Will's marriage and that the drying shed had been converted to their living quarters. In the darkness of the early morning hours, the two women spoke of many things. Most of all, they talked of their love, and they promised each other they would be together always.

Catherine recounted the events that took place at Briarcrest after Lydia left for Wickingham in the middle of the night. She told her of her father's reaction upon hearing of her death and of his visit to the grave site. "There was a young man there. You know him, Lydia. He carried you upstairs on the litter when you were not well enough to walk yet."

"Little James," Lydia said, her mind wandering back to childhood days.

"*Little* James?" Catherine said, surprised.

"Oh, I know he isn't little in stature, but it's what he is called. It's because he is still so childlike in his mind. When he was younger, the children used to torment him. During the children's party one May feast, the others wouldn't allow him near the table filled with treats and gifts. When I saw it, I made all of them step back and let him have first choice of anything he wanted. Being treated in so special a way made him so happy.

"Afterwards, I explained to the children that Little James was not as quick a thinker as they were, but he had other good qualities and they should try to see them. When I asked them to think about how they would feel if they were Little James, they felt remorseful. Some of them even became his friends after that and looked out for him. One boy has remained his very good friend. He was the other young man who carried me upstairs. After that incident, Little James and I continued to have a special bond. He always came to visit me whenever he heard that Marian and I were at Briarcrest."

Suddenly Lydia sat upright in alarm. "Oh, no. I must tell Beatrice that she will have to sit down with him and try to explain that I am well. If I go back to Briarcrest and he sees me, he will think he's seeing a ghost and will be afraid. I would never want to frighten him. He's such a dear thing."

"I am sure Beatrice will be happy to talk to the boy for you, Lydia," Catherine comforted.

"Yes, you're right. I must ask her to inform all of the people of Briarcrest that I am alive and well. They will all need to know. You should have seen Guy's face when he saw me. I thought he would collapse from the shock."

Both women laughed at the thought of the stalwart knight's reaction at seeing Lydia alive.

Catherine continued her story. "Well, when we took your father to the gravesite, Little James was kneeling there, crying. He was so tender when he placed a little bunch of flowers on the pile of earth. It was because of his grief that your father finally believed it was all true. Otherwise, he might well have had the grave dug up and found that your coffin was filled with stones that Beatrice, Hilary and I placed there before sealing it up."

Lydia said softly, "I shall have to thank Little James one day. I owe my life to him, as well as to the Ladies of Briarcrest. Most of all, though, I owe my life...to you, Catherine."

The breaking dawn faintly illuminated the room. Feeling self-conscious, Catherine sought a diversion. She threw off the covers and went to the carved chest at the foot of the bed. Opening the lid, she picked up something small and dove back into bed quickly again to avoid the morning chill. Nuzzling close to Lydia, Catherine sheepishly held out a small cloth pouch. Lydia opened the bag slowly and discovered a medallion on a cord.

"What is this, Catherine? Why do you give me a gift?"

"You once told me that, when it was too warm for you to wear the cloak I made for you, you would miss it. I said I would have to think of something else for you to wear without concern for the time of year. When I returned home from Briarcrest, I had Edward make this so that I could give it to you when we were together again. I pray we shall never be parted, but even when we are about our daily duties, we shall hold each other close. I have my medallion from you and you shall have this one."

Lydia turned the pendant toward the early morning light until she could see the image. It was the figure of the Green Lady. She drew in her breath. "Oh, it is beautiful!" Swallowing back her tears and clutching the medallion to her heart, she whispered, "Thank you."

They held each other until the sun rose over the rooftops. The storm of the evening had passed and the day promised to be bright and warm.

CATHERINE STIRRED THE embers in the fireplace. The fire caught and flared. Catherine added some wood until it was crackling. The kitchen warmed. It felt pleasant. As Catherine put on a kettle of water, Lydia stole up behind her and wrapped her arms around Catherine, holding her close. "It feels so good to be here," she murmured into Catherine's shoulder.

Catherine turned around in Lydia's embrace. "It feels so good to be *home*," she corrected. "This is your home, now — our home, Lydia."

Lydia closed her eyes and smiled, savoring the words. "Mmm, yes, it rings true."

Catherine held Lydia's face in her hands. Lydia opened her eyes to meet Catherine's and the fire erupted again. With some difficulty, they tore themselves away and forced themselves to concentrate on breakfast preparations.

Henry arrived to say goodbye. He was glad of the pleasant day, he said, for he knew the journey home with the carriage would be difficult enough after the earlier storms. Catherine and Lydia tried to talk him into staying, but he finally admitted that he was anxious to get back to Briarcrest and his family.

Soon after Henry left, Sarah came into the kitchen through the back door and squealed with delight at the sight of Lydia. All three women chirped merrily together. Against the fireplace wall, Catherine's shadow looked as if it was leaning back enjoying the scene immensely.

By mid-morning, the women were busy working in the shop. To Catherine, it felt as if Lydia had never left. Yet in other ways, it felt very different now that Lydia was home to stay. That evening, the newly wed couple ate dinner with Catherine and Lydia.

Day followed day and night followed night. They came and went, Will to Lord Pembroke's shop and Sarah to work with Catherine and Lydia. They all settled into their new lives — Sarah and Will, Catherine and Lydia.

Chapter
Thirty-four

Early Spring, 1460
Willowglen

WITH THE BLOOMING of the first buds on the trees of Willowglen came an invitation from Briarcrest to attend the May Celebration. Catherine asked Sarah if she would tend to the shop while she and Lydia traveled to Briarcrest. Sarah was pleased to hear of their plans and consented. She had only one request: that Catherine and Lydia convey Sarah's deepest gratitude for the lovely wedding gift that the Ladies of Briarcrest had sent. Catherine assured Sarah that she would relay the message as soon as they set foot in Briarcrest Hall.

The Eve of the May Feast
April 30, 1460
Briarcrest

BEATRICE AND HILARY welcomed Catherine and Lydia as if they were daughters returning home. The last time the Ladies of Briarcrest had seen Lydia, she was still weak and recovering from her wounds, disguised as a peasant woman in an old work cart with Henry at her side. Now, it gladdened the older women's hearts to see her looking so healthy and happy. The spring sun had already tanned Lydia's once-milky skin as she worked in the garden behind the spice shop. Her delicate body had become firm and muscular. They sat in the garden drinking mint tea that first afternoon of their return to Briarcrest and Beatrice asked the two younger women to join Hilary and her in their chambers that evening for a bath.

"It's now a new tradition," laughed Beatrice. Then she added with a twinkle in her eye, "You will find everything about the May feast quite different from last year, I think. You have been through a great deal together."

Lydia gave Catherine a knowing glance. Catherine agreed, smiling silently.

IT PROVED TO be a different May feast indeed. During their bath that evening, as Beatrice sprinkled some crushed lavender and bay leaves into the water, Lydia moved into Catherine's arms. Beatrice and Hilary seemed to take no notice, but in truth, they did. They only pretended it was the fragrance and warmth of the water that made them smile.

As they sat in the soothing water, Beatrice poured cups of mead for each of them. Then she said she had a request of the younger women.

Eager to do whatever the Duchess asked of them, Catherine and Lydia assured her they would try to honor her request. They were dumbfounded to learn that Beatrice and Hilary wanted them to assume the duty of crowning the May Queen.

Catherine recovered from her surprise and responded. "Oh, Beatrice, we could not do such a thing. Surely it is a great honor that should be reserved for the Ladies of this house."

"Which brings us to another topic, my dears," Beatrice said with a mischievous sparkle in her eyes. "One day, Hilary and I will be too old to carry out the household duties of Briarcrest, you know — "

"Aunt Beatrice, that will not be for a very long time," Lydia protested.

"Be that as it may," Beatrice replied, "we feel this matter must be attended to before that time comes. Since we have no children who will take possession of Briarcrest, we would like it to become your home. We can draw up the papers and have them recorded and sanctioned in the court of London. No one will be able to dispute your claim to Briarcrest and its lands once it's done. It will give us peace knowing that Briarcrest Hall will continue as it has these past years. Will you agree?"

"I...we...are not sure, Aunt Beatrice," stammered Lydia.

"Promise you will at least think about it? Both of you?"

Lydia and Catherine looked at each other, wide-eyed.

Catherine finally responded, "We promise to think about it, Beatrice. It is the least we can do."

Lydia nodded in agreement.

The May Feast
May 1, 1460
Briarcrest

THE MORNING SUN warmed the room as Lydia and Catherine lay in the tapestry-curtained bed, indulging themselves in the luxury of their late rising. Catherine had been lying with her eyes closed, trying to suppress a smile, for she knew Lydia was watching her.

At last, she said, "Do you intend to stare at me like that every morning while we are at Briarcrest, My Lady?"

Lydia replied innocently, "No, only on the days that I do not wake you by kissing you all over your body, Mistress."

"Lydia!"

Lydia rolled toward Catherine and looked into her eyes. She called softly, "Catherine, it's the May feast. Come, I shall give you your heart's desire..."

BY THE TIME they entered the forest that morning, everyone was well into the celebration. Lydia and Catherine visited the meadow first. Standing silently amid the tall, fragrant grass, they reverenced it as if it were a sacred site. Afterward they went to the clearing in the woods to join in the festivities. Among the guests this year were Father Giles and Robert, Lord of Greencastle, with his companion, Sir Phillip.

Late in the afternoon, a gong sounded and two forms appeared dressed in matching embroidered robes. In their hair, each woman wore pine boughs and golden streamers. A hush fell on the crowd as they entered the clearing and approached the larger-than-life leafy form sitting on her wooden throne. Carrying the golden crown, Lydia ascended the steps. Catherine accompanied her. After Lydia placed the crown on the Queen's head, the women turned to face the gathering and Catherine announced in a clear, resonant voice, "Behold the Queen of the May."

The crowd raised their cups and tankards and shouted, "Huzzah, huzzah!"

The feast continued. Lydia and Catherine joined Beatrice and Hilary at the head of the table.

When the revelers returned to Briarcrest Hall late that afternoon, they were entertained by Madame Toussants. This year, she, too, had attended the festivities in the woods. Sensing that something remarkable, something powerful, had transpired during the past year, Madame Toussants made an inquiry of the

Ladies. They told her briefly of the events that had transpired during the past year. Finally, Madame Toussants said, "So, ze torch, it is passed on, no?"

Hilary replied, "It still remains to be seen, Yvette. The invitation has been extended, but we cannot make the decision for them. They will have to make it for themselves. However, I think it's a good sign that they are hesitant. If they were too eager, I might worry."

Beatrice added, "They must think long and hard about their future. That's why we decided to pose the question early. They can take as long as they need to consider our proposal. Briarcrest is theirs *if* they say yes."

"*When* they say yes," Hilary corrected.

"Perhaps," said Beatrice.

"Hmmm," added Madame Toussants.

Catherine and Lydia came and sat beside the trio to catch their breath from dancing around the hall. The young women exchanged whispers. Then they threw back their heads, laughing merrily.

"Hmmm," repeated Madame Toussants. Glancing at Beatrice and Hilary, she looked as if she understood a great mystery.

Epilogue

The days and months turned into years. Time passed far too quickly. The herb, spice and fine linen shop in Willowglen flourished. Catherine and Lydia's lives were rich and full. The day Lydia was admitted to the Guild, Catherine was ready with a new sign. Hanging outside, above the shop door, it now read:

Hawkins & Wellington
Herbs, spices & fine linens

The people of Willowglen had known Mistress Catherine all of her life. They had come to respect her as a healer and as a shop owner. It did not take long before Lydia gained the same respect for herself. As Catherine treated people in their illnesses, Lydia assisted her. They were thought odd by some, but Catherine was accustomed to it, and Lydia seemed to take no notice.

Year after year at the May feast, Lydia and Catherine donned the robes of the celebration to crown the May Queen while Beatrice and Hilary stood beaming. The ladies of Briarcrest never repeated their request for Lydia and Catherine to take over the management of Briarcrest. Instead, they waited, anticipating the day when the younger women would be ready to speak of it again.

Sarah took over the shop each year while Catherine and Lydia went to Briarcrest for the May feast. After Little Will was born, he toddled among the herbs "helping" his mother. His father was no longer an apprentice to Lord Pembroke. He was, rather, his assistant. That business, too, flourished and the couple moved into a larger cottage at the edge of town. In the spring of 1465, a daughter was born to Sarah and Will. The couple named her Catherine Lydia.

ON A COOL, spring evening as the May feast drew near, Lydia and Catherine sat in the garden surrounded by new growth. The light of a full moon hanging high in the night sky illuminated the garden.

Lydia whispered, "Catherine, I have been thinking."

"About what, Lydia?"

"About Beatrice and Hilary, Briarcrest...and us. About the request they made of us—do you realize that it was fourteen May feasts ago? If we do not agree to oversee Briarcrest, what will become of it? What will become of the people? And what of Beatrice and Hilary as they grow older?"

"I... have been waiting, Lydia."

"For what?"

"For you to bring it up," replied Catherine.

"Have you thought about it, also?" asked Lydia.

"Often," responded Catherine.

"So have I. What do you think?"

"I am still not sure, Lydia, but now that you have brought it up, I think we must ponder it together," Catherine said.

"Yes, I think you are right." Lydia was silent for a moment, then she asked, "Would it be difficult for you, Catherine?"

"Difficult?"

"To give up the shop, I mean."

"I used to think it would be impossible, but I'm not so sure of late. I think that if we decide it's the right thing, leaving the shop won't matter," replied Catherine.

Lydia said, "Things are changing—even in Willowglen. This afternoon at the Governor's Hall, I heard that the Inquisition comes closer and closer every day. They are saying that the Church will no longer tolerate those of us who use herbs for healing. They have killed some women, Catherine. They said they were—of the devil."

Catherine sighed and asked, "Would we be protected from it if we take over Briarcrest, Lydia?"

"Who can say, Catherine. Still, I feel as though the time has come. Perhaps when we go to Briarcrest this year, we should speak of it to Beatrice and Hilary."

"Yes, I think we should, Lydia."

The two women sat absorbed in their thoughts. The stillness of the evening was only broken by the cricket-song coming from the garden.

Catherine's eyes wandered to the old drying shed and she thought aloud, "It seems like only yesterday that Sarah and Will lived back here."

Lydia added, "Like yesterday and, at the same time, like a

lifetime ago, Catherine. Sometimes I wonder where the time has
gone."

They sighed in unison. The night air started to chill.

Catherine asked, "Are you ready to go in, Lydia?"

"Yes," Lydia answered.

The two women looked into each other's eyes. By the light
of the full moon, it seemed as if they could see into each other's
souls. They each reached out a hand and the fire ignited.
Upstairs in the bedchamber above the spice shop, they expressed
their hearts' desire as they had done so many times over the
years.

Anna Furtado is a California transplant from New England. She lives with her partner and two fur-people of Scottish Terrier descent. Her first publications were on the Web writing pet care articles for www.petfoodexpress.com and LesbiaNation.com. She was a first-place winner in the Writers' Market 24-Hour Short Story Contest. *The Heart's Desire*, the first book in the trilogy, *The Briarcrest Chronicles*, is her first work of lesbian fiction.

Printed in the United States
49620LVS00005B/198